'What is it, Russell? What troubles you?'

'Nothing,' he said abruptly. 'Only that I am selfish to tease you so, and to jump on you just now, without warning. Whatever could you think of me?'

Honesty won, as it usually did with Mary. 'I thought how much I was enjoying being jumped on. I suppose that means I wasn't really thinking of anything at all. Until I remembered our situation.'

Russell began to laugh and his whole body began to behave itself. He remembered one of the reasons why he had loved Mary was her transparent honesty—which made her subsequent behaviour so surprising.

'You did not find me repellent, then?'

Truth won again. 'No, I never did.'

The smile which she gave him served to set his recovering body on edge once more. This would never do...

Dear Reader

I thought that it might interest myself and my readers if I wrote two novels about twin brothers who were not at all alike, either in looks or in character: the elder, Russell, being carefree, gallant and fair, and the younger, Ritchie, being quiet, serious and dark. I decided that Russell would be the heir to an earldom while Ritchie, who had wanted to be a scholar, was ordered into the army by their father. Ritchie's story is told in *Major Chancellor's Mission*.

In this second story Russell, who has always been aware that his father favoured his younger brother, grows tired of his idle life and his father's dismissal of him as a lightweight. In an attempt to prove himself he goes north to his father's estate in Northumberland and in doing so travels not only into his own past, but also that of his father. By meeting again his lost love, Mary Wardour, Russell not only discovers why he lost her, but finds his own true self and true love into the bargain.

I hope you enjoy Russell's story in *Lord Hadleigh's Rebellion*.

Paula Marshall

LORD HADLEIGH'S REBELLION

Paula Marshall

First published in Great Britain 2001
Large Print edition 2002
Harlequin Mills & Boon Limited,
Eton House, 18-24 Paradise Road, Richmond, Surrey TW9 1SR

© Paula Marshall 2001

ISBN 0 263 17210 4

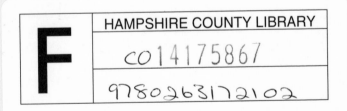
Set in Times Roman 14½ on 15½ pt.
42-0602-87293

Printed and bound in Great Britain
by Antony Rowe Ltd, Chippenham, Wiltshire

LORD HADLEIGH'S REBELLION

Prologue

Spring, 1817

'Oh, damn and blast everything,' Russell Chancellor, Lord Hadleigh, exclaimed aloud as he walked along Bruton Street, causing several passers-by to look at him in some alarm.

The more he thought about his current errand, the worse he felt. It wasn't as though he hadn't been thinking recently of breaking off his long connection with Caroline Fawcett, but he had hoped to do so gradually so that when the end came it would not be too much of a shock for her.

Instead, though, that very morning his father, the Earl of Bretford, had issued an ultimatum to him in such strong terms that there was no denying him—unless he were ready to find himself turned into the street, penniless, with only his title left to him and nothing else...

He had arrived home from the Coal Hole just before dawn, thoroughly out of sorts with himself, having drunk too much and, for once, gambled too much.

He had scarcely had time to lay his throbbing head on the pillow before Pickering, his valet, was shaking him awake.

'What the devil are you at, man?' he exclaimed. 'Don't you know that I arrived home only an hour ago?'

'Yes, m'lord, but your father sent for me not five minutes gone, saying that the matter he wished to discuss with you was urgent. He demanded that I inform you that he wishes to see you in his study immediately and will not brook any delay.'

'Did he, indeed?' Russell swung his legs out of bed, which set his poor head protesting in the most unkind way. 'Have you any notion of what has brought this about?'

'None, m'lord, except...' and his valet hesitated.

'Except what, Pickering? For God's sake, have you caught my father's habit of being unable to finish his sentences?'

'No, m'lord, only that he seemed to be rather more angry with the way the world wags than usual.'

At this dire news, for his father's foul temper was notorious throughout society, Russell gave a slight moan before allowing Pickering to help him to dress. On the way out of the room he caught sight of himself in the looking-glass on the tall-boy opposite to his bed, and decided that he looked more fit for the grave than enduring the roasting which he was sure his father was going to give him.

I'm over thirty years old and he treats me as though I were a boy in his teens, was his last unhappy thought before the footman opened the double doors to the study where his father was impatiently pacing the room. It was small wonder that the carpet was showing such visible signs of wear.

'There you are, Hadleigh. By God, at the rate you're going your rowdy life will soon begin to show on your face—' He stopped abruptly before adding, 'I never cease to wonder how unlike you are to your brother, Richard—'

He stopped again.

The sense of being second rate, a disappointment and a failure, was so strong in him that Russell could not prevent himself from filling the gap which his father had created.

'I am not so far gone that I cannot remember my brother's name, sir. Nor that I am somewhat surprised that you should send for me at this ungodly hour to tell me what I already know.'

At this weary piece of impudence his father's face turned from red to purple.

'You are pleased to be insolent, Hadleigh. I have had enough of you. You are so lost to everything but pleasure that I tremble to think of what might happen to the estate when I am called to my last rest and you inherit. Although there is no male entail attached to the estate, it has always been the custom of the Chancellors to pass it on to the elder son without a quibble. I, however, am beginning to quibble. Nay, more than that—' He stopped again.

'More than what, sir? I am all agog to learn the end of the sentence.'

Remembering his unpleasant riposte later, Russell flushed with shame. At the time his disgust with himself seemed to have translated itself into a disgust with everything.

'It is this, Hadleigh. I am serving you with an ultimatum. I wish you to marry and settle down. To begin with, you are to dismiss that woman you have been keeping, immediately, this morning, if possible. I would have you marry some decent young woman—someone like your brother's wife, Pandora. His judgement in marrying her is as sound as yours is faulty. If you refuse me in this, I shall immediately send for the lawyers and arrange matters so that Richard inherits everything but the title. I shall also at that point discontinue your allowance. You would then have to fend for yourself.

'I am not, Hadleigh, about to condemn you out of hand. I shall give you three months to marry someone who will bring honour to our name, provide the Chancellor family with more male heirs, and settle down to bring honour to it yourself. Failing that, I shall turn you away.'

White to the lips, Russell asked, 'Does Ritchie know of this, sir? After all, he has already provided you with a male heir.'

'Indeed not. It would not be proper that he learn of it before you have had a chance to redeem yourself. As for him providing me with a male heir—you know as well as I do that a man of sense would wish to have as many grandsons as possible, the death rate among little boys being what it is.'

Ritchie had once said to Russell that he had lived in his older twin brother's shadow all his life. The truth, he thought, was somewhat different: he had lived in Ritchie's. Ritchie, who had become his father's darling, Ritchie, the soldier-hero, the serious man, the man of duty. Ritchie, who had already fathered a son.

'I wish I had been the younger twin of whom nothing was expected,' burst from Russell's lips almost without him willing the words.

'That, Hadleigh, is what I complain of—your innate frivolity. I have no more to say to you, except that I expect you to do as I ask—or face the consequences. I have been corresponding with my friend, General Markham, whose only child is a daughter and consequently his heiress. He and I hope to arrange a match between the pair of you. He is giving a house-party at Markham Hall next week, and I would wish you to join it so that you might become acquainted with her. I hope you grasp that the matter is urgent. I am not prepared to allow you to continue your irresponsible way of life any longer.

'You may leave. I want no verbal assurances from you, only deeds.'

His father sat down and began to write, lifting his head up only to say, 'You know where the door is, Hadleigh. Kindly use it. I have no wish to see you again until you have done all that I have just asked of you.'

So, here he was, several hours later, about to give Caroline her *congé*, not as he had once imagined, at his wish, but at his father's. If I had any courage at all I would have told him to go to the devil and set out to make my own fortune. But how? I am trained for nothing. I wanted to be a soldier. That was denied me. I was the heir, Ritchie was to be the soldier. I asked my father to allow me to manage our estates at Eddington in Northumberland, but was told that that was cousin Arthur Shaw's job. What's more, he said, he had no wish to deprive him of it in favour of an untrained, overgrown schoolboy.

Russell's unhappy train of thought stopped at this point. He had no mind to revive for himself the misery which had resulted from his father's other brutal interference in his life thirteen years ago. Not that that was entirely his father's fault, but had he been kinder then...who knows, things might have been different.

No, I will not think of that... The past is dead and gone and that time will not return again. What time *had* done was to bring him to Caroline's door before he was ready to face her. The unhappy truth was that he disliked the notion of telling her that he wished to end their liaison so much that he had continually put it off. Now his father had forced his hand and he must bite the bullet.

Somewhat to his surprise there was a hackney carriage standing in the street outside and Caroline's little page was loading bags into its boot. He ran briskly up the steps, his door key in his hand and let himself in, calling her name with an urgency which surprised him. He was even more surprised when the drawing room door opened and Caroline, looking as lovely as ever, walked into the hall, dressed for the street and carrying a large leather bag.

'You?' she exclaimed. 'I thought that you had forgotten that I lived here. Have you any notion of how long it is since you last visited me?'

Shame struck Russell all over again. It was truly his day to feel like a cur! Oh, he would pay her off with a lump sum, but the cruel fact remained that he was casting her off.

'Not lately, I know,' he almost stammered. He had stammered as a boy until a tutor with a cane had banished it—lately it had begun to come back again.

'True,' she said, smiling at him coldly. 'Well, I will relieve you of the need to visit me again. I have tired of your capriciousness and have decided to leave you. I was about to post you a letter informing you of my departure. Fortunately that will no longer be necessary since I can now tell you so in person.'

'Leave me?' he heard himself saying witlessly.

'Yes, leave you. It has been borne in upon me for some time that you have tired of me and did not know how to tell me so. I entered on our liaison for the foolish reason that I was in love with you. Oh, I knew that you would never marry me, but you assured me that you had decided that you would never marry anyone. I stupidly believed that that meant that we could play house together until we became Darby and Joan. I am still in love with you, but I refuse to be a millstone around your neck. I have recently met a worthy merchant who has decided to make an honest woman of me. We are to marry next week.

'And, no, I want no farewell presents from you of any kind. The one wish that I have to leave you with is that I hope that you may never suffer as I have done in loving someone as hopelessly as I have loved you. Farewell, Lord Hadleigh. Let us remember the happy days we had together and wish each other well. Now I must leave. The carriage, and my new life, awaits me.'

'No,' he said. 'Not like this.'

'You mean that you would have preferred to cast me off, and not me you?'

'No,' he said again, but, of course, she was right.

She reached up to pat his cheek with her gloved hand. 'Remember me a little, is all I ask.'

With that she was gone, out of the house and out of his life.

The decision had been made for him, but Russell felt no better for that—only worse, seeing that this was the second occasion on which a woman had abandoned him. Between his father and his mistress he had been shown a vision of himself with all his shortcomings made plain. All that remained was for him to go to Markham Hall to court a woman whom he had no wish to marry in order to recover his father's favour. Woman was perhaps a misnomer. He seemed to recall that Angelica Markham was only eighteen years old.

He arrived home to find that his father was out, so he could not inform him that his long-standing affair with Caroline Fawcett was over. At a loose end—as usual, he thought bitterly—he wandered into his father's study, intending to ask his secretary, Mr Graves, when he would return. The secretary was not there, either. He began to leave, but something, he never knew quite what, led him to walk to the secretary's tall desk, which stood before the window, to examine the papers on it.

There was a small pile of them that contained the accounts and the other details of the family estate at Eddington. Moved, again by he knew not what, he began to inspect them, the accounts first.

When he was at Oxford he had discovered that he had a bent for mathematics. Where others of his age found the subject boring and spent more time either amusing themselves or preparing for a political life by concentrating on the classics, he had played with numbers. They had always fascinated him. He remembered Dr Beauregard saying...

No, forget that, forget everything to do with Dr Beauregard, particularly his daughter.

He could not, alas, forget what lay before him while he rapidly totted up the lines of figures. Now, having done so, he thought, nay, he was sure, that something was wrong. He added them up again, to reach the same answer and to turn back to an earlier sheet. He had just finished checking that when the door opened and Graves came in.

'Ah, m'lord, were you looking for me, or your father?'

'My father, but I find that I do have a question for you about these accounts.'

'Indeed, m'lord. I wonder what you think that you have found.'

'If I am not mistaken, Graves, there are some discrepancies here which I ought, perhaps, to discuss with you.'

Graves, who was well aware of the lack of consideration and respect which the Earl had for his heir, always addressed Russell in a manner which showed that he shared his master's opinion of him. He shook his head and there was a slight hint of mockery in his answer.

'I, too, have checked these figures and have discovered nothing untoward. I fear that you must be mistaken.'

'I, however, fear that I am not,' returned Russell in a voice which Graves had never heard before. 'You will do me the courtesy—'

Graves did the unforgivable: he not only interrupted his superior, but refused to do as he had been ordered. 'I am a busy man, m'lord. I have gone through these accounts and reports most carefully and find nothing wrong with them. May I suggest that you raise this matter with your father, who, I assure you, has the utmost faith in my ability and my integrity. He, too, always checks my work, and that done for him by Mr Arthur Shaw, his agent at Eddington, and so far all has been to his satisfaction.'

For a moment Russell was tempted to seize the impudent swine before him by his cravat and threaten to throttle him if he continued to refuse to discuss the matter. Only the thought that his father would be sure to take Graves's part prevented him. Yes, he would speak to his father, but he knew full well that his answer would be the same as his secretary's: a refusal to listen to what his son might have to say.

And so it proved.

His father had been quite jovial at dinner, so much so that over their port at the end Russell had felt able to lean forward and remark, 'By chance, sir, I saw the accounts from our estate at Eddington. I thought that I detected evidence of something wrong there. I wonder if you would allow me to—'

He stopped. His father's face was rapidly turning purple with anger, as it had done so often when he had been a boy, and his old helplessness in the face of that anger had returned to plague him.

'Come, Hadleigh, what do you have to say to me that is so urgent that you see fit to badger me over a glass of port? Why do you hesitate? Pray continue.'

'I was wondering, sir, whether you would allow me to go there and see if all is well. As I recall, neither you nor any other member of the family has visited Eddington, preferring our home in Norfolk instead. Perhaps it is time that one of us did. You are occupied in government, Ritchie is reorganising the estate he has inherited, so that leaves me.'

'So it does, Hadleigh, and why in the world you think yourself fit to go to Eddington and trouble my good agent there is beyond me.'

'But I am your heir. My name is Hadleigh, which is taken from a village not ten miles from Eddington and I have reason to believe, from looking at Mr Shaw's reports, that it might be useful if I visited the land to which I owe my name.'

Russell knew, by the expression on his father's face, that it was hopeless to continue: his final words confirmed that he was right.

'Confine yourself to matters of which you might know something,' his father almost snarled. 'Arthur Shaw is a good, hard-working fellow—unlike yourself—and I will not have him distressed by your meddling in affairs with which you have nothing to do, and of which you know nothing. That is my last word to you, sir.'

Russell was tempted to try to continue to plead his case. Unfortunately his scrutiny of the accounts and reports had been cut short by Graves so that he had been unable to gather enough evidence to convince his father that he had right on his side. He was also dismally aware that even if he had his father would continue to snub him. To press the matter further might, he feared, result in him saying something unforgivable, but what would be the point of that in the face of his father's intractability?

Fortunately he would shortly be out of the house for some little time, even if the errand he was sent on to Markham Hall was not one which he would have chosen. At least, while he was there, he might forget for a time that he was not only unloved, but also despised.

Mary Wardour moved a chess piece on the board which stood beside her before beginning to fill yet another sheet of papers with numbers and arcane signs. She was halfway down it before there was a respectful knock on the door.

She sighed. Gibbs, the butler, of course. What was it *now*? Was she never to have a whole afternoon of quiet and peace?

'Come in,' she called, laying down her quill pen on the stand before her.

Gibbs entered, looking rather more solemn than usual. 'A lady to see you, madam,' he began, but got no further before the lady in question pushed urgently past him.

'No fuss,' she trilled. 'I will announce myself. You may leave us.'

Mary gave an inward groan. Of all the people in the world who had to interrupt her just when she had thought that she was about to solve the tricky problem of the knight's move, this particular woman was the last she would have welcomed.

'Lady Leominster,' she said, rising. 'Pray be seated. I quite understand that your fame is such that you need no announcing.'

The Lady chose to interpret this as a compliment.

'Oh,' she declaimed, 'and I am sure that you will be delighted to have a short rest from your labours. I am, I own, a little surprised that you should frowst indoors on such a fine sunny day. But no matter, I have come to reprimand you, you naughty thing. It is a godmother's privilege, after all. You so seldom go into society these days that you are in danger of becoming that strange thing, a female hermit. This will never do. To that end I have prevailed on my cousin Markham to invite you to his grand house-party next week.'

Mary's expression was so mutinous that she raised her gloved hand. 'No, do not refuse me. It is high time that you married again.'

She put her head on one side and studied Mary's face as though it were a fine painting brought out for her to admire.

'Quite lovely,' she murmured. 'Yes, quite lovely. With that complexion, those dark eyes and even darker hair, any man would be proud to call you wife. And your fortune, of course. We mustn't forget that.'

How many more of society's taboos could the old trout ignore or break? Wasn't it enough that she had burst into the room without so much as a by your leave when Gibbs must have assured her that the mistress was not at home?

'Yes,' said the Lady, and then, as though issuing an order from on high, 'Yes, of course, you must marry again. Thirty is not such a great age for a widow.'

'Heaven forbid,' exclaimed Mary and goodness, where had that come from? After all, her marriage to Dr Henry Wardour had not been an unhappy one, despite the great difference in their ages and that it had been arranged between him and her father and presented to her as a *fait accompli*.

'Do admit that it must have been off-putting' exclaimed her tormentor, 'to marry an old fellow like Dean Wardour. I suppose that is why you feel condemned to carry on his work.' She waved a disparaging hand at Mary's pile of papers and the chessboard, having ignored another taboo—that one did not raise such intimate matters as the nature of a couple's married life with one of the partners in it.

She was so determined to make her point that she leaned over and struck Mary smartly on her writing hand with her glove before continuing with increased vigour. 'It's all very well for an old codger to trouble himself with such abstruse matters as mathematics.

A handsome young man would soon give you other things than *that* to think about. All the more reason, then, to accept the General's invitation.'

The only reason which Mary could think of which would make her accept the invitation was that it might enable her to dismiss the old harpy sitting opposite to her so that she could get back to continuing her late husband's work—which was also her work.

'How long would I be expected to remain at Markham Hall? Not too long, I trust.' If that grudging acceptance made her sound nearly as elderly as her late husband, then so be it. Fortunately it seemed to please the harpy if her crocodile's smile was any guide. And there's a couple of mixed metaphors which would have set my late husband grieving if he had heard me utter them!

'My dear, I am up in the boughs, I do assure you. I will inform the General myself that you will be delighted to renew your acquaintance with him and dear Angelica. You do remember dear Angelica, don't you?'

If dear Angelica was the girl who had sulked and moped her way through her come-out party, which Mary had unwillingly attended only after another session of bullying from the formidable lady opposite to her, then Mary remembered dear Angelica.

'Oh, yes, Lady Leominster. Of course I remember her.'

Who, indeed, could forget her tantrums? One could only pity the unfortunate man who might lead her to the altar. Fortunately again, the Lady took her utterance at face value, leaving Mary to regret being such a cat when thinking about, and speaking to, others, but happy that she was able to disguise her true feelings.

Her reward was a smacking kiss from the Lady, who rose and announced dramatically that she was off to persuade—by which she meant bully—her niece Phoebe Carstairs to visit Markham Hall as well. 'Another gel who does not know what's best for her,' she sighed.

If I knew what was best for me, then I wouldn't even consider putting a foot in Markham Hall, let alone visit it, was Mary's rebellious thought before resuming her work with a brain that was now more concerned with how she was to endure a week of total inanity when she might be enjoying herself by finally getting this confounded white knight to behave itself.

The black knight had been much more obliging.

Chapter One

Markham Hall was a truly beautiful building. It dated back to early Tudor times and was a dream of rich crimson and gold bricks and mellowed stone. All the later improvements, designed to increase the comfort of the family and the family's guests, had been added at the back so as not to spoil the illusion that the Hall was still an Early Tudor fortress that had been transformed into a mansion.

It was said that good Queen Bess had lived here for a short time when her Catholic sister Mary had been on the throne, but no proof of this had ever been offered except a contemporary portrait of her as a young woman which hung in a prominent place in the Great Hall.

A large number of visitors were arriving that late April afternoon. There were several carriages on the gravel sweep before the main doorway, which was actually a gate which opened on to a quadrangle around which the original house had been built. A bevy of footmen, grooms, coachmen and various servants were carrying luggage into the Hall.

Two footmen, one of them carrying a large green umbrella, ran forward to greet Mary's driver and to open the door of her chaise for her so that she might descend and be escorted indoors, together with her maid, Jennie, and her companion, Miss Eliza Truman, away from the light rain which had begun to fall.

Inside all was beauty and comfort. Mary's suite of rooms overlooked the rolling countryside where a folly in the shape of a ruined miniature tower stood high on a hill. Peter's Place, it was called, after a fabulous huntsman who had run with the Quorn Hunt, Leicestershire's pride, two hundred years ago.

Mary had scarcely time to change out of her travelling clothes into a light mauve gown and settle herself on the sofa in her little withdrawing room before the butler and a footman arrived with the tea-board.

'Lady Markham thought that you might care for some refreshment after your journey from Oxford. We dine late here in the Great Hall. The General likes to call it supper. The family and the guests assemble in the Stuart room at the sounding of the first bell and meet to converse before the meal.'

'Very civilised,' murmured Mary, eyeing the teapot and the biscuits known as Bosworth Jumbles.

The butler bowed. 'The General and his Lady send word that they hope that you will enjoy your first visit to Markham Hall. They are looking forward to meeting you again. Should any of your wants remain unsatisfied, then you have only to ring for the house-keeper, Mrs Marsden, and she will look after you.'

'Well,' said Miss Truman when the butler had bowed himself out, 'I have encountered less state when my late patron visited royalty. The tea, however, is most welcome.'

Mary had forgotten what visiting her wealthy contemporaries was like. She was not sure that she wished to live a life of such formality, if only for a fortnight. She had brought her work with her, but doubted whether she would ever find time to solve the latest problem which she had encountered. Her companion, though, obviously revelled in being waited upon so assiduously, suggesting that they might ring the housekeeper for more hot water when they had drunk their first cup.

The rain outside had stopped and the sun was shining. Mary said, 'Do so, by all means, but I should wish to take a walk in the grounds. If *you* wish to rest after our journey, there is no necessity for you to accompany me.'

'At least take your maid with you. It will be expected.'

Mary sighed. Peace and quiet was all that she wanted. 'Indeed, no,' she replied gently. 'I am sure that I shall be perfectly safe.'

'But who will carry your umbrella?'

'Why, I shall. Now, will you please excuse me? I shall not be long.'

Her umbrella in her hand, a short jacket over her dress, Mary made her way downstairs and out into the open after asking a somewhat surprised footman the best way into the gardens. He escorted her to a large door at the back. One path from it led to the stables, another to a series of formal gardens before taking a sharp turn into the Park itself.

The gardens had been improved during the last century, almost certainly by Capability Brown, Mary decided, before she ventured into the Park where she admired in turn the ornamental bridges, the artfully placed stands of trees, and the lake and its miniature stone quay where two small pleasure boats were moored.

Mary was compelled to admit that everything she saw pleased her, particularly the fact that she was the only person present to admire the unfolding vistas which Brown had so carefully devised. The scene before her was so beautiful that she began to wish that she had not left her sketchbook and water-colour paints at home. For a time she sat on a rustic bench placed exactly where the view before her was at its most lovely, and it was with a sigh that she rose and returned to the Hall.

A different route back through the formal gardens seemed a good idea until she heard men's voices coming from one of them when she approached the trellised archway which led into it. She was about to turn and retrace her steps in order to avoid them when she heard a voice which memory told her was familiar.

No! It could not be him! It could not!

He spoke again, and laughed at the end of a remark which set the rest of those present laughing, and this time she was sure that she recognised the voice of the man who had made it. Whatever the cost she must find out if her supposition was correct so that she might be prepared when she met him later at dinner. To have come upon him without warning would have challenged even her own calm self-control which was legendary among those who knew her.

She moved forward in order to look into the en-closed garden so that she might see the company as-sembled there, but not be seen by them. And yes, it was indeed Russell Hadleigh whom she thought that she had heard, whose pleasant baritone voice she had immediately recognised, even though it had been thirteen years since she had last listened to him speaking.

He was seated among a group of young men before an iron table on which stood, not tea, but bottles of port, Madeira and white wine. Unbuttoned might be the best word to describe them all, including Russell, Mary thought wryly, especially, perhaps, Russell. She also recognised Peregrine Markham, her host's son and heir, but the other young bloods were un-known to her. It was, perhaps, fortunate, she thought later, that she was not near enough to hear what they were saying—which, judging by the nature of their laughter, was not very proper.

Peregrine Markham suddenly stood up, which set her moving away before she could be seen and recognised. She had no wish to speak to any of them, let alone Russell Hadleigh, before she had had time to compose herself. Indeed, how she made her way safely back to her room she never knew, her brain was in such a whirl.

Mary had hoped never to see him again, and had she known that he, too, was going to be a visitor at Markham Hall, she would never have given in to Lady Leominster's bullying and agreed to go there. By great good luck, though, seeing him without his being aware of her presence meant that she could prepare herself for the inevitable moment when they would meet before dinner. It was essential that he should not know how much the mere sight of him still had the power to dis turb her.

The disturbance was, of course, ridiculous. How could his betrayal of her thirteen years ago still have the power to upset her? Worse than that, how could the mere glimpse of him set her heart beating so rapidly as though it were only a day since he had last walked away from her after giving her such a loving kiss?

The Judas kiss of treachery, she had thought later. The memory of it had caused her so many bitter tears until, as the years passed, she began to forget him and his broken promises—which made her present strong reaction to him so unexpected.

I grow maudlin, to allow him to affect me so powerfully. Why, I even started to ask myself whether he would recognise me, as I recognised him. Oh, he has changed. He is no longer a handsome, slim boy, but a man with a cynical face, all that charming innocence which he once possessed has quite gone.

'My dear, have you been over-exerting yourself?' asked her companion when she re-entered their drawing-room. 'You look quite flushed. I do believe that it was a mistake to undertake a walk after a hard day's travelling.'

'Not at all,' Mary replied, a little distressed that her recent experience had overset her to the degree that Miss Truman was able to remark upon it. 'What you are seeing is merely the glow of exercise'—and *what a lie that was!* 'The grounds are quite remarkable and worthy of the brush of a master painter.'

'Indeed,' said Miss Truman, quite deceived by this explanation. 'I have read about their excellence, and now I am privileged to enjoy it. I have also heard that the General's chef is known for his excellence and I am looking forward to dinner—or supper, as always he calls it—with the keenest anticipation.'

Would that I were, was Mary's internal reaction to that!

Russell Hadleigh was not feeling much keen anticipation, either. He had not yet met the young woman whom his father, and hers, intended that he should marry, but was shortly about to do so. He had met her brother, Peregrine, always known to his associates as Perry, several times before, and had taken him in mild dislike. The notion of him as a brother-in-law did not attract.

Perry Markham was a gambler who took losing badly. Despite his recent bout at the tables, gambling was not an addiction with Russell. He could take it or leave it. It occasionally served to relieve a little his boredom with his empty existence. He could not understand a man allowing it to dominate his life as Perry Markham allowed it to dominate his. He wondered whether the General knew exactly how much his son was losing at the tables—and how much he was drinking to cover the pain of his losses there.

Russell had forsworn drinking that afternoon for the amusement of watching the others indulge themselves overmuch. It was during a pause in the idle conversation of young fellows with too much time on their hands, and too little to do in it, that he had seen a female hovering near the arch which led into the garden in which they sat. He could not quite see her face, but he thought that she looked young—or had he hoped that?

He *had* hoped that she might enter and bring a little brightness to an afternoon which was dull despite the sun which had begun to smile on them all. Alas, the sight of so many young fools—and he counted himself among them—must have caused her to turn away and deprive them of the pleasure of her presence.

Now his valet was dressing him for the evening with his usual loving care. It was an odd existence, he thought, which turned so much on dress and the other minor minutiae of a man's existence. He had recently asked his father if, when the next election came along, he might be allowed to stand at one of the seats which the family controlled—a small borough whose name gave him his title. To become an MP would give him an interest in life and allow him to bring some experience of power and management to the time when he finally inherited.

'You are not ready to do that, sir. Nor steady enough,' his father had growled at him.

'I am older than Lord Granville was when he first went into Parliament, and quite as steady,' he had replied.

'But you are not Lord Granville,' his father had snorted.

What could he say to that, other than, 'But I understand that he was only in his early twenties when he became an MP and I am over thirty. By then he had been an Ambassador to Russia.'

This did not answer, either. He wondered afterwards why his father had taken him in such dislike that he would not give him the opportunities which other heirs to noble names had been offered. Had what had happened thirteen years ago been enough to damn him as a serious person? Surely not—but the thought was always there.

Instead he was at Markham Hall to propose marriage to a young woman whom the *on dits* said was a frivolous, flighty piece—and that solely to please his father and not himself. Well, he was about to find out whether the *on dits* spoke truly or were simply baseless rumours.

Downstairs he found himself before the Tudor drawing room which opened on to the Great Hall where the General and Lady Markham, Perry and Angelica standing beside them, were receiving their guests. Angelica was pretty enough and fortunately bore little resemblance to her brother Perry, whose looks were not of the first stare, to say the least.

'I understand that you are acquainted with my son, Peregrine,' the General said, 'but I believe that you have not yet been introduced to my daughter, Angelica.'

Russell allowed that he had not and turned his attention to her—to find that she was a beauty in the current mode, with bright blue eyes, flaxen ringlets and a prettily rounded figure beneath a pink silk frock decorated with cream rosebuds. She offered a curtsy to his low bow and simpered at him, saying in a little girl's fluting voice, 'So happy to meet you at last, Lord Hadleigh. I have heard much of you from my brother.'

Had she, indeed? And was that a recommendation or not?

'And I am delighted to meet you, Miss Markham.'

'Oh, please call her Angelica,' interrupted Lady Markham cordially. 'We are all friends here, I trust.'

'Angelica.' He smiled and bowed again. 'So I must be Russell.'

It was the least he could say. He could only wonder what her conversation would be like. Well, he would shortly find out, for his valet had informed him that the Servants' Hall had it that he was to sit next to her at dinner. Her conversation? Had he run mad? Persons of his rank married young women for their dowry, not their conversation.

He gave a bow and a nod to Perry, who also simpered at him. After the General and his Lady's enthusiastic reception of him, Russell dismally realised that they, and his father, and now Perry, had settled between them that he was to marry Angelica. He wondered what all the hurry was about.

At last he was free to enter the drawing room, which was rapidly filling up with the General's guests, most of whom knew one another. It was his duty to be pleasant to the other guests, and one thing which Russell did know was how to be pleasant. He thought that he might even be able to do it in his sleep!

It was when he had finished talking to the Honourable Mrs Robert Chevenix, whose husband was a crony of his father's, that he saw a young woman sitting beside a middle-aged female who was obviously her companion. The young woman's dark head was turned away from him, but there was something strangely familiar about her whole posture. It was not until she turned towards him, and he at last saw her face, that he knew who she was.

Mary Beauregard! Mary, his lost love whom he had last seen thirteen years ago. Somewhat to his surprise, she was still very much like the young girl he had once known. Oh, her face had matured, but in the doing had served only to add to her quiet beauty, not detract from it. Her skin was as creamy as he remembered it, and her dark eyes...

Those dark eyes in which he had once drowned— he would never forget them. Those eyes that, alas, were faithless like the lips which had promised him eternal love when he had last seen her. An eternal love which had only lasted a week.

Now, thirteen years later, he ought to be able to look at her coldly without the sight of her enchanting him as it had once done, but he couldn't, and what sort of man did that make of him? It was a question which he did not immediately answer, because at that moment she saw him. Instead, a new question sprang into his mind.

What did she see when she looked at him?

Was she as inwardly disturbed as he was?

Only the eye of love, or of hate, could detect the faintest quiver of her mouth, or the hand which shook when she raised it to smooth down the fichu of her dowdy dress, but Russell saw both telltale signs and wondered which of the two contrary emotions was afflicting him and, quite possibly, her.

He bowed, his face, usually so mobile, a mask— the impassive mask which he wore when he chose to play cards. He said as coolly and distantly as common politeness would allow, no more, no less, 'Mrs Wardour, I believe. We meet again after many years.'

Mary looked up at him. Near to, as he had seen the changes time had wrought in her, she saw more plainly those which had altered him. One thing that struck her again was the cynicism written on his face, in the curl of his lip, in the knowing eyes which looked at her, and seemed to dismiss her.

'Yes,' she replied, as cool as he. 'I am, however, now the widow of Dr Henry Wardour.'

This statement shocked Russell out of his deliberately chosen indifference to her and the company in which they found themselves.

'I must commiserate with you upon his death, he must have been a good age.'

'But not so very old,' she riposted. Mary would never have supposed that she could outface her one-time love to the point where she retained her self-control and he did not. 'He was only in his early fifties. Such a difference in age on marriage is a commonplace in our society. Indeed, I gather that you are here invited here as a possible suitor for Miss Markham so I find your surprise at my marriage a little misplaced.'

What in the world had happened to the ardent young woman whom he had once loved that she could speak to him in the tones of a cold shrew?

'Your rebuke is a just one,' he admitted, and could not say more, for at that point they were joined by Perry Markham, since the Markhams' reception line had ended and dinner was almost upon them.

'So, Hadleigh, you have already made yourself known to Mrs Wardour, but then, no pretty woman ever fails to gain your attention, eh,' and he poked a stiff finger into Russell's ribs which set him moving away.

'You mistake, Markham. Mrs Wardour and I knew one another many years ago—and we were renewing an old acquaintance, were we not?'

Mary's response to that was to offer both men a stiff smile.

'Too many years ago for us to be able to claim that we are old friends,' she said.

If this frosty answer surprised Perry Markham it did not surprise Russell.

'Well, in that case, old fellow,' went on Perry, smiling at Mary, 'I shall not be encroaching on a long-time friendship if I inform you that I am to escort Mrs Wardour into dinner. But fear not, you are to take in my sister Angelica, who cannot wait to further her acquaintance with you. She will be along any moment to claim you, so you will forgive me if I ask Mrs Wardour to join me so that I may show her my father's famous collection of porcelain.'

Both Russell and Mary were only too pleased to end their unwanted and unhappy tête-à-tête—with the exception that Mary had no wish to become more intimate with Perry, and Russell was not greatly looking forward to squiring Angelica, whom he suspected was exactly the kind of vacuous young creature whom he had always tried to avoid.

However, they both separately thought that in an imperfect world one cannot always have exactly what one wants—which was a conclusion which they both took into dinner with them!

The Great Hall was justly named. It was hung with faded banners covered with the honours of bygone battles. The dining table ran the length of the room before a giant hearth. On the wall facing the hearth were placed antique Tudor settles before low wooden tables. Flambeaux provided light even on this spring evening for the Hall's windows were high and small and their glass panes were dull with age. All in all it was scarcely a friendly place, and the formality which seemed a feature of the Markham household was very present in it.

Matters were not helped for Russell by Angelica having been placed on his left hand and Mary on his right. Mary had Perry Markham on her right and he was monopolising her attention while Angelica was doing the same for Russell. Unfortunately, her conversational powers were as limited as he had feared.

Having assured her that he had been to Astley's Amphitheatre, the home of horses, and acrobatics, but not lately, he then had to confess that he had not been overly impressed with Master Betty, the famous boy actor. Yes, he had seen the ballet at the Opera House, but no, he was not greatly taken by that either.

'What, then, do you prefer?' she simpered at him.

'Shakespeare,' he told her, 'in particular when Kemble plays the great parts, such as Othello, Hamlet and Macbeth, but his brother Charles is also admirable in lighter roles.'

'Oh, Shakespeare!' She pouted. 'I was taken to see *Macbeth* in my come-out year. What a disappointment! Everyone was ranting at everyone else and people were being killed on stage. I wonder that anyone should pay to go to see such dreadful things.'

She ended with a delicate shudder and a widening of her blue eyes. 'On the other hand, I quite liked *As You Like It* when they made it into a pantomime. The clowns were so funny, much better than all that boring talk. Have you visited the Prince Regent's home at Brighton? They say it is most fantastic. I confess that I was greatly surprised when I was presented to him. He was so fat and ugly—and so old. I cannot abide old men and women.'

'Yes,' Russell said, 'I have visited the Pavilion and quite like it. As for the Regent being old, I fear that, if we live long enough, we all come to that in the end.'

Angelica's shudder was a prolonged one this time. 'Pray do not let us speak of it. Tell me, have you read *The Secret of Harrenden Castle*? Now there is a horrid book which I do like—you never actually *see* the bodies in it.'

So this was the woman whom his father wished him to marry! Had he given up his lively Caroline for this vacuous young thing? He thought of his brother's wife Pandora with her frank ways and her keen interest in everything about her. Now *there* was a treasure if there ever was one, even if she were something of a surprising treasure for quiet Ritchie to have won.

Angelica, who, to give her her due, was finding it as difficult to talk to Lord Hadleigh as Lord Hadleigh was finding it difficult to listen to her, gave up at this point. Why did her papa wish her to marry this dull old man? She had imagined that he might be a jolly fellow like Perry and his friends, but no such thing. He was as solemn as a judge and as dreary as the parson on Sunday morning when he was droning on and on in his sermon.

All in all, it was a great relief for them both when the dinner ended and the ladies withdrew to leave the gentlemen to their cigars and their port. But not before Russell, the devil prompting him, had leaned sideways to whisper in Mary's pretty little ear, 'Are you finding all this as tedious as I am?'

Mary, who had been as bored by Perry as Russell had been by his sister, said sharply, 'Indeed not, and if I were it would be a gross insult to our hosts' hospitality to say so.'

Russell bowed his head and murmured, 'Rightly rebuked. You were always much more aware of the niceties of life than I was.'

'Was I, m'lord? I fear that I have quite forgot the details of any conversations which we might once have had,' and she turned away from him to address Perry again, as though to speak to him was wearisome.

The anger which seemed to overcome Russell these days was upon him again. He murmured to her back, 'Now, madam, that I do not believe, nor should you ask me to believe it.'

Mary's head swung sharply round. 'What you might believe, m'lord, is a matter of total indifference to me. Pray allow that to terminate our conversation,' and she turned away from him again to address a bemused Perry.

'I had not understood that you were so well-acquainted with Lord Hadleigh, Mrs Wardour.'

'Once, long ago,' she replied as carelessly as she could, and, more to punish Russell than because she wished to ingratiate herself with Perry Markham, added, most graciously, 'Pray call me Mary, Mr Markham.'

'Only if you will address me as Perry,' he responded gallantly.

Angelica had found the young Honourable Thomas Bertram, known by his friends as the Hon. Tom, to be a more amusing dinner companion than Russell, who now whispered into Mary's ear, 'If we are all to be so informal, Mrs Wardour, then you might oblige me by calling me Russell—as you once did.'

She swung round again, to murmur under her breath so that Perry might not catch what she was saying, 'Certainly not, you forfeited that right long ago. Pray cease to badger me: it is not the act of a gentleman to twit a lady so mercilessly.'

Well, that was that, was it not? And Russell, who was already regretting his baiting of Mary, said slowly, 'I apologise, Mrs Wardour, but the temptation to address you as I might once have done was too great for me.'

How dare he? How dare he after he had treated her so lightly all those years ago! Mary turned away from him for the last time, saying, 'I would be extremely happy, m'lord, if you refrained from addressing me at all,' and gave Perry her whole attention for the rest of the dinner.

She would not be drawn into conversation with him, not now, or ever again. He deserved nothing from her, and nothing was all that he would get. She had done her duty to her hosts by speaking to him at all and from this evening onward she would be careful to avoid his company.

Russell ate the rest of his dinner in silence and it might as well have been straw that he was consuming. Angelica offered him the odd word now and then, and it was a great relief when the meal ended, the ladies retired, cigars were offered, and the port began to circulate.

Talk became general, and, as Mary had earlier thought, the men being alone together it became unbuttoned. The younger men at the bottom of the table began to talk prize-fighting, their seniors, politics. Russell, caught between the two, said nothing.

Presently Perry, avoiding his father's eye, leaned forward and said to his fellows, *sub rosa*, as it were, 'To avoid the stifling dullness of the Leicestershire countryside in spring I have two diversions to offer you, gentlemen. Tomorrow a Luddite is to be hanged at Loughborough for an attempt on the life of a local mill-owner. I thought that we might make up a party and compare how these matters are organised in the country compared with those in town.

'On the following day there is to be a mill not far from here between two bruisers, both from London. One is Sam Tottridge, who gave Tom Cribb a hard time before he lost—and Tom's a tough customer, being champion of England. T'other is a man of colour, known as Yankee Samson because he comes from some godforsaken corner of the States. What say we make up another party to watch that? I'll run a book on the match if that is agreeable to you all.'

He turned to Russell, who had sat there quietly trying to make his one glass of port last until it was time to join the ladies. 'How about you, Hadleigh? Are you game?'

'Not for the hanging,' said Russell as coolly as he could in an effort not to give offence to his host's son. 'I find no pleasure in watching a man being strangled to death to the cheers of his fellows, particularly when the man in question is a poor devil who has lost his livelihood. As for the boxing match, I shall decide that on the day. I prefer to put the gloves on myself occasionally rather than applaud a man who does it for me.'

'Oh, well, suit yourself, Hadleigh. Tottridge is worth watching, believe me, and the black has a good reputation, too. As for murdering Luddites, I beg to disagree with you there. Hanging's too good for them. Not turning parson, are you?'

It was plain that Perry Markham had drunk more than he ought. Russell smiled. 'Not at all. Merely growing old, I suppose.'

'Doesn't seem to take others that way. Never mind, though. You can always stay at home with the ladies and play backgammon and help to wind their wool for them.'

Several of Perry's hangers-on laughed sycophantically at this. Russell merely smiled, and answered him, again pleasantly, 'What a splendid notion, Markham. I thank you for your suggestions on how to pass my time. You have, I believe, a good library, and that might serve to catch my interest.'

Several of his hearers sniggered at this, and Russell was relieved that the General ended this rather unpleasant conversation by announcing briskly, 'Time to join the ladies. They will be wondering what has become of us.'

I doubt that, thought Russell, watching the rest of the party stagger rather uncertainly towards the drawing room, although some of them might welcome our arrival to save them from boredom.

I also wonder whether Mary will be kinder to me after dinner than she was during it!

Chapter Two

Russell was among the last to arrive in the drawing room where some of the ladies were busily talking, others were playing a hand of whist, and the quieter souls were happily engaged in their canvas work, Mary Wardour among them.

There was a chair near to her and on impulse he walked towards it, and pulled it round so that he half-faced her and her companion, who was also stitching purposefully away. Thus placed, he had quite deliberately trapped her into a situation where their conversation would be so public that she would be loath to rebuke or reprimand him as she had done at dinner.

'Mrs Wardour,' he said, smiling at her.

Mary looked up at him and, despite herself, it was as though something wrenched inside her. She was a girl of seventeen again and her young lover was smiling at her: his mouth had a little curl at the end and his eyes...

She shook her head. What in the world was she thinking of? Lord Hadleigh was no longer her young lover and she had tried to forget him and all his

46

works. Alas, here in this crowded room, surrounded by the curious, careless and the malicious, she must say and do nothing which would damage her own reputation.

'Lord Hadleigh?' she said and inclined her head.

'Mrs Wardour,' he said again, as though he were memorising her name, 'we were well-acquainted long ago, I believe, and we meet again after many years. I think that we should be doing one another a kindness if, from now on, we behaved as though we were meeting for the first time.'

Was he drunk, to make such a monstrous proposition to her? He looked and sounded sober, unlike Perry Markham, who had obviously over-indulged and was lurching into the room and now trying to avoid her, probably as the result of finding her a dull partner at dinner since she had shown no interest in racing or the delights of the London stage.

Russell Hadleigh was plainly waiting for an answer from her. What could she say to him? Not what she wished to, here in public, that was for sure. To have exclaimed, 'Go away and cease to trouble me,' would certainly set society's tongues a-wagging, and no mistake!

Instead she said, as coolly as she could. 'If that is what you wish, m'lord, it would only be civil of me to agree to such a polite request.'

'Splendid,' was Russell's answer to this rather cold concession. He leaned forward a little confidentially, adding as he did so, 'Then if I proposed that we should take a circuit of the picture gallery together, you would not refuse me, I trust. I understand that you have visited Markham Hall before and would surely be qualified to show its treasures to me.'

'I, m'lord?' Mary could not help replying. 'Would it not be more appropriate for you to ask Miss Markham to display the family treasures? After all, I gather that she is the real reason you are here.'

Good God! Had rumour already given Angelica Markham to him as a bride? Rumour also said that Mary Wardour had been invited for Perry Markham's sake. Was that as false as the one relating to Angelica? If he had been dubious about making her Lady Hadleigh before he had met her, now that he had, any dubiety he had previously experienced had been reinforced: he had not the slightest intention of marrying the girl. He was only too happy that the moment the Hon. Tom Bertram had arrived in the drawing room Angelica had made a dead set at him. They were each well suited to the other.

'Oh,' he said, as carelessly as he could, 'you should take no note of gossip of that nature. I am here—why am I here?' he continued. 'I am not quite sure, but looking for a bride is far from my mind at the moment,' and he gave her his most dazzling smile again, a smile which poor Mary remembered only too well.

'Nor am I looking for a husband,' returned Mary shrewdly, for she knew full well why she had been invited and Perry Markham was certainly not to her taste.

Miss Truman, who had been listening to their odd conversation with some interest, now took a hand in it.

'I think, my dear,' she said to Mary, a light note in her voice, 'that it would only be proper to introduce me to Lord Hadleigh, seeing that you have had such a long acquaintance with him.'

Now, what to say to that? was Mary's somewhat frantic thought. She could scarcely tell her companion the unhappy truth of her first acquaintance with Russell, who had now risen to his feet, waiting for the introduction which would inevitably follow.

The rapport between him and Mary, once so strong, but now almost forgotten, was strongly revived. He grasped that she was somewhat overset by her companion's innocently made remark and, however badly she might have treated him in the past, he had no desire to embarrass her in the present.

He bowed to both women. 'My friendship with Mrs Wardour was long ago, when we were little more than children. We have, alas, seen nothing of one another for many years, until this very day.'

Mary and Miss Truman both rose on that, and Mary, thankful for Russell's intervention, if for nothing else, did the pretty by making her companion known to him.

'I believe, m'lord,' Miss Truman said, 'that I had the honour, some years ago, of being for a short time the companion of your brother Richard's wife, then Miss Pandora Compton. Circumstances parted us and we lost touch. I trust that she is in health.'

'Very much so. She is now the mother of a lively and handsome boy.'

'Which does not surprise me,' Miss Truman said, 'since my dear Pandora is both lively and handsome herself.'

Russell gave a smile of such pleasure on hearing this that Mary was bitten by a sudden sharp and unwanted pang. What in the world would make her indulge in such folly as being jealous of the unknown Pandora Chancellor? she asked herself furiously. Lord Hadleigh could compliment the whole female sex and bed whom he chose. It was no business of hers if he admired his brother's wife. But, alas, it seemed it still was, since she was being weak-minded enough to allow him to charm her all over again. It was as though thirteen years had never passed.

'Indeed,' he replied, serious now.

'And I am sure that my dear Mary would be happy to show you the picture gallery. She is extremely knowledgeable about such matters. You could not have a better guide.'

It was quite plain to both her hearers that Miss Truman was busy matchmaking. She had already decided that Perry Markham was not a person whom she could recommend her employer to marry. Lord Hadleigh, now, was quite a different matter. Not only was he handsome, but she had already been informed that he had been decent enough to refuse to join the party which was attending the hanging on the morrow while, on the other hand, the wretched Perry was the ringleader in the unhappy affair.

As for Mary, after such a recommendation from Miss Truman, she had no choice but to agree to Russell Hadleigh's wish to have her as his escort and the pair of them rose to carry out Miss Truman's bidding.

The eyes of most of the room watched them leave it. Later, General Markham was to say fiercely to his son when he cornered him in his room, 'You must know how essential it is that you offer for Mary Wardour. Most of our problems would be solved by such a marriage. But instead of fixing your sights on her, you fool about with a pack of young men whom you have brought here against my wishes. As a result of that, you have allowed Hadleigh to corner her when I wished to fix his interest on Angelica. Do you wish to live permanently in Queer Street?'

Perry hissed back at his father, 'May I remind you, sir, that it was not I who lost the family's money by gambling on Boney winning at Waterloo, but it is I who will have to pay for it by marrying a bluestocking of a widow who is older than I am and has no interest in any of the things which amuse me.'

'Delay much longer in offering for her,' his father exclaimed, trying to goad his son into doing as he wished, 'and the whole world will soon know that we are bankrupt. So far I have been successful in staving off ruin, but my creditors are growing weary of waiting for pay day.

'As for her lack of interest in your idle life, what has that to do with not wishing to marry her? Get her with an heir or two and you and she may go your own separate ways. No need to wish to play Romeo and Juliet together. After all, I am the heir to my cousin, Viscount Bulcote, and since, unfortunately, he is as poor as a church mouse, too, we have no salvation there. On the other hand, Mrs Wardour might care to be called Lady Bulcote—if Russell Hadleigh hasn't snapped her up first.'

Russell Hadleigh wasn't snapping anyone up, least of all Mary Wardour. In fact, he wasn't sure exactly what he was about. He had told himself to avoid her, that he had nothing more to say to her, nor could she have anything to say to him, and yet, when dinner was over, the mere sight of her had set him mooning after her as though he had been twenty again!

Once they were out of the room and in the vast Entrance Hall, one door of which led to the picture gallery, Mary turned to him and said in the frostiest tones she could summon up. 'You can really have little wish to spend the next half-hour in my company inspecting paintings about which you must care little. May I suggest that we part—possibly to return to our suites and then, after a decent interval, to the drawing room.'

'Indeed not,' was his answer to that. 'Not only do I have no wish to return to the drawing room, other than in your company, but I do wish to see the General's paintings. I missed the Grand Tour because of the war, my Oxford education was ended prematurely for a reason of which you are well aware, and, as I grow older, I have become determined to fix my interest on other pursuits than gambling, drinking and attending race meetings and boxing mills. An idle life is beginning to tire me.'

Whatever could he mean by speaking of his education ending prematurely for a reason which she well knew? Had he not ended it himself when he had abandoned her so cruelly?

She was about to tell him that in no uncertain terms when something about him stopped her. The empathy for her which Russell had experienced a little while ago—that memory of their lost happy time together—now overcame her. Whatever else, she knew that he was not lying to her. After all these years he wanted her company. Not only that, his interest in the paintings was genuine, not a trick to enable him to begin deceiving her all over again.

'Very well, since you put it so movingly, Lord Hadleigh, I will do as you ask. You must, however, remember your request that we meet as strangers and practise a self-denying ordinance, as the saying has it. Refer to the past again—however remotely—and I will leave you at once.'

'So noted,' he replied in a comic parody of a clerk registering the commands of his superior, and again it was as though the years had rolled back and he was teasing her as he had done then. 'Lead on, Mrs Wardour. You may begin my education.'

He had not been lying to her when he had said that he wished to see the contents of the picture gallery, or else he was a superb actor. He showed a keen interest in the paintings, which ranged from a fourteenth-century panel of the Madonna and Child by a pupil of Duccio to the latest works of the English masters. Lawrence had painted the General himself and they debated briefly whether he deserved to stand alongside the great masters of the past.

'Reynolds, perhaps, or Gainsborough at his best may merit such an honour,' was Russell's verdict, 'but Lawrence is an extremely competent journeyman, no more.'

'I think that you know more about painting, Lord Hadleigh, than you suggested earlier.'

'That is my brother Ritchie's influence,' he confessed. 'He is a gifted water-colourist—but then he is a gifted everything, unlike his slightly older brother.'

There was no bitterness in Russell's words, nor in his voice, but there was something there which told Mary not of envy or of jealousy, but of a certain wistfulness, of something missed and lost.

'I have not had the good fortune to meet your brother,' Mary said, surprised at how easy talking to Russell had become. 'I remember that he went to Oxford a few years before you when I was still little more than a child.

'Oh, few people have met him. He resigned from the Army after Waterloo in order to restore the estate which had been left him while he was still a serving officer. He spends most of his time in the country and visits London rarely. As for Oxford, he was excessively precocious and was only fifteen when he matriculated. My father also thought it best that we did not attend there at the same time.'

Again there was that odd note when he referred to his brother. A mixture of pride and something else, hard to judge.

By now they had completed their tour. Russell motioned to a long sofa which stood in front of one of the glories of the collection: a Tintoretto showing the god Jupiter in the shape of a bull abducting Io. The sky above them was a miracle of colour.

Once seated, Russell stared at the painting and a thought which was difficult to resist popped into his head. I ought to have behaved like Jupiter all those years ago and carried Mary off before she had time to change her mind about me. Had I done so, we should not now be sitting primly side by side—and like Ritchie I might be starting a little family of my own.

What would happen if I tried to kiss her now— which would be much less than Jupiter did to Io, of course—but it would serve for a new beginning with her. Merely to sit by her has my unrepentant body behaving as though I am twenty again.

No, I must not! I promised to behave myself, and behave myself I will.

Mary, seated beside him, her hands in her lap, and her mind a whirl of conflicting sensations, was also affected by the painting's subject. She tried to drive both memory and desire from her. In an effort to banish the unwanted feelings which were beginning to overwhelm her, she turned towards Russell in order to say something banal to him which would return her wandering senses to their proper condition of calm self-control.

She began to speak.

Only to discover that Russell was also turning to her and also beginning to speak.

What they were about to say was never to be known.

As many times before in their lost past when they had found themselves similarly afflicted, they began to laugh. Laughter released them from the unnatural state in which they had been living since they had found one another again.

Russell gave a little cry, something between a moan and an exclamation of exaltation, and put one arm around her. With the other he tipped her face towards him and began to kiss her on the lips. Mary responded by kissing him ardently back. The kiss, which had, at first, been a gentle one, began to change its nature and ascend into passion. That, and their sudden unwanted recollection that they were in a public room where they might be discovered by their fellow guests at any moment, ended the kiss abruptly and left them staring into each other's eyes aghast.

Laughter and passion had alike flown away.

'Forgive me,' said Russell hoarsely.

'I cannot forgive myself, let alone you,' Mary said breathlessly. 'Whatever possessed me to make me start kissing you back? No, do not speak of the past,' she went on, 'I see by your expression that you are about to.'

Well, that was true enough, particularly since the present had become unbearable. It was a long time since merely the presence of a woman had roused Russell so rapidly. Even with Caroline true passion had been missing—something which explained why their relationship had deteriorated so rapidly.

He thought of Ritchie's eyes following Pandora around the room: his rapt expression when she had been cuddling their child. He cursed himself. What was the matter with him that Ritchie and his doings seemed to exist as some kind of reproach to his own empty existence?

Mary saw his face change and, before she could stop herself, put a hand on his arm.

'What is it, Russell? What troubles you?'

'Nothing,' he said abruptly. 'Only that I am selfish to tease you so, and to jump on you just now, without warning. Whatever could you think of me?'

Honesty won, as it usually did with Mary. 'I thought how much I was enjoying being jumped on.

I suppose that means that I wasn't really thinking of anything at all. Until I remembered our situation.'

Russell began to laugh and his body began to behave itself. He remembered that one of the reasons why he had loved Mary was her transparent honesty—which made her subsequent behaviour so surprising.

'You did not find me repellent, then?'

Truth won again. 'No, I never did.'

The smile which she gave him served to set his recovering body on edge once more.

This would never do. Russell rose, put out his right hand, said, 'Allow me,' and lifted her. 'Is it your wish that I escort you to the drawing room?'

Before Mary could answer him, the door to the gallery was opened by Perry Markham, followed by the Hon. Tom Bertram and a giggling Angelica.

Perry made straight for them, saying, his voice lurching like his walk, 'We have come to see what could be occupying you so. Not the paintings apparently, Hadleigh, since you had your back to them.'

'On the contrary,' said Russell, raising the quizzing glass which he rarely used and inspecting Perry through it. 'I have been admiring your Duccio, a very rare specimen that, and the Tintoretto behind me. That, too, is a nonpareil, or so both my brother and Mrs Wardour assure me. For my part, I prefer something less showy, like the tiny Watteau—a great favourite of yours, I dare swear.'

Perry goggled at him. Dutch O, What HO, and Tint O—whoever he was! What in the world was the fellow spouting about? Perry Markham might be the heir to rooms full of rare paintings, but he knew nothing about any of them.

'You see how well Mrs Wardour has been instructing me,' continued Russell sweetly, using all the charm for which he was justly famous. 'Pray do tell me, which is *your* favourite painting? I would be delighted to inspect it.'

Perry gazed wildly around the room before pointing at a Fragonard oil of a pretty courtesan and saying, 'Oh, that, I suppose.'

'Really,' teased Russell, swinging around and bringing his glass to bear on it. 'I can't read the painter's name from here. Do tell me who he is.'

Perry continued to goggle helplessly at him. Mary, to save the poor wretch from further embarrassment, said helpfully, 'It's by Fragonard and its title is *Girl with One Slipper.*'

The Hon. Tom, not so fuddled as his host's son, exclaimed, 'I like it, but it's a trifle warm, is it not? Shouldn't be hung where the ladies can see it.'

'Really!' exclaimed a tittering Angelica, who was behaving as though she, too, had spent the evening drinking, 'Do let me look,' and she swayed over to the painting, past the amused Russell and inspected it closely.

'It looks quite ordinary,' she announced disappointedly.

Mary, whose attempt to spare Perry from Russell's naughtiness had backfired badly, and who was determined to reprimand him in private for roasting the poor ignoramus so mercilessly, announced, 'Oh, dear, Lord Hadleigh, I am most dreadfully thirsty. I should imagine that by now lemonade and other light refreshments will be being served.'

'Quite so,' agreed the Hon. Tom. 'We came here to get away from them.'

Russell, bent towards her and put out a gallant arm. 'Allow me, Mrs Wardour. I, too, feel in need of light refreshments. I have no wish to be overset by the heavy.'

'Stop it,' Mary hissed furiously into his ear when she took his arm. 'I am having difficulty in keeping a straight face while you engage in your nonsense— and he is our host's son.'

'Delighted to oblige you,' Russell almost carolled, so pleased was he that Mary was at last treating him as a fellow human being and not an obstruction in her path. 'You must continue to instruct me in proper conduct during the remainder of my stay here, most improving, exactly what I need.'

'Did he really mean that?' asked a baffled Angelica when Russell and Mary had disappeared through the door. She was the only one who had heard Russell's reply to Mary. Fortunately, she had not heard Mary's remark which had provoked it.

'Mean what?' asked Perry, who was now fuddled in a double sense. Firstly through the amount he had drunk and secondly through Russell's nonsense about painting and artists.

'About Mrs Wardour instructing him.'

Perry shook his head—and then wished he hadn't. He thought that it might be about to fall off. The Hon. Tom, who was uneducated, but not a fool, said slowly, 'He didn't mean any of it. He was roasting us.'

'Was he, by God!' exclaimed Perry making a staggering run for the door. 'I'll teach him what's what and no mistake.'

'No, you won't,' said the Hon. Tom. 'In the condition you're in he'd make mincemeat of you. They say he's as good with the gloves, the foils and the pistols as that brother of his. Besides, you'd only be proclaiming that he'd riled you. Refuse him the satisfaction. What's more, your pa wouldn't like it.'

'Pa never likes anything Perry does,' offered Angelica helpfully.

'There!' said the Hon. Tom. 'Leave it. You'll have forgotten everything by morning, I dare swear.'

'He always has done before,' was Angelica's brutal finale to the whole unhappy encounter. Did they really want her to marry someone who spent his time admiring paintings?

Which, if Mary and Russell had heard her, would have had them agreeing that it was the most sensible thing anyone by the name of Markham had said, or thought, all night!

* * *

'That was really exceedingly naughty of you,' Mary told Russell reprovingly, once they were safely out of the picture gallery. 'You must have gathered by now what a nodcock Perry Markham is, but there was no need to have made a fool of him quite so mercilessly.'

'No?' replied Russell, haughty eyebrows raised. 'He began the whole wretched business by jeering at me and mocking me, most mercilessly, after dinner for not wishing to see that poor wretch hanged tomorrow. I was only giving him a taste of his own medicine—and before two others, not before the entire assembled men of the company. I consider that he got off lightly—but I promise not to do it again if it distressed you.'

'And you really are not going to watch the hanging tomorrow?'

'By no means. I take no pleasure in behaving like the ancient Romans in the Colosseum who cheerfully watched gladiators slaughter one another, even if I do admire their architecture and their writings. By the by, I hope that none of the ladies will be in the party, although I suspect that quite a number of women will be present.'

Mary shuddered. 'It is bad enough speaking about it without being there. Will all the men be going?'

'Most, I suspect. But let us speak of more pleasant things before we rejoin the others.'

'Indeed. There is one question which I should dearly like to ask you, and that is, did you ever meet

Lord Byron before he started out on his travels again?'

'Several times. I heard him make his speech in the Lords on behalf of the hand-loom weavers who were losing their livelihood because of the new machines. I thought it very fine. I also think it is a great pity that he never bent his energies more towards politics than pleasure. After all, he is his own man, unlike others who have their choices made for them. I agree that he writes some immortal poetry, but his private life of unbridled pleasure does not bear inspection. I gather that now he is in Europe he still mixes writing divine poetry with living a sybaritic life.'

How easy, Mary mused later, while retiring for the night, it had been for them to fall back into the half-serious, half-jesting mode of conversation which they had enjoyed before their affair had come to its sorry end. There was no doubt that their minds worked in harmony. Earlier that evening Miss Truman had commented that Lord Hadleigh had the reputation of being a lightweight in life and love.

After talking with him again, Mary thought that she was wrong. She was, however, gaining the impression that something was awry in Russell Hadleigh's life, and that he envied his younger twin, Ritchie, not only for his happy marriage but for having a settled aim and career. He must also have watched Ritchie achieve a certain amount of justly earned fame for his exploits as a soldier, leaving the

Army with the rank of colonel and a reputation for courage and enterprise.

She shook her head. Why should she waste her time thinking about the problems of her one-time lover, however much, if truth were told, he still attracted her?

But the past was the past and must remain dead. A thought which she took to bed with her after reading a little of one of Mr 'Monk' Lewis's lurid romances, a Tale of Terror called *Feudal Tyrants*. Mary had a passion for such novels, which had shocked her husband whose taste in literature was fixed on the arid and the philosophical. He considered it to be her one weakness.

Whether it was Mr Lewis's vivid descriptions of past times which excited her brain, or whether it was meeting Russell Hadleigh again that did the damage Mary could not decide on the following morning. Whichever it was, during the night—was it in a dream?—she found herself walking in the gardens of her father's home in Oxford. She was seventeen again and beside her was a handsome young man who had arrived that morning to be her father's pupil.

Dr Beauregard was not one of Oxford's official dons, but he was a mathematician with a European-wide reputation and it was a habit of some of the professors to send their brighter pupils to him for further training.

'I am expecting a new young man this morning, Mary,' her father had earlier told her, 'so I am afraid that you must forgo your work with me today. Wilkinson thinks that he has a very good mind and would profit from spending some time in my company. What is surprising about him is that he is a young nobleman—it is not often that they display such rarefied talents, although one must not forget Henry Cavendish, of course.'

He was, Mary knew, referring to Henry Cavendish, the grandson of the second Duke of Devonshire, who had made some remarkable discoveries in chemistry.

'No, Father,' she replied, teasing him gently. 'No, I promise not to forget Henry Cavendish.'

He fixed her with a stern eye. 'See that you do not, my dear. Knowledge must always be treasured and never lost. The young man to whom I have referred is the heir of the Earl of Bretford. His name is Russell, Lord Hadleigh, so you must address him as m'lord. He has a courtesy Viscountcy, I understand. I think, that after I have assessed him today, it is likely that you may both profit from taking your lessons together with me. We shall see.'

Lord Hadleigh! What a delightful name. It was like those in the Tales of Terror which her father grudgingly allowed her to read. 'All work and no play makes Jane a dull girl,' he had said once.

Well, she wouldn't be a dull girl with Lord Hadleigh as a fellow pupil—although whether she would enjoy taking her lessons with him was quite another thing! She had learned—to her distress—that if she ever told anyone, male or female, of any age, that her papa was teaching her advanced mathematics and that delightful piece of arcane mystery, calculus, they were sure to look at her as though she had sprouted two heads.

Aunt Charlotte Beauregard had once told her never, ever, to let any young man know how clever she was, for that was sure to end any chance of marriage for her. Years later, Mary learned that an extremely clever mathematician and geometer named Annabelle Milbanke had succeeded in marrying Lord Byron despite that; but since the marriage had proved to be an absolute disaster, perhaps Aunt Charlotte had been right.

At the time of Lord Hadleigh's arrival, however, such warnings troubled Mary not at all. When their maid, Polly, arrived in her room to tell her that her papa wanted to see her in his study downstairs, Mary had run down eagerly, knocked on the study door and found her papa seated behind his desk. A tall young man was standing facing him.

He turned and bowed when Mary entered. She was immediately struck dumb at the sight of him. He was so extraordinarily handsome: a cross between the statues of the young Hercules and the God Apollo who stood in the entrance hall of the Beauregards' home.

But Russell, Lord Hadleigh, possessed one great advantage over them: he was warm flesh and blood, not cold stone. He had fair waving hair—he had removed his mortar-board with its nobleman's gold tassel when she had entered—and bright blue eyes above his classically handsome face.

Her father was saying something: introducing him, no doubt. Mary curtsied in a kind of daze. She thought that he was informing m'lord that he and she were to study together with him and, if so, how would she ever be able to say anything sensible before such masculine perfection?

It was almost as though he knew how overthrown she was, for he was saying in a voice as beautiful as he was, 'I am delighted to meet your daughter, Dr Beauregard. It is rare to find such intellect as she must possess and such beauty combined in one person,' and he bowed to her at the end of his speech.

'No doubt,' said her father drily, 'but, if you are to study together, looks must give place to diligence and, dare I say it, inspiration. Mathematics needs that as much as poetry or painting.'

Lord Hadleigh nodded solemnly. 'Indeed, sir, and it shall be a pleasure to try to discover it from your teaching.'

That was the beginning. Lord Hadleigh was to arrive on the following morning for an hour's teaching for as many weeks as her father cared to instruct him. He was not so advanced as Mary was, but it was amazing, she thought, how quickly he caught her up. He did not pass her. They cantered together along the paths which earlier mathematicians had laid down for them. Isaac Newton was Dr Beauregard's God. Once he had hoped to surpass him. Now he devoted his life to trying to find someone who might overtop even Newton.

The morning of Mary's walk with Lord Hadleigh he had rubbed his eyes halfway through the lesson and exclaimed, 'At the rate we are progressing I fear that the pupils may yet outclass the master. Perhaps that is not surprising: after all, Newton was a very young man when he had his most original ideas. Mary, my love, I grow tired. Take Lord Hadleigh on a tour of the gardens; by the time you return I shall doubtless be refreshed.'

When she recalled this detail of her dream Mary grasped, for the first time, that her father was beginning to succumb to the illness which was, in due course, to carry him away from her forever. In her dream, though, which was not really a dream but time recalled, she thought nothing of this, only that she would be alone with her new friend.

He was, however, already more than a friend. They had sometimes been playfully naughty in their supposedly serious discussions with her father. At first he had reprimanded them; later he had encouraged them, for in it he could see forming the inspiration which had left him, but which he hoped he was passing on to them. So, on that late spring morning, walking in the garden, something more than scholastic inspiration was beginning to pass between the pretty seventeen-year-old girl and the handsome twenty-year-old boy.

They walked down a pleached alley to a herb garden, where later all the scents of summer would fill the air, but which, like the pair of them at present, only offered hints of a beautiful maturity.

Lord Hadleigh duly admired everything, although an older Mary ruefully knew that her father's garden was but a miniature of those gardens he must have known which surrounded his father's great country houses.

They looked into one another's eyes. Russell, for so she was coming to think of him, was not innocent. He had already learned the delights which came from pleasuring women—and being pleasured by them. But Mary was, and knowing that he went slowly with her. Not only had he no wish to seduce his tutor's daughter, but he was beginning to care for her for her own sake. Such charming innocence, allied to such remarkable learning, was not to be besmirched. Both were to be respected.

So he sat by her on a rustic bench and they talked together of small things. She asked him what it was like to belong to a family since she was an only child whose mother had died young.

'A large family?' he replied, and there was a note in his voice similar to that which sounded when the older and more disillusioned Russell Hadleigh spoke of his brother and of his sister, long married to a Scots laird and long lost to him. 'My father is not what is known as a family man, you understand. Ritchie and I were friends when we were boys, but he saw fit to part us when we grew older. Twins should not be over-dependent on one another, he said, but must learn to live alone in the world.'

'I would wish to have had a sister, or a brother,' she told him. 'Someone to whom I could talk freely.' She gave him a shy glance. 'As freely as I find that I can talk to you.'

Something happened to Russell then, she was sure. For his face grew shuttered and what he then said surprised her at the time, although later she understood, or thought that she understood his unspoken meaning. 'I do not wish to be your brother.'

This declaration, she remembered, saddened her a little at the time, but she continued to talk to him. He had a dog at home, he told her, one Rufus, which had grown old and which he had left behind when he came to Oxford.

'Father will not allow me to have a dog or a cat,' she said sadly. 'He does not approve of pets. He calls it light-minded to wish for one.'

'And you do wish for one?'

'Yes, very much.' She wanted to add, I should not feel so lonely, but thought that it might be weak-minded of her to confess such a thing.

'If I were your papa,' he said, smiling at her, 'I would allow you to have any kind of pet you wanted. A bird, perhaps. Ritchie had a parrot until it died of old age. Being Ritchie, he taught it to speak a little.'

'How kind you are,' she told him, before looking at the little watch which hung from her waist. 'I think that it is time that we returned. Papa considers punctuality to be one of the great virtues. He says that most females do not treasure it.'

'Nor most males, either,' returned Russell, which set her laughing and saying,

'You see, that is what a kind brother would say.'

Mary did not remember exactly what had happened on that long-ago spring afternoon, only that it was the start of something which in the end became more than friendship, more than the love of brother and sister, but which ultimately became more powerful and dangerous than either.

Now, older and wiser, she contemplated the day ahead. The women of the party, deserted by their men, had arranged to visit a neighbour who had recently improved his gardens. Rumour claimed that they were magnificent, including not only a cataract tumbling down an artificial hill, but also not one, but three, follies.

I'm not really in the mood for follies, Mary thought. Instead I'll cry off and spend a quiet day in the library with my chess set for company. I grow tired of female small talk. Once there she could hide away from everything, including a past whose happiness had not yet been touched by pain.

Chapter Three

Russell Hadleigh yawned and put down his book. The morning was not yet half-gone. He had arrived down to a late breakfast to find that, for once, the other men in the house party had forestalled him. They were all agog and all eager to be off to the hanging. Thinking of it certainly wasn't putting them off their fodder, the Honourable Thomas told Russell a trifle gloomily.

'Put you off yours, has it?' asked Russell, contemplating the Honourable Thomas's half-empty plate.

'Doesn't do to say so,' was the rueful reply. 'A fellow's supposed to look forward to such things. I'd cry off if I could, but they'd all jeer at me for being lily-livered.'

'Well, by that I am lily-livered,' said Russell. 'For, as you know, I've no intention of joining the party.'

'Well, you're Hadleigh, Bretford's heir, and even if Perry does come on a bit strong with you, you're grand enough to do as you please. I'm only a wretched younger son, tolerated because I'm one of the crowd who makes up the numbers. Doesn't do to offend—though I suppose I might kick over the traces one day.'

Enter assorted gentlemen, thought Russell, remembering the instructions in various stage plays: courtiers and hangers-on of the great, the rich and the powerful. He shivered a little. I suppose that I have them, too—or would if I liked the notion of a crowd of sycophants walking around me all day. He disliked the thought: it was yet another thing which Ritchie didn't have to trouble about since he was a younger son who did have money—but not enough to attract the parasites.

'So there it is,' moaned the Hon. Tom dolefully, adding another slice of ham to his plate. 'What will you do while we are junketing?'

'Read a little, walk a little, ride a little: admire the scenery.'

'Leicestershire doesn't have scenery,' said the Hon. Tom. 'It only has countryside. Countryside ain't scenery.'

With this last remark he wandered off towards where Perry was holding court: something which he would not be able to do if his father were to be gazetted bankrupt.

Really, Russell thought gloomily, all that he was doing at Markham Hall was practising idleness in different surroundings from those he was used to.

His valet fetched him nuncheon some time after noon, and he ate it in his room, looking out over the park and towards some low hills in the distance.

I am becoming solitary. I think I'll go and be solitary in the library.

Yes, the library *was* solitary. Not a soul was in it. It was a typical gentleman's collection, he saw, his eyes roving along the shelves and his hands thrust in his pockets. He was bored with himself and, to that degree, was bored with life—until he reached the table in the window.

On it stood a small and exquisite chessboard, whose finely wrought miniature men were set out as though in the middle of a game. On one side of it was a pile of unused paper, on the other, another, smaller pile on which had been written lines of what appeared to be mathematical symbols.

Intrigued, Russell picked them up and studied them. It soon became plain to him, although it would not have done to many, that the symbols were the complete record of the game on the board until it had been abandoned for the time being.

The piece that was being studied on the last page was the white knight, and the calculations on the paper showed all the different consequences of moving it from its present position on the board—and the consequences for all the other pieces if each possible move it could make was analysed!

Russell could not prevent himself from picking up a clean sheet of paper and the pencil which had been left on the table and begin to list the further changes which followed on from those on the last sheet of paper. He was so absorbed in this task that he did not hear the door open and someone enter.

A cool voice said in his ear, 'Pray, what are you doing with my work, m'lord?'

Russell started up. It was Mary standing beside him, Mary who had left the chessboard in the library, secure in the knowledge that no one would visit it, or, if they did, would stare goggle-eyed and uncomprehendingly at both the board and her papers.

'Nothing,' he said, his mind still on the ramifications of the latest move. 'I am merely doing my own work—and not interfering with yours.'

She gave a little laugh which was neither kind, nor unkind, but neutral. 'Then you haven't forgotten our numbers since we worked together with my father.'

'Indeed not, Mary, although I own I am a little rusty—but the rust is fast disappearing as I begin to work with them again. And pray call me Russell as you used to when we last played with numbers.'

'I was not playing with numbers today, *m'lord*, I was working with them.'

Mary's stress on the word *m'lord* was slow and deliberate. This troubled Russell not at all. Since he had sat down in front of the chess board something had happened to him, something which he had not felt for years. He felt not only liberated, but full of a sense of power, of achievement. The ennui which had marred his recent life had disappeared. He felt himself equal to anything.

'Nor am I playing with numbers today, Mary. I am fascinated by what you have been doing, which is, I suppose, trying to work out a logical means of countering every move your opponent makes in a real game. That, if you could succeed, would be an achievement worthy of Newton or Pascal themselves. I have, in my own small way, been trying to see if I could join you in your exercise.'

His face was so eager, so alight with interest that for a moment time disappeared and they were boy and girl in her father's study again. Time re-ordered itself, but the effect of that brief spasm was to set Mary answering him as she would have done then.

'Perhaps you would allow me to examine your work, Russell?'

Russell! He had seen the slight quiver that had passed across her face before she answered him—and then she had called him Russell! He had said, or done, something which had unwittingly restored some of the rapport which they had once shared.

'Willingly,' he said, and handed her the sheets of paper which he had filled with his calculations.

Mary sat down beside him and began to inspect them. Presently she laid the papers carefully down on the table and looked at him for a long moment before saying slowly, 'How long did it take you to do that, Russell—I mean, m'lord? I have only been absent a short time—' She stopped and shook her head.

Russell was suddenly overwhelmed by a great sense of anticlimax. He took Mary's shaking head to mean that she was disappointed by what he had done. The feeling was the more acute because he thought that what he had written down was worthwhile, the logical conclusion of her own calculations.

'I'm sorry,' he said humbly, 'if what I have just done was all a nonsense. It is a long time since I did any serious work with numbers...' Mary, her eyes shining, had put her hand on his arm to stop him from explaining himself.

'Not at all,' she exclaimed. 'If you haven't done anything like this lately then what you have accomplished here is remarkable. I could not have done all this in twice the time. It is an area where you always surpassed me in the past. I was better at looking at the principles involved, you were more accomplished with the detail. That is why Father said that we made such a good team: our strengths differed.'

She was speaking with all the eagerness of the girl who had sat by him in her father's study. It was as though for Russell, too, that time had returned. He leaned forward, sharing her eagerness, saying, 'You really mean that, Mary? You are not deceiving me to keep me in countenance?'

'Not at all. Oh, if we could only work together again...what could we not do.' Now it was her turn to stop briefly, before saying, 'Forgive me. I am talking nonsense. You have a life of your own and we parted for good long ago.'

He wanted to say, I have no life which holds any meaning. Instead, without thinking, he took the hand which she had used to check him earlier and kissed it.

'Tell me the ultimate of what you are trying to do, Mary, and perhaps, while we are at Markham Hall, we might find time to work together again.' She made no attempt to resist him, but the light which had filled her face and make her look almost a child again was gradually fading.

Mary said sorrowfully, 'You know full well, m'lord, why we may not do that. Any opportunity we once had to work together disappeared long ago.'

'That was then, Mary, this is now.'

Russell's ardour was all the greater because the strange combination of mathematics, the presence of Mary, and the notion that they could be together again, was having a profoundly erotic effect on him. He knew that most men and women would be amused by the notion that anything so dry, so abstract, as the higher mathematics could rouse a man as he was now roused!

Later he was to tell himself that power, and the sense of power, is an aphrodisiac, and if excelling at playing games with numbers made him feel powerful, then it was neither strange nor unnatural, but only to be expected, that he should become roused. When, added to all that, the woman who was with him was, in her quiet way, as beautiful as she was clever, it was no wonder that his breathing had begun to shorten dramatically.

He was a boy again and the world was opening up before him as it had done then.

'You have just said that you were favourably impressed by what I have already done—how much more, then, could we not do if we worked together? Before we do, however, I think that we ought to play one another at chess. I have to confess that it is many years since I last engaged in a game.'

The sad truth was that after Mary had left him the mere sight of a chess board had been enough to distress him. They had played so many happy games together, encouraged by her father who thought that the brain was excited by it: that it acted as a form of inspiration.

What to say? He looked so eager, so pathetically eager, and if the truth were told she was remembering that the game which had once been such a source of pleasure to her had become just another chore, an intellectual puzzle to be solved. To sit opposite to him again would be like revisiting her lost girlhood. On the other hand, if she allowed him to tempt her into giving way on this, was she simply paving the way for yet another piece of treachery on his part?

Why she agreed to play against him Mary never knew.

'Very well, but it will only be one game, I am not promising anything more than that.'

It *was* a surrender, though, and they both knew that it was.

'Allow me to record the state of the current game first,' she said and, taking his answer for granted, rapidly wrote it down before rearranging the pieces.

'You may have white,' he said, once the pieces were rearranged.

'Indeed, not,' said Mary haughtily. 'I want no favours from you.'

Russell laughed. 'How that takes me back. I remember that you never did. Shall we let chance settle the matter?' He took a coin from his pocket and saying 'Heads or tails? I say heads,' he prepared to toss it up.

'No,' said Mary, laughing across at him as she had done so long ago. 'Allow me to inspect the coin first. I seem to remember that you had two and one of them possessed two heads and the other two tails. You played that trick on me once, but never again.'

'Oh, ye of little faith,' Russell grinned back at her and threw the coin to her. 'It is a good one and you may do the tossing. Am I right to trust you?'

Oh, yes, it was just like the old days when laughter and banter had filled their time together after the hard work of study was over.

Mary said reprovingly, 'You know that I never cheated you. There,' and she tossed the coin up, caught it on the palm of one hand and covered it with the palm of her other.

The smile she gave him when she exclaimed, 'Now, Lord Hadleigh, which is it? Heads or tails?' nearly destroyed him.

'Tails,' he finally achieved.

'Tails it is,' she announced, lifting her hand. 'Why is it that you always win, even when you are not cheating me?'

He could not prevent himself from saying, now suddenly sober, 'Now Mary, you know as well as I do, that I did not always win.'

Either she did not take his meaning—that she had ended their affair and married another—or she preferred not to. She swung the board around to give him the white pieces and said quite simply, 'Let the battle begin.'

That, too, was said in memory of the old days and with the same calm amusement which she had used then. It was for her beautiful quiet that he had always loved her. He had been a noisy boy—unlike Ritchie—and he was fascinated by her calm self-control and wished that he possessed it.

Time and the passing years had sobered him, and he was not sure that it had been for the better. Meeting Mary again, though, had revived some of his old exuberance, his zest for life, the sense that anything was possible for him if only he put his mind to it.

'Prepare to be dealt with as the Romans dealt with Hannibal,' he announced grandly, 'particularly as you have no elephants.'

'But I have knights instead,' and she moved the Black one—to which Russell countered with his White—and battle was fairly joined.

The afternoon flew by. Early on someone—who?—looked in on them and retreated at the sight of their rapt faces, at the fair head and the dark bent over the board.

Once Russell raised his head to stare into Mary's eyes. 'You are bamming me,' he said accusingly as she moved a minor pawn. 'What the devil—if I may be so frank—did you do that for?'

'Since you read my notes you should know exactly why—and the devil had little to do with it.'

Oh, but he had, thought Russell a few moves later. He desperately wanted to win this game. To prove what? That he might have lost to her years ago, but he could not lose now—although it seemed likely that he was just about to do exactly that.

And then he saw a way out of his dilemma when he was on the point of being mated. Mated! There was a double meaning there, was there not? Mate in chess meant death—but in life it meant the possibility of birth. Which one was this? And if he were not to win, for he could not, might he not force a draw and in the doing hold both death and life in balance: the perfect equilibrium! He moved his White knight for the last time.

'Stalemate!' he announced triumphantly.

And so it was.

Neither of them had won—or lost.

The perfect ending.

Mary did not think so. 'That was not supposed to happen,' she exclaimed, indignant for once. 'I must have made an error in my calculations.'

'Ah,' said Russell, laughter on his face. 'But then you were playing yourself, not me. I think the ending is perfect, for neither of us have lost face.'

'Or both of us have,' countered Mary, beginning to smile herself. 'I wonder what Father would have said.'

'That we are well matched, but then, we always were.'

Mary's smile disappeared. 'I think that we ought to stop now,' she said. 'The others will be returning at any moment.'

'But you will give me a game again tomorrow, will you not? And allow me to assist you with your calculations?'

His face when he said this was as earnest and serious as he could make it. To be with her again was all and more than he might have expected. It was not simply that she stirred him as no other woman had, but their meeting of minds was something that he had never experienced with anyone other than Ritchie when they had been boys together.

She could not refuse him. Forgetting everything which had earlier passed between them, she remembered only the exhilaration of the last two hours—and gave him the reply which he so dearly wanted.

'If you promise to behave yourself and not pester me about the past, then yes, we may do as you wish, only providing that you are reasonably discreet.'

'Bravo!' was his response to that. 'As we have already noted, the men of the party are preparing to journey to the boxing mill so we might as well agree to meet here at two of the clock. I see that there is a chess set and board on one of the cupboards which looks as though no one has used it for years. I propose to take it to my room and engage in a little useful practice. You will not find me such an easy mark tomorrow, I hope.'

'That remains to be seen,' returned Mary saucily. 'For the present then, adieu. I shall expect you here on the hour tomorrow,' and she left him to pick up the spare chessmen and the board, wondering what kind of a fool she was to put him in a position where he could let her down all over again.

Eliza Truman was waiting for her in their suite. She said nothing at first, but after Mary had rung for the tea-board to be brought up to them, she remarked, her voice as neutral as she could make it, 'By chance I visited the library and saw you there with Lord Hadleigh, playing chess. It is not for me to advise you—you are, after all a widow, no longer in the first stare of your youth—but are you wise to allow him to cultivate you? His reputation is that of a man who has no wish to settle down.'

'In that,' returned Mary, 'he is like many others.'

'Indeed, but those others are not pursuing you.'

Mary sat down and stared at her companion. 'What makes you believe that *he* is pursuing me?'

'The way he looks for you—and after you. And you are surely not pursuing him.'

Mary's answer was not as totally honest a one as those she usually made. 'I am not sure what his motives are for seeking me out. Other than that in our long-ago acquaintanceship we frequently played chess together and, since he was at a loose end, as I was, we agreed to play a game. That is all.'

But enough, perhaps, was a comment which Miss Truman was wise enough not to make. Instead she asked, a little pointedly, perhaps, 'May I enquire who won this suddenly decided-upon match?'

'No one. It was a draw. Ah, splendid, here comes the tea-board, now we may refresh ourselves,' which, Mary thought, was as good a way as any other to put an end to that line of conversation.

Before dinner, Perry Markham, in high spirits after the hanging, was entertaining a few of his cronies in his room. It was quite a merry affair since port and wine were circulating freely. 'Can't wait until after dinner to down a few glasses, can we?' being part of Perry's cheerful invitation to his small court. 'Hanging's thirsty work. Astonishing how many of the plebs were drunk before it began, wasn't it? It's a wonder they were wide awake enough to enjoy themselves when the fun started.'

The Hon. Tom, who had been quietly sick in the middle of the so-called fun, had blamed his own malaise at the hanging on too much ale in order to keep up his reputation for being part of Perry's hard-living set. In consequence he had felt compelled to refuse to drink in the evening. He sat in a large armchair looking woebegone.

'Not too set down to miss picking a few pockets, though,' he said mournfully. 'I lost my purse and my handkerchief.'

'Oh, come on, Tom, do cheer up,' roared Perry. 'I've a fine piece of news, hot from my man Dawson, to pass on to you all. It seems that m'lord of Hadleigh, who was too fine and delicate-minded a gentleman to come to Loughborough with us, spent the afternoon with Mrs Wardour playing chess—in the library of all places. Didn't know anyone used it these days.'

This, as he intended, drew a great deal of appreciative and already tipsy laughter.

'Thought she was invited here for you, not him,' said one would-be know-all, 'and that Angelica was his target. Not like you, Perry, to let another put his oar in before you.'

'Game's not over yet,' spluttered Perry, 'and it's not chess I'm talking about. As for Angelica, she's more interested in Tom, isn't she? But there's no hope for you there, old chap—the General wants a richer prize than your good self, more's the pity. I'd prefer you as a brother-in-law rather than that high-minded ass, Hadleigh, who looks down his nose at me every time we meet.'

The ringing of the first bell for dinner, informing the guests that they were to meet in the drawing room, ended this Parliament of Fools. There was a rush for the door as a result of which the Hon. Tom was last out, still nursing his grievances against life and hoping that the sight and sound of Angelica would cheer him up.

He was lucky. Angelica was standing before the hearth, admiring herself in the huge mirror which stood above it, while ostensibly chit-chatting with Mary. She saw the Honourable Thomas reflected in it when he came through the door. Ignoring all the conventions relating to politeness and good manners, she broke off her conversation with Mary in mid-sentence, turned and almost ran to him.

'So there you are, at last. I thought that the hanging was over before noon. We all expected your party back in the mid-afternoon, but no such thing. It has been a most boring day. I have seen enough gardens and follies to last me for the rest of my life!'

'Come to that, my dear girl, I never want to witness another hanging, but we won't tell your brother so, will we?'

'Mrs Wardour must have had a dull day, too. Or at least a dull afternoon. I gather, that of all things, she spent it playing chess against Lord Hadleigh.'

The Hon. Tom was left to reflect how rapidly gossip ran round a country house. He wondered uneasily whether his pursuit of Angelica had been watched closely enough for the news to reach her father. It wouldn't do for him to open a real campaign for her hand until Lord Hadleigh had left without making an offer for it.

Lord Hadleigh had watched Miss Angelica with a mixture of amusement and relief. Thank God he was not her target, and that she had made it easy for him to approach Mary, whom she had left at a loose end, since Perry Markham was too far gone to remember his duty to his father, and the estate, to seize the opportunity to charm her.

'I think that I am more than happy that you didn't go to watch the hanging today,' Mary whispered to Russell, 'since most of those who did go have arrived back on their very worst behaviour. Does it usually have such an effect?'

'Oh, I think that it was the drink before, during and after, which has made them all so infernally jolly,' Russell whispered back. 'Don't look, but the General has a face like thunder this evening. Expect lightning during dinner, if not before.'

Before was the truest word Russell had spoken. The General, after a word with his wife, walked up to Perry and began to expostulate with him in a whisper—which was not the best mode of speech to employ with his overset son.

Finally the General seized Perry by the elbow and gently tried to urge him to the door.

'I think,' announced the General loudly enough for the rest of the company to hear him, 'that you and your friends who went to Loughborough today might like to dine in the Small Hall and join the men after the ladies have left us. I shall ask the butler to arrange matters. In the meantime, you might wish to adjourn to the small drawing room.'

He did not add, if you can still walk, although Russell, amused, considered it likely that Perry and his friends might be legless after they had dined on their own—if not before.

Only the Hon. Tom was unhappy at this turn. He was stone-cold sober and still to be deprived of Angelica's company. It was too bad, but he—and Perry and the others—still retained enough sense to do as the General bid them, even if they grumbled gently all the way to their new rendezvous. Only Russell, of the younger members of the party, was left to join his elders, something which did not trouble him in the least. This was particularly true after the General had informed them that dinner would be delayed for a short time while the table was re-laid.

He was right not to be troubled. He had Mary on his right, and she had no Perry on her left to try to monopolise her, only elderly Brigadier Sykes, who was slightly deaf and whose conversation was limited to military matters and asking women how their children were faring. Neither of these conversational ploys would serve to enable him to entertain Mary for more than a few moments.

'My lucky day,' Russell whispered to Mary, 'since I have been gifted with your company during most of it.'

'We must behave ourselves,' Mary whispered back. 'You must not ignore Angelica and I must try to convince the Brigadier that although I am Mrs Wardour I have neither children nor a husband. He seems to be having some difficulty in grasping the nature of a widow.'

'Point taken,' responded Russell in his best Parliamentary manner before turning to Angelica and asking her how she had enjoyed her afternoon.

'Not at all,' she pouted. 'I was the only lady present who wasn't married or past her last prayers. Our hostess seemed to think that it would entertain us to learn all the Latin names of her plants and animals. She had a small menagerie of rather smelly monkeys and a creature called a hamster: a horrid little thing which resembled nothing more than an over-sized rat with nasty front teeth. She actually offered it to me to hold.'

'Really?' asked Russell, intrigued by this sad recital. 'And what did you do when she handed it to you?'

'Screamed and dropped the wretched animal—and then there was an awful to-do with everyone running round trying either to dodge it or catch it. The gardener finally picked it up—and then, of all things, *he* tried to give it to me. At that point I fainted and a footman carried me into the house where they restored me with tea. I'm sure that I shan't have any appetite tonight.'

How he kept his face straight during this mournful tale, Russell never knew, particularly since Angelica was attacking her dinner as though she had been starving for weeks. He heard Mary stifle a muffled giggle, and to cover it, remarked, 'Perhaps the animal was as frightened of you as you were of it.'

'Surely not,' exclaimed Angelica, between spoonfuls of asparagus soup. 'One good thing came out of it, though. I was able to remain in the house and was spared any further lectures or possible attacks by ravening beasts.'

'There was that,' agreed Russell solemnly.

His duty being done, he turned towards Mary, who was scarlet-faced from suppressing her laughter, and said in as low a voice as possible, 'Do you remember the day that I introduced you to a guinea pig?'

'Indeed I do. I was so entranced by it that you had difficulty in taking it away again with the result that Father came home before you had gone and raised the roof about the inadvisability of keeping pets. Once you—and the guinea pig—had been banished, he made me go and have a bath in case I had caught some dreadful disease from it.'

'He and Angelica would have a great deal of common ground there, if they had none elsewhere,' Russell could not resist remarking. Yes, it was just like old times again when they had teased one another unmercifully.

'I said that we must behave ourselves,' Mary told him severely after that. 'To that end you must entertain Angelica again, and I will ask the Brigadier about the campaigns he engaged in during the last war. That is another of his favourite topics for conversation.'

So, it was all downhill, particularly when, once dinner was over, Mary and the women departed and the refugees from the hanging returned to the dining room in their place. Their presence was enough to drive a man to drink and no mistake. Fortunately Russell's newly made resolution not to overdo things held good and he returned to the drawing room quite sober and ready for another bout of jousting with Mary.

Unfortunately, Mrs Markham, in the good cause of persuading Lord Hadleigh to offer for her daughter, button-holed him the moment he was through the door and rounded him up for a game of spillikins with Angelica and some other youthful members of the party who had arrived at Markham Hall not long before dinner.

It was all enough, thought Russell morosely, playing the mindless game with several giggling girls and the Hon. Tom, to make him wish that he had broken his resolution and was in no better state than Perry, who slouched in an armchair in the corner of the room, his legs spread out before him and his head on one side, like a drunken idler who had escaped from Hogarth's great series of prints: *Marriage à la Mode.*

By the time that the noisy game had ended, Mary, and her companion, had gone to bed—a place to which Russell finally retired. He would have gone there much more cheerfully, was his final judgement after a night of so-called merriment at Markham Hall, if Mary had been waiting for him in it.

Alas, Russell's stay at Markham Hall improved not a jot. Both the General and Mrs. Markham were determined to throw Angelica at him, and short of being rude to his host and hostess there was nothing he could do about it. The one thing which kept him from inventing some reason for leaving was Mary's presence.

Even that, though, was soon to be denied him. One afternoon, in the library, to which they repaired whenever they could escape the iron clutches of the Markhams—for Mary was also being relentlessly pursued on Perry's behalf—she had bad news for him.

She had just trapped his Black King in the inescapable corner to which she had driven him when she announced mournfully, 'This game must be our last for the time being. I have just received a letter from my Aunt Charlotte Beauregard, in the north, asking me if I would visit her as soon as possible.'

Russell stared at her, dumbstruck. He had begun to congratulate himself that, little by little, he was melting the ice around Mary's heart. Yesterday, for instance, she had laughed up into his face, and put a congratulatory hand on his when a clever move on his part had driven *her* King into a fatal position.

He had taken the hand and kissed the palm of it, and she had made no move to reprimand him. On the contrary, she had left her hand in his so that he had kissed it again, his eyes fixed on hers.

'Mary,' he had said hoarsely, 'it is time we spoke of the past. We cannot go on pretending that what happened, did not happen...'

'No,' she told him, but she did not take back her hand which he kissed again. 'It was you who suggested this prohibition. Without it we cannot go on.'

'*I* cannot go on like this,' he murmured. 'It is killing me. What I felt for you when I was little more than a boy is as nothing to what I am feeling now.'

'No,' she had replied, at last retrieving her hand. 'We are friends now, not lovers. Let us remain so.'

'Alas, Mary, I can never be merely your friend.'

Had she not been so determined that she would not mention the past she would have replied, Then you must have changed greatly, since if in the past you were more than my friend, you would not have abandoned me so lightly.

But since she was so determined, she said nothing although, if she had, the trouble which lay between them might immediately have been resolved. As it was she merely smiled and shook her head so that Russell, despite his growing desire for her to be to him what she had once been, fell silent also. If he could have nothing else from her, then he might be able to live with her friendship, however barren that might seem to one who loved her so ardently.

'Aunt Charlotte was my father's sister,' she explained to him when telling him that she must leave. 'She is one of my few relatives, but she lives so far away—near Newcastle, in fact—that we rarely meet. Consequently when she asks me as a favour to visit her as soon as possible I feel it to be my duty to go.'

Russell was struck by this piece of news. 'Near Newcastle, you say—exactly where?'

'By some coincidence, not far from the little town which gives you your name. I suppose you know it well.'

'I don't know it at all,' he was compelled to confess. 'For some reason my father never visits Eddington House, our country house there, and neither Ritchie nor I have ever been further north than Doncaster, where he has a small country house which is used once a year to visit the races there. My father is passionately devoted to the breeding and running of racehorses.'

Something in the tone of his voice set Mary remarking, 'And you are not?'

'Not to the exclusion of everything else.' He did not say that it was a pity that some of the affection which his father showered on his horses might have been better employed in caring more for his children.

Mary did not pursue the topic and they spent the rest of the afternoon in experimenting with the chess set, working out all the different moves which might result from the moving of minor pawns.

'I shall be lonely when you have gone,' he told her before they parted. 'I shall have to think of some excuse for leaving. If you thought that I was invited here so that I might make an offer for Angelica, you were right. Since it is plain that we have nothing in common, I must not remain to raise false hopes in the General's breast.'

'Well, I was invited for Perry,' returned Mary frankly. 'And a less suitable match for me I cannot imagine. However, I am my own mistress and so nothing can compel me to marry someone whom I dislike.'

'If, by that, you mean that I am not my own master, then you have hit the nail on the head once again. I came here at my father's behest; he thinks that it is time that I married. What he does not know is that the one woman whom I might wish to marry has decided to remain merely my friend. I fear that he will be most displeased when I return without fixing myself on Angelica.'

Mary scarcely knew how to answer him, so decided to say nothing.

They sat for a moment in silence. Mary was collecting the chess pieces, Russell was arranging the sheaf of notes which they had made between them, preparatory to handing them to her.

He said suddenly, apropos of apparently nothing, 'In two days' time I think that I shall make my adieux

and pay a visit to my brother. He is the most sensible
creature I know and his advice is always worth having. What I will ask you to do is give me your northern address so that I may write to you. I promise that
the letters will be those of a friend. I will also send
you some further calculations about the chess game
after I have begged, borrowed or stolen Ritchie's set.'

Mary hesitated; Russell thought that she was about
to refuse him.

'At least grant me this,' he said earnestly. 'It is
little enough.'

She nodded. It was another surrender. Later, much
later after he had left Markham Hall, Mary decided
that Russell was behaving like the Roman general,
Fabius Maximus. Fabius, always known as the
Cunctator, or The Delayer, had defeated the invading
Hannibal by withdrawing before him, destroying his
position little by little, leading him on until he had
defeated the invader in one last great battle.

Would there be one last great battle between herself and Russell, and if so, who would win it? More
to the point, what would either winning, or losing,
really mean?

Chapter Four

More than once, on his way to Ritchie's home at Liscombe Manor, Russell asked himself if he had taken the coward's way out by deserting Mary before she had left and before matters had been resolved between them.

On the other hand, he had, almost without knowing it, allowed the influence she still possessed over him to lead him to make up his mind to do something about the bad blood which existed between him and his father.

Whether it was her renewed admiration of his mathematical and philosophical powers, which, despite the length of time during which he had not practised them, were still there if only he cared to call on them, or whether it was the memory of the bright future that he had thought he once had with her which had done the trick, Russell could not decide.

What he *did* know was that, rightly or wrongly, Ritchie might be able to give him the kind of advice which would set him on the way to ending the pointless life to which his father's treatment had condemned him.

Ritchie was in the stables when he arrived at the Manor. He was breaking in a young horse, but was doing so without the brutality usually inflicted on the animal. He must have seen Russell arrive, but made him wait while he patiently whispered in the horse's ear, led him gently around the yard, and then mounted him in one easy movement.

After that he cantered slowly around, raising the whip which he never once used, to acknowledge Russell's presence before dismounting, handing the animal over to a watching stable lad and greeting his twin with an uncharacteristic and demonstrative arm thrown round his shoulders.

'You look done up,' he said calmly. 'Surely the journey from Markham Hall wasn't quite so demanding.'

'Not at all,' Russell riposted, standing back, 'but...' and he shrugged his shoulders '...I am at a kind of *point non plus*, and it is beginning to trouble me. I thought that you might be able to help me.'

'Point taken,' said Ritchie, punning a little in his dry way. 'But not here and not now. Later, after dinner, unbuttoned and a bottle of port between us, would be more suitable. For the meantime, come in and meet Pandora and the brat. I have a horrid feeling that he's going to look more like you than me. On the other hand, he behaves like me, quiet and contemplative. Nurse says that she's never known such a well-behaved child, most unnatural.'

'And on the other hand, again,' quipped Russell, walking beside his brother into the sprawling Tudor building, 'I'm sure that you're happy that he doesn't look like you, and behave like me. I seem to remember that I was always a noisy boy.'

'To say the least, and point taken again.'

He was leading Russell into a large room with an old-fashioned fireplace, above which was an intricately carved representation in wood of herons in flight. Pandora sat before it with a sleeping child on her knee. Motherhood had made her lovelier than ever and had given her a new steadiness.

'Welcome,' she mouthed at him, waving a hand at the child who stirred a little and turned his face into her breast. 'I've just finished feeding Will. Nurse has gone to fetch him a shawl before she puts him down for his afternoon sleep.'

No wet-nurse for Mrs Ritchie Chancellor then, thought Russell, somewhat amused, but the amusement was mixed with jealousy. Ritchie had married his true love, but he had been denied his. And the result was the handsome boy on his wife's knee.

As if he had known what his brother had been thinking, Ritchie said gently, 'Why not give Uncle Russell the brat to hold, my love? A little practice for him would not come amiss.'

'Surely,' said Pandora with a grin, 'but if he wakes, then he must do the soothing.'

Will did not wake, and Russell found himself doing something which he had not foreseen when he had left Markham Hall: holding a warm male infant, and—most surprisingly—wishing that the little bundle was his.

'Well, what is it that brings you here?' asked Ritchie when Pandora had left them to their port that evening. 'I thought, from Father's letter, that you were off making an offer for young Miss at Markham Hall.'

'Not I,' said Russell fervently. 'She was to my father's taste, not mine, so I am doomed to disappoint him once again. How I am to tell him without the heavens falling on me is at least one part of my worries.'

Ritchie held his port up to the light and stared at it.

'May I enquire who, if anyone, is to your taste?'

'Mary Beauregard, who is now the Widow Wardour. I don't suppose that you remember her.'

'Just, although I never met her. She is back in your life, then?'

'Yes, but that is not what I particularly wish to speak to you of, delighted though I am to meet her again. It's Father. What the devil is it that I have to do to satisfy him?'

'He gives me no responsibility, leaves me to rot in idleness and when, by accident, I thought that I had found that there was something odd about the reports and accounts from Eddington he sent me away with a flea in my ear. I'm damned sick of it all and I don't know how to remedy matters. I may be his heir, but...' and he shrugged his shoulders again. 'Perhaps you might be able to tell me what I could do to please him.'

'Nothing,' said Ritchie. 'He's determined not to be pleased by you. Why not try pleasing yourself? That's more to the point we keep running around.'

'That's easy for you to say. You're of independent means, I'm not.'

'Agreed.' Ritchie was thoughtful. 'Of course, you could throw everything up and enlist as a private soldier—but I wouldn't recommend it.'

'Exceedingly helpful of you, I'm sure,' sniffed Russell. 'I'm absolutely sure that something is going badly wrong up north—but I'm helpless...'

His voice trailed off. Why was Ritchie looking at him like that?

'Really?' said Ritchie. 'Tell me, are you going to spend the rest of your life feeling sorry for yourself? It's time you defied the old man, took the initiative.'

'Now, how the devil do you propose that I do that? He's warned me off.'

Ritchie looked sideways at him. Oh, Russell knew that look. He'd seen it often enough when they were boys.

'Your trouble,' his twin told him, 'is that you're too easy-going. You want people to like you. I don't. You're so good and truthful it's almost nauseating.

Why don't you go up north, to Eddington, and try to find out what is happening there? Question old Shaw, ferret about. After all, you are the heir. Tell him that you're Father's agent, or emissary, what you will. Smile at him and ask him to show you round, explain things, go over the books.'

'But suppose he refuses to oblige me and asks for evidence? A letter from Father giving me the power to question him, for instance.'

'So, tell him that as you're the heir you don't need one.'

'But that would be lying,' said Russell, staring at Ritchie who, his face impassive, was carefully inspecting the ceiling.

'So lie, then. If I hadn't told a good few in my time I wouldn't be sitting here trying to advise my Don Quixote of a brother—I'd be six feet under. Everyone lies if it's in their interest. Go to the House of Commons and listen to them doing it all day long. Why should you be the only honest fool in the world? Try being a dishonest one for a change: it usually answers better.'

Russell was fascinated. Was this Ritchie speaking? Of course it was. He'd been one of Wellington's agents in Spain, had single-handed broken up a smuggling ring in Sussex and had doubtless done more beside. That he always looked as if butter wouldn't melt in his mild mouth must invariably have been an asset in the dangerous life he had led.

'My life has always been too easy,' he said at last. 'Being the heir, I've never really had to try, have I?'

'True,' said Ritchie, transferring his attention from the ceiling to Russell's face via his glass of port.

'So I go north and pretend I'm you?'

'If you like. Trying to be the man you might have been if our father hadn't unmanned you somewhat might be better. We are alike in some things, but not in all. I'm a rogue, you're not. On the other hand, your honesty might just be an asset in certain circumstances. You'll have to work out for yourself which they are.'

Russell, whose glass was empty, poured himself a large jorum of port. 'I think, little brother, I'll get halfway drunk as a preparation for being halfway honest.'

'Excellent,' said Ritchie. 'I'll drink to that, too.'

Russell was remembering this conversation when he was being driven north. After a happy fortnight spent with Ritchie, he had arranged to leave all his retinue—such as it was—behind at Liscombe, taking only his valet, Pickering, with him and his elderly coachman, Needham, who had known him since he was a lad. It would look odd if he were to travel completely on his own, but the less everyone knew of what he was about to do, the better.

'I'll send you the bill if they eat me out of house and home,' Ritchie had murmured as a last fond farewell—adding 'Good luck,' before Russell climbed into the heavily loaded post-chaise. The other chaise he had with him was left, together with its driver, with his accommodating twin.

The journey north was uneventful until they reached a small posting inn on the far side of York. Another chaise stood in the yard. A stable lad was leading its horses away. Pickering, sent to commandeer a room for his master, returned with a rueful look on his face.

'It seems, m'lord, that the best rooms have already been taken by a lady and her retinue, travelling north.' He hesitated, coughed and added. 'I enquired as to her identity and was informed that she was a Mrs. Wardour, a lady of substance. She is on her way to Ancoates, near Corbridge.'

'The Mrs Wardour who is travelling from Markham Hall, I trust?' said Russell. Well, he might have lost the best rooms in the inn, but he was going to have the bonus of meeting Mary again.

'Indeed, sir. I saw her lady's maid myself. A fine young woman with whom I became acquainted at Markham Hall.'

'Very fortuitous, then,' said Russell with a grin. It seemed that both master and man were in luck.

Pickering inclined a respectful head. 'True, m'lord. I have asked for supper to be served at not too late an hour.'

'Splendid—and while you're about it, see if there is a post-boy available to help Needham, who is feeling distinctly under the weather.'

So, Mary was here! Russell's worries about what to do when Eddington was reached flew away. He was on the verge of whistling when he entered the inn, but restrained himself. Persons of his standing were expected to maintain a due decorum—on public, at least.

He wondered how long it would be before he would meet her, and once again he was in luck. Walking into the parlour, he found that she was already seated there, her maid by her side. It was the maid who saw him first. She bent her head and whispered to her mistress, who rose in one graceful movement.

'Lord Hadleigh. I am surprised to see you here. I had thought that you had returned to London after visiting your brother.'

Russell bowed. 'That was my original intention, I do own. However, I changed my mind and decided to visit Eddington. You may remember that I spoke of it. I had a mind to see the place, particularly since I have never travelled further north than Doncaster.'

He did not add that another reason was the thought that he might see her again since her destination was so near his—although their present meeting was, gratifyingly, much sooner than he might have expected.

'Then we shall be near to one another once we reach journey's end,' murmured Mary. She was not sure how to greet this news. On the other hand, she could not deny that the moment she had seen him her heart had begun to beat faster and the journey north, hitherto rather dull, now took on a different complexion.

Russell, as if picking up her thoughts, offered, 'We could do it in tandem, could we not? I have been feeling rather bored with no company other than Pickering who, good fellow though he is, is rather lacking in the conversational line.'

'Why not?' agreed Mary, wondering what she was letting herself in for. Was this another part of his campaign to charm her again—something which she had sternly told herself after she had left Markham Hall that she would not allow him to succeed in?

Making decisions in his absence was one thing: holding on to them when she met him again was quite another.

'And since we are both lodging here this evening, would it be too much to ask that we might take supper together? It would be easier for the landlord and more pleasant for the pair of us. I know that Pickering will certainly be sharing his with your little maid.'

What could she say but yes when he smiled down at her in that winning way? If he had been charming in youth, he was overwhelming in maturity. Russell was simultaneously thinking the same thing of Mary. Even a tiring and lengthy journey north had not dimmed her attractions.

The landlord was only too happy to accommodate them at the same table. The food he supplied was, like his rooms, plain, but excellent. Roast beef, followed by a syllabub, with a bottle of excellent wine, were the perfect ending to a tiring day. The only thing lacking, Russell thought, was that Mary would not be sharing the bedroom with him.

Whether it was the food or the wine which was the cause, her manner to him had never been so easy. They laughed and talked like old friends who had not seen one another for years rather than the fortnight which had elapsed since he had left Markham Hall. It was as though they were young again, experiencing the new delights which leaving childhood behind had brought them.

'Miss Truman is not with you, I collect.'

'Unfortunately, no. Just before we were about to leave Markham Hall she received a letter from her elder sister—or rather from her elder sister's lawyer. It seemed that she was on the point of death and it was essential that Miss Truman should repair at once to Norfolk, where her family has lived for some generations. She was reluctant to leave me, but I pointed out that my maid could take her place on the journey and that my coachman and my footman would guard us both. Besides, once I had arrived at my Aunt's home, I should not lack for company. Were you lonely on your journey? I see that you have not brought along with you the grand train which was yours at Markham Hall.'

'Sometimes I'm quite happy to be alone,' replied Russell truthfully. 'Particularly since I have recently been taking stock of my idle life and deciding to do something about it. Discovering at Markham Hall that I had not lost my mathematical bent was a useful beginning.'

'You have not entered Parliament, then? Heirs to great names often do.'

He shook his head. He could not tell her of his father's contemptuous dismissal of that wish. Instead he murmured, 'Somehow, it never seemed ...àpropos.'

Mary was shrewd. 'To you—or to your father?'

She knew at once that, somehow, she had said the wrong thing. He looked away, and the subtle rapport which, despite all, they still shared, told her that she had said something to disturb him.

He turned his head towards her again and smiled his beautiful smile. 'Both, perhaps,' which was as far as he dare go. He was not about to whine to her about his miserable life. Ritchie had told him to lie whenever it was convenient, and so he would offer Mary half a lie.

But he did not think that he had deceived her.

Silence fell.

The meal was ended, the small fire which had been laid for them was dying down and it was time to retire.

Mary was the first to rise. She picked up the shawl which she had discarded during the meal and prepared to make her adieux before leaving. Russell rose, too. For a moment they were face to face before the door.

She licked her lips nervously. Russell took a deep breath at the sight, and before he could stop himself took her into his arms, bent his head and kissed her, not as once before on the lips, but oh, so gently, on the cheek. Some instinct told him not to frighten her. As before, merely to touch her roused him.

Mary's response was even more eager than the last time—but her behaviour at the end of a few stolen moments was exactly the same. She drew back, placing her right hand over his mouth and saying, 'No. You no longer have the right to do that—nor do I wish it.'

Russell, his eyes hard on hers, knew that if he had uttered half a lie a few moments ago, Mary was now offering him a whole one. Her tongue said one thing, her face and the posture of her whole body told him another.

'No,' he said, and his 'no' was quite different from hers. 'You do not mean that. You love me still—as I love you.'

'You forfeited my love.' She was trembling as she spoke and looked away from him lest the mere, and dear, sight of him broke her resolve. 'You said that we were to be friends, only friends. More than that I do not want and cannot give. Break that resolve and we must part, never to meet again. Now, pray allow me to leave. I have had a long and difficult day—as have you.'

Russell swallowed. 'Very well. Let us meet again at breakfast—as friends.'

She inclined her head, hiding her glorious eyes from him. 'If you will behave yourself.'

He said, and it was, in some odd way, the hardest thing he had ever had to say, 'Yes, I will behave myself, at breakfast—and all the other breakfasts and suppers until we take our separate ways at journey's end.'

'If you will—but only and always as friends.'

Russell bowed to her. He had given way and in the doing a strange thought crossed his mind. He had never really asked himself exactly what had happened, what had been said, and done, that she should have thrown him off all those long years ago and which had left her so obdurate where he was concerned. Tonight, when he reached his room, he would attempt to recall those long-lost days and so discover what had caused her change of heart.

Once alone, though, his memory refused to obey him. He had tried so hard to wipe out his love for Mary that to live again those idyllic days was almost impossible. In the end he lay down to sleep, distressed. He had always prided himself on his memory—even Ritchie could not excel him there: in that, they were equals. He had never thought that it would let him down so badly.

For a time he dozed before falling into a restless sleep from which he awoke some time in the small hours, just before the summer's dawn. He stared at the opposite wall—he had not drawn the bed-curtains, and suddenly his memory, hitherto so lack-lustre, returned in full force and in full colour, unlike many of his dreams which were in dreary black and white.

Her father had driven them to a great house not far from Oxford in order to meet a savant, a learned man, whose great-grandfather had been a friend of Isaac Newton. Mary's father had boasted to the savant about his two youthful prodigies and he had asked to meet them.

After a happy morning spent displaying their skills, the savant, whose name still eluded Russell, said, 'Now I wish to talk of private matters to my learned friend, Dr Beauregard, so perhaps the young people might like to repair to the library. It's not a suggestion which I would make to many of their age, but I believe that they might enjoy themselves.

'I have an Orrery there, and laid out on the library table some plans, calculations and diagrams which I have drawn up in an attempt to build a clockwork machine which would be able to add, subtract, multiply and divide, thus saving our brains as well as our energy. We would then have more time to engage in important work based on what our mechanical servant has already accomplished for us. I would value their opinion on my efforts.'

Thus dismissed, they had walked down a long corridor filled with the portraits of the learned man's ancestors—and what the devil had his name been? No matter, they had arrived at the library and did, indeed, enjoy the time they spent there—if not always quite in the way which their host had intended. They had played with the Orrery, watching the planets, including their own, revolve around the central sun, before examining the savant's work and marvelling at its complexity.

'Do you think that we could ever be able to do anything which might rival this?' Mary had asked him.

Russell, whose time had been spent between admiring the savant's intellectual prowess and Mary's face, alight with eager interest, answered her with, 'Why not? I doubt whether he was any more advanced in his skills when he was our age than we are now.'

He felt a dreadful shame on remembering his answer. What had he, Russell Hadleigh, done but neglect the skills which he had acquired in early youth, wasting his time in pleasure instead? Inevitably, since he was at bottom a man of sense, aimless pleasure had begun to pall, leaving him with nothing since his father had closed before him every avenue which he might have explored. Had he continued with his studies as Mary had done, who knows what he might have accomplished? Instead, once she had thrown him off, they had seemed barren, a symbol of all that he had lost—and wished to forget.

At this confrontation of the past Russell Hadleigh with the present one, his mind almost betrayed him. His revived memory began to slip away in a haze of regret and pain. To regain it he admonished himself sternly. What had she said then? How had she answered him? Immediately he was with her in that book-lined room and once more her voice was in his ear, as clear and youthfully excited as though he had truly recovered that lost time. He saw her face again, alight with the joy which had sprung out of their mutual intellectual passion.

'I think,' she was saying, 'that if we continue to work together there is nothing that we might not do.'

His other passion for her, which had been growing during the weeks which they had spent together, came into full flower at that moment.

'Oh, Mary,' he exclaimed, 'I know that you are speaking of our studies, but is there not also something else lying between us?—this, for instance,' and he leaned across the table to kiss her on the brow.

'Tell me, I beg of you, my darling girl, that you have come to feel for me, as I feel for you.'

He had drawn back so that he might speak to her from the heart, and she, her eyes, shining like stars, which told him as much as any words that he was not alone even before she said, 'I had not dared to hope...I, too...'

She stopped.

The older Russell, remembering this, knew that Mary had led a quiet life, away from the society of those of her own age and consequently the feelings which she then had for him were so new to her that she did not know quite what to make of them.

Was it normal, or usual, she must have asked her-self, for a young woman to feel such strange excite-ment in the presence of a young man; to long to see him when they were apart; to have such a lift of the heart when he came into the room? Russell knew of her inexperience and was tender with her. He had no wish to exploit it in any way. To have done so, to have played with her feelings, even if he had stopped short of seducing her, would have been the act of a cur.

More than that, though, was his own understanding that what he was beginning to feel for her was more than simple lust, but something deeper. It was an un-derstanding that here was the other half of himself whom he had been fortunate enough to meet before he had wasted his youth dallying with other women after whom he might lust—but never love.

He remembered that, mesmerised, they had stared at one another across the table.

'Perhaps I should not have said that—' she began.

He would not let her finish.

'No, Mary, you're wrong. When I told you what I felt for you I was neither lying, nor flirting, nor pass-ing an idle moment by trying to please the young woman I was with. I truly meant it. When we are both a little older I shall ask my father—and yours—for their permission to marry you. That is, my dar-ling, if that is what you wish.'

Her face told him that his wish was granted, before her words.

'In the meantime,' he said slowly, 'we must behave ourselves. Your father trusts us, and we must not betray that trust. We have all our lives before us, and we must remember that if we are tempted to anticipate our love.'

Oh, what a pompous young ass he had been! Yet he had meant every word he had said, particularly since he was convinced that the world lay all before the pair of them. If he had forgotten his father's demeaning of him, or that Dr Beauregard might have other plans for his daughter, glorious though a marriage to Bretford's heir might be, that was the privilege of his eager, innocent youth, not his disillusioned maturity.

A little chaste loving which might not rouse him overmuch seemed now in order, and so he kissed her gently, put his arms round her and petted her as innocently as he could, so that she turned her starstruck eyes up to him, and stroked his cheek in her turn.

Fortunately, they both drew apart before matters became too ecstatic, and when Dr Beauregard and the savant returned to talk to them of the savant's plans, they were behaving themselves. Mary was inspecting one piece of paper, and Russell another—and there, for the time being, his memories ended.

Were they memories? Or was it a dream? Russell was to ask himself these questions the next morning. Or was it a mixture of both, since immediately before

he fell into a deep and contented sleep, he remembered the name of the savant: it was Dr Henry
Wardour.

What he had not yet remembered was all that had
led up to that dreadful day when he had learned of
her betrayal, but he would—he was sure that, given
time, he would.

Chapter Five

Mary had thought that breakfasting with Russell might be different, but no such thing. To her surprise they were as easy together as though they had been Darby and Joan themselves, the mythical husband and wife whose marital bliss had been a by-word.

Pickering, Russell's post-boy and the two drivers had already had a self-important conference in which they had agreed the route north until they were near Newcastle upon Tyne. The post-boy had been able to advise them on the best inns, and which shortcuts to avoid.

He had put a grimy finger by his nose and told them to avoid all the minor roads: it was safer on the main ones.

'Less likely to be attacked by the gentlemen of the road—or stray Luddites trying to stop and loot a passing coach,' he had finished.

Told of this by Pickering, Russell remembered that Ritchie had handed him a pair of pistols and an elegant-looking, but deadly, French sporting gun for protection. 'Better be safe than sorry,' had been his farewell words.

'These days even the Home Secretary carries a brace of pistols in his carriage when driving around London—and you will be driving across the moors both before and after York. Keep them with you so that you can use them in an emergency.'

'Come on, brother,' Russell had protested. 'I'm not off to the wilds of Spain and having to worry about dodging Napoleon's army.'

'True, but these days travelling in England is not as safe as it was, believe me. If it were ever really safe, that is.'

So far, at least, he had met nothing untoward on his journey north other than small crowds of ragged boys running and shouting after the chaise once it had left the stable-yard of the post-house. He would be sure to rag Ritchie about his dooming once he had arrived safely at Eddington.

In the meantime, they drove north in tandem so that the journey became for both Russell and Mary something out of time. In the evenings they played chess and renewed their friendly rivalry in the world of numbers to the bemusement of their fellows in the common room of whatever post-house they were lodging in. Neither Russell nor Mary dared trust themselves to seek privacy in the other's bedroom. Simply being together, even in company, was disturbing enough without tempting fate further.

Pickering, for one, could not believe what was happening to his master.

'Can't think what's come over him, never seen him so happy before,' he confided to Mary's driver with a knowing wink, 'unless it's your missis, of course. Not that he suffers from the blue devils, you understand,' he added hastily, 'just not very cheerful. Always considerate, though, many aren't.'

'You're right there,' said the driver. 'My missis is a good 'un, too.'

It was on their way from the last post-house before their roads diverged that Mary and Russell's time in Arcadia ended. The previous evening Mary had come to believe that perhaps, after all, she might consider forgiving Russell for his past behaviour.

Her marriage had been happy enough, even though Dr Wardour had been old enough to be her father, but it had only been a meeting of minds. If she were honest she had endured his love-making, tepid as it was, rather than enjoyed it. With Russell, though, she was beginning to grasp that their relationship was so powerful that it encompassed both the mind and the body.

If their hands touched over the chessboard, it was, indeed, as though their whole bodies were engaged. If Russell so much as looked at her in a particular way, with his startlingly blue eyes hooded, her response to him was strong enough to frighten her. From his behaviour Mary was compelled to believe that she was having the same effect on him. It was all quite different from her sober games of chess with Henry Wardour!

If they were both so profoundly moved by such slight things as these, what would happen if they were to engage in the final act itself? She had listened to other women talking, and had been surprised that they could find such pleasure in it—but now she found herself wondering what it would be like if she and Russell...

At this point in her musings Mary put up her hands to cover her hot face. What had come over her that she should think such things?

But she knew.

It was meeting Russell Hadleigh again and discovering that the current which ran between them was so strong that if she ventured into it, she would drown, as surely as she would drown if she walked into the Thames in London. But if drowning there brought death and oblivion, what would drowning with Russell Hadleigh bring her?

Sleep that night was long in coming, and her dreams took her into the past again, the past where they had walked in the garden together, happy in each other's company. She would not allow herself the nightmare of reliving the past where she had lost him, but would remember only the happy, earlier part of it and the increasingly joyful present.

And if she were a fool to indulge herself in that, then she was a fool and so be it.

'There will be no chess game for us tonight since our roads divide this afternoon,' Russell said at breakfast, 'but when we reach our destination we shall not be so far apart that we may not arrange another, either at Eddington or at Ancoates. The road between them is not too difficult for a chaise. Or a man on horseback.'

'True,' agreed Mary. 'And that being so, we must arrange a meeting as soon as we are settled in.'

Russell thought that these were the kindest words which she had spoken to him, seeing that it was the first time that she had initiated a meeting between them.

'Indeed,' he said eagerly. 'As soon as possible, although I am not quite sure what kind of welcome I shall get when I reach Eddington.'

Mary's rather surprised expression told him that he needed to explain himself a little.

'I fear that they have had no warning that I am coming. It was a spur-of-the-moment arrangement— but it is strongly approved of by my brother Ritchie. He thinks that I need occupation and that visiting Eddington, and learning how it is managed, will be of use to me.'

This was another half-lie, but he did not wish to tell Mary of his suspicions about the running of the Eddington estate until he had had time to inspect it. It would not be right to criticise Shaw if he were mistaken—although he was pretty certain that he was not.

* * *

Their chaises were being made ready for the journey in the stable yard. Both Mary and Russell were finding it difficult to say goodbye. Russell dearly wished to kiss her before they parted, and Mary was, to her own surprise, wishing that he would take the initiative and do so. After all, he had twice kissed her without any encouragement from her, and now, after almost living together for several days, they had fallen into the carefree camaraderie, if not to say love, which they had enjoyed in youth.

'Soon,' said Russell, bowing over her hand. 'I shall arrange to visit you soon. You will allow that, I trust?'

'So long as you do not take advantage of me when you do.'

'No, indeed, you will be quite safe since your aunt will play duenna.'

Still they did not move away, and still Russell held on to her hand. The post-boy gave a preliminary toot on his horn to recall them to the rigours of the day.

'Adieu,' he said at last, and this time he did kiss her, on the hand—but the effect on them both was as strong as if he had kissed her on the lips. Only after that did he, reluctantly, release her hand, and Mary, equally reluctantly, moved away.

'Until we meet again,' he breathed, before allowing Pickering to come up to him and say briskly,

'Time we left m'lord. We have a somewhat longer journey than Mrs Wardour after she takes the by-road to Ancoates.'

Reluctantly they parted. Even the knowledge that they might meet again soon was not enough for either of them. Mary resumed her seat in the chaise, filled with a vague unhappiness. The certainty that they would not meet again that evening weighed on her mind as heavily as a burden she had taken up would lie on her shoulders.

Again and again in her musings she returned to the same conclusion: how strong must their mutual passion be if the passing years had not been sufficient to dim it? Once they had met one another again, the miseries of her forsaken past had been swept away. The quiet life which she had lived with Henry Wardour seemed empty and barren—even though when she was living it it had seemed sufficient to her needs.

Russell was experiencing similar feelings. He must, he decided, clear up this odd business at Eddington quickly so that he could concentrate on winning Mary back again. With her by his side, stalwart and true, he believed that he could face anything, including his unloving father.

Halfway between the post-house and the parting of their ways one of Russell's horses fell slightly lame and slowed them down, with the result that Mary's chaise, which had started ahead of them, was soon out of sight. Needham and the post-boy decided that they would take on a sound horse at the next inn they reached—which would delay them even further.

Russell had half-hoped for yet another farewell at the moment of their final parting—and having taken on a nag which looked distinctly seedy, but proved to have unexpected stamina, he was still in hopes that Mary might wait for him to catch her up, even if it delayed her quite considerably.

He was surprised, however, when after a sharp bend in the road, her carriage came into view, and even more surprised to find that it had ended up in the ditch, half on its side. Its two horses had been cut loose by a pair of ill-favoured fellows who were leading them away. The driver was lying on his back in the road and the post-boy was nowhere to be seen.

Mary and her maid were standing in the middle of the road, being harangued by another ill-looking fellow who, Russell saw when his own chaise neared the scene, was threatening them with a pistol.

His chaise jerked to a stop before he could even give an order for it to do so. Russell's post-boy had seen what was happening even before he did, and was, Russell was to discover later, already reaching for a rusty blunderbuss which he always carried with him.

Russell leaned forward to take his own pistols from where they had been stored for easy use. He handed one to the startled Pickering, put his own into the waistband of his breeches and picked up the French sporting gun which Ritchie had lent him. Seen at a distance, it looked exactly like one of the new Baker rifles which the British Army had adopted.

'Enough to strike terror in anyone's heart,' Ritchie had said in his quiet way.

Russell jumped out of the chaise. Pickering followed him as he had been instructed before they left Liscombe: he was gingerly holding his pistol away from him as though it might, by accident, fire in his direction rather than at the enemy.

Russell strolled leisurely forward, the sporting gun at the ready, stopping some distance away from the armed man so that his likelihood of being shot by him would be low since the robber's pistol looked more like an antique than a dangerous weapon.

He could see that it was Mary and her maid who were in the most immediate danger so he knew that he must go carefully. He was ruefully aware that he was appearing to be much braver than he actually was in trying to act as he thought that his twin might when in a tight corner.

'What's this, then?' he asked in as unthreatening a manner as possible—but keeping the rifle trained on the armed robber.

'What does it look like?' snarled the robber, backing away a little. 'We wants the missis's money and her hosses. Yours, too, as well.'

'This says you won't get either,' drawled Russell, raising his sporting gun and sighting along its long, elaborately carved barrel.

'Try to fire that and I'll shoot the missis,' threatened the robber, pointing his pistol at Mary. Had he seized her, and then made the threat, Russell would have had no alternative but to give way at this point and try to work out another stratagem for rescuing her, but the robber could see what Russell could not.

Not only had Pickering, following his master's example, raised his pistol menacingly, but Russell's post-boy was also advancing on him, his blunderbuss in his hand. Worse than that, the robber's two cohorts had decided to save themselves by mounting the horses they had been holding, and were riding rapidly across the scrub which lined the by-way and into the trees, away from possible death or capture.

Deserted by his accomplices, the robber still tried to hold his ground, waving his pistol between Mary and Russell, who was busy holding *his* ground.

Mary, without turning her head towards him, shouted, 'Be careful, Russell, he might kill you instead of me.'

'Yes, do be careful,' mimicked the robber. 'It's a pretty choice for me, ain't it?'

'*Point non plus,*' murmured Russell to himself. Aloud he said, 'Don't be a fool, man. It's a hanging matter if you kill any of us—and all for nothing. If you kill the lady with your one bullet, I shall certainly shoot you. On the other hand, if you kill me, then my servant here will shoot you. Not a pretty choice at all, I would say.'

'Damn you!' howled the robber. 'What have I to lose? It's a hanging matter or death whatever I do. I *will* kill the doxy,' but before he could swing his pistol in her direction Russell tightened his finger on the trigger of his gun and fired himself.

The robber dropped to the ground, his pistol still in his hand. Blood was pouring from his shoulder. He tried to sit up, but failed. Russell walked forward, kicked his pistol away, and turned to Mary, who was white-faced and trembling, but who had remained quite calm during her ordeal.

'You're neither of you hurt?' he asked, stopping himself with a great effort from taking her into his arms to comfort her. 'I shouldn't have let you go on unescorted.'

Mary said, her voice shaking, 'No, but I was very frightened—until you came.'

She looked down at the man on the ground. 'Russell, he's going to bleed to death unless we do something for him.'

'So, as one might expect,' Russell said, 'you are merciful as well as brave. Pickering,' he shouted, 'you can put down that pistol, get one of my shirts from my luggage and we'll see if between us we can't make some impromptu bandages. Needham, go and see if you can do anything for Mrs Wardour's driver. Meantime I'll take Mrs Wardour and her maid to the chaise and open the bottle of brandy I always keep in it for emergencies. That should put some colour in their cheeks.'

Mary gave a strangled laugh at this sally designed, she was sure, to steady her shattered nerves. Her maid, over whom Pickering had been hovering protectively, and who had said nothing so far, murmured, 'You were very brave, m'lord.'

'Not I,' said Russell, leading them over to where his chaise waited, the post-boy standing by the horses. 'I was lucky rather, and need to thank my brother who armed me so well.'

Presently, after he and Pickering had bandaged the would-be robber, Russell checked with Needham that Mary's driver was slowly recovering from the fall he had taken when the shot from the robber's first pistol had killed one of their horses, thus landing him—and the chaise—in the ditch. The chaise had lost one of its wheels and would have to be abandoned for the time being.

'But never mind that,' Russell said, continuing to take charge and order matters clearly and lucidly after a fashion which surprised him when he thought about it later and which impressed Mary at the time. 'One way or another I'll see that you reach Ancoates—but what are we to do with our murderous friend?' He pointed at the robber whom Pickering had propped up against one wheel of Russell's chaise.

'Nothing,' the man moaned. 'You've done for me, now leave me here to die. I'm only an old sojer, turned off after Waterloo. Who's to care about me?'

Russell looked down at him—and thought of the distance, and difference between them. There was no sentimentality in his conclusions: the man had threatened to kill both him and Mary, but he felt compelled to ask himself how he would have coped with the bad hand which fate had dealt to the man before him had he been in his position.

His own worries about his life seemed mean and stupid in the face of this. Starvation and ruin would never be his lot: his life had been cushioned from birth. He had never even had to contemplate what Ritchie must have done daily when he was in Spain: his own death or mutilation.

Nevertheless, the man had threatened to kill Mary and he must be handed over to the authorities to be dealt with.

The post-boy, who had shown remarkable presence of mind during the whole wretched business, and who possessed a great deal of local knowledge, took a hand again by solving the problem of where to deliver the robber.

'There's a post-house back on the road north in a village not far from here where the Squire has his big house in the main street,' he offered eagerly. 'I mind me that he's a magistrate. If you allow me to drive you there, you can hand this fellow over to him. Mr Needham and Mr Pickering can look after the ladies and Mrs Wardour's injured driver if you leave some of your arms with them.'

'Excellent,' said Russell. 'I am supposing that once we arrive at the post-house we can hire a chaise to come back and pick them up. One thing is for sure, my chaise isn't big enough to hold everyone—even merely to take them to this village. Besides that, we shall certainly need another post-chaise if I am to escort Mrs Wardour, her servants and her luggage safely to Ancoates, seeing that her own is so badly damaged. We shall also need to hire labourers from the village to pull her coach out of the ditch so that we can unload it.'

Mary had walked over to Russell's chaise, her maid following.

'If you could leave two of your rugs behind, Lord Hadleigh,' she said, 'We could use one of them to sit on the grass by the road while you are gone and my poor driver, who still seems overset, could lie down on the other until he recovers. I am sure that both Pickering and Needham will be able to keep guard for myself, Jennie and my driver until you return.'

'You could, of course, come with us to the inn,' Russell offered. 'I do have room for just one more.'

'I haven't the slightest intention of deserting Jennie and the others,' she announced. 'The weather is fine, and the scenery, now that I have the time to inspect it, is wildly beautiful and well worth a more prolonged look. I suggest that you make all speed to this village and settle matters there.'

She was rewarded with Russell's most brilliant smile. 'I should have known that you would always consider others before yourself,' he murmured. 'I have no doubt that you are being a most splendid influence on me.'

Her smile for him was equally dazzling. 'I have to say, Lord Hadleigh, that judging by your recent behaviour you really need no guidance on how to act both bravely and promptly. Here comes Pickering with the rugs. Now you may safely leave us.'

Between them Pickering and Russell manoeuvred the barely conscious robber into the chaise where he lay full length along the seat opposite to Russell's, moaning gently all the way back to the main road and from thence to the village of Coatsburn, which was, as the post-boy had said, at no great distance from the attempted robbery.

The Squire's house was indeed in the centre of the village, facing the Market Cross. Its gardens were all behind it and ran down to a tributary of the Tyne. A supercilious butler answered the door and stared at Russell as though he were a hawker come to sell pins and needles.

'Yes?' he enquired, his lip curling.

'You may inform your master—whoever he might be—that Lord Hadleigh of Eddington wishes to speak to him on a most urgent matter. Since speed is of the essence here, I trust that you will not delay further.'

'Of course, m'lord, pray enter.'

Before the butler had time to leave the entrance hall, a door at the side opened and a large gentleman in country clothing entered and stared at them both.

'What is it, Peters? And please introduce me to this gentleman before you begin any explanations.'

'I have the honour to introduce my master, Sir Ralph Cheyney, to you, m'lord Hadleigh. Lord

Hadleigh says that he wishes to speak to you most urgently, Sir Ralph.'

The large gentleman, who appeared to be in his middle fifties, said drily, 'Does he, indeed? Pray, what can I do for you, m'lord?'

'I am sorry to intrude,' Russell began, 'but I regret to inform you that an attempt was made to rob a lady travelling north, apparently on her own. I was travelling a little behind her, and was sufficiently fortunate to prevent the attempt from succeeding. I have in my chaise one of the robbers who was badly injured when I fired at him to prevent him injuring the lady. On being informed that you were a magistrate, I have taken the liberty of driving the wretch here and asking you to dispose of him. I could scarcely leave him bleeding to death on the road.'

'No, indeed,' replied Sir Ralph, again dry. 'Most messy—and inconsiderate for other travellers, too. Peters,' he said to the butler, 'ask Mr Williams to come to the study. Please, m'lord, do me the honour of accompanying me there so that we may make arrangements to dispose of your prisoner. A Luddite, perhaps?'

Russell shook his head. 'No, Sir Ralph, an old soldier turned off after Waterloo.'

Sir Ralph shook his head. 'That's too bad, but he shouldn't have turned robber—but who knows, he perhaps had no other skills.'

'Possibly not.' They were now in Sir Ralph's study, where a large desk stood in front of a magnificent hearth flanked by bookshelves which were filled from the floor to the ceiling with imposing-looking tomes.

'We magistrates meet here,' Sir Ralph explained. 'Now, m'lord, is there anything else I might do for you?'

Russell told him of Mary's predicament, and how he proposed to deal with it, Sir Ralph nodding the while.

'I think that I might be able to help you here. I will send my wheelwright and a carpenter to examine the chaise and find out whether it is repairable. Unfortunately, the only post-house in the village is a poor one. It may be able to supply you with fresh horses, but the accommodation it offers is most un-satisfactory. It would please me to entertain you and the lady overnight—she must be suffering from shock and a night's stay would be a great restorative.'

He looked hard at Russell. 'I knew your father, Lord Bretford, long ago when we were young to-gether. You are not very like him. We might have been relatives once—but that is an old story. Since you are still Lord Hadleigh, I take it that he is alive and well.'

'Indeed,' Russell replied. He had heard his father speak several times of old friends of his youth, but he had never mentioned a Ralph Cheyney. 'It is kind of you to offer shelter and I am immediately prepared to accept it on behalf of myself and the lady. She is Mrs Mary Wardour, the niece of Miss Charlotte

Beauregard who, I gather, is settled not far from here.'

'Yes, indeed. I have met the lady and will be pleased to assist her niece.'

Russell told Sir Ralph that Mary was waiting patiently by the roadside. Sir Ralph immediately arranged for his own coach to be sent forth on the instant to bring the whole party to Cheyney Court, as his home was called.

'After that, m'lord, I will arrange to have nuncheon served. Nothing like good food to soothe the nerves, eh? Do you wish to accompany the coach and direct my man to where your party is to be found?'

Russell allowed that he did. Sir Ralph, who seemed to be a bustling gentleman, next turned his organising energies on Mr Williams, and made arrangements for the robber to be removed from Russell's chaise and transported to the local gaol where a doctor would examine him. 'Mustn't have him die on us,' he roared cheerfully, 'before we hang him.'

If he hadn't been given such a talking to by Ritchie about his soft-heartedness, Russell would have deplored Sir Ralph's cheerful coarseness: as it was he found himself being amused by it.

'Quite so,' he said, his face as straight as he could make it. Wouldn't do to antagonise such a helpful fellow who was making sure that not only would he be able to rescue Mary without delay, but was also offering her shelter for the night.

*   *   *

Mary was prepared for a long wait and could only hope that the robbers would not return to finish what they had started. She was not overly worried for, even if Pickering seemed a trifle unhappy about his role as her protector, both her driver and her post-boy seemed quite cheerful now that they had been left armed with the reloaded sporting gun and the two pistols. On the contrary, her driver kept muttering that if they reappeared he was ready and waiting for them this time.

What had surprised her about their recent adventure—or misadventure, she was not sure which it was—was the speed and courage which Russell had shown from the moment he had arrived on the scene.

He had told Jennie that he had not been brave, but he had strolled forward, holding his gun at the ready, as though it were something he was used to doing every day. All his charming indolence of manner had disappeared. He had told her that his brother had been a soldier, and he had behaved just as she might have expected one to behave.

After he had shot the robber he had organised matters so briskly that she was not surprised to see his chaise returning after a very short time, followed by a wagon and a rather elderly, if splendid, coach with equally splendid armorial bearings on the side. The motto beneath the arms was in English, not Latin, and proudly proclaimed 'Always Ready'!

Russell leaped out of his chaise—there was no doubt that he was ready, too—and advanced towards her, saying, 'We have had a piece of great good luck to counterbalance the bad one we have just suffered. Sir Ralph Cheyney, the local Squire, turned out to be an old friend of my father's and is offering us not only a meal, but also lodging for the night—and possibly longer if your chaise needs a great deal of repairing. Two of his men are in the wagon and will start work at once to pull it out of the ditch in order to discover how badly it is damaged.'

She had never seen him so animated, so happy. Since she had met him again there had always been a faint aura of restraint about him, almost as though he were not sure of himself. In that he had been quite different from the eager boy she had once known.

'How extremely fortunate we have been,' she exclaimed, once matters had been arranged and she was seated in Russell's chaise being driven back to Cheyney Court. 'We might have been compelled to spend the night in an indifferent post-house. You have not been very long, either. I had imagined that it might be quite some time before you returned.'

'Oh, Sir Ralph is a managing kind of man and was highly indignant at the notion that a lady of quality should be put to any distress by a pack of thieves! He would hang all the highwaymen at his gate-post if he thought that would deter others, were his last words to me before I left. Moreover, since he has had the goodness to put himself and his people about so much, I have arranged that we shall be equally brisk in our return—particularly since he has ordered nuncheon to be prepared for everyone from your good self down to the junior of the two post-boys. I think that we have quite made his day.'

'Oh, the robbers, highwaymen, call them what you will, did that,' Mary riposted, 'except that…' and she hesitated '…except that I am sorry to learn that the wounded man is an old soldier, turned away and left to fend for himself after defending our country. Can that really be true?'

Russell's face was grave. 'I fear so. My brother spoke about it and said that if I had become an MP he would have asked me to raise the matter in the House—he considered it to be a great scandal and a shame.'

'Did you wish to be an MP?'

A shadow passed over his mobile face when he replied, 'I would like to have become one, but my father had other notions about who should sit for the seat he controls. Unfortunately, I'm not sufficiently well known to be able to gain adoption at the few which become vacant and are neither Rotten Boroughs nor in the gift of the great—like my father.'

Mary said robustly, 'My late husband was of the opinion that too few people were eligible to vote. He also thought it was quite wrong that a single person—such as the Duke of Newcastle—would not only be able to compel his workmen to vote for his candidate, but that he also had the gift of a number of

Parliamentary seats so that even those who could vote were deprived of choice.'

Russell made a wry face this time. 'I suppose that someone like myself, trained for nothing, is hardly the stuff of a good MP.'

'Nonsense. You have a very good mind—but forgive me if I inform you that something tells me that you have not used it overmuch in the years which we have spent apart.'

Mary thought for a moment that she had gone too far. She was not in a position to offer him such an implied rebuke. Their re-acquaintance was too short for her to judge him without his resenting her frankness. He was so silent after she had finished speaking that she opened her mouth to apologise—only to have him say in a slow, heavy voice, 'You are quite right. I have wasted my time—and it is only recently that I have come to understand that, for my own good, my life must change.

'You are the second person in the last few weeks to tell me as much, and I have resolved to reform myself. In future I shall trust in my own judgement and not depend on that of others.'

He meant by that his father, but he could not tell her so, for that would be a betrayal of them both.

Mary's reply was a measured one. 'I needed to learn that after my husband died,' she told him. 'While he was alive he made all the decisions for the pair of us, even down to what he wanted for dinner and how the house was to be run. I was left to be…not an idle decoration, for he expected me to continue to work on mathematical problems, but someone who obeyed his every wish without question.

'At first, once he was no longer there to direct me, I found it difficult to make my mind up about anything, but after a time I began to find it exciting to be in charge of myself. Although he left me his money and his estate in a trust for me, the income from it is more than enough to enable me to live in comfort, and I find that I like being my own mistress.'

She was not surprised to hear him say, his expression a trifle wry, 'Does that mean that you do not wish to marry again, but would prefer to remain a wealthy widow?'

What could she say to that? She was rapidly growing to believe that she might like to be Lady Hadleigh since Lord Hadleigh was distinguished, among other things, by his kindness, but the past lay between them and would not die. For the first time Mary felt that it was a mistake to pretend that what had happened all those years ago had not happened, that it might be better if they spoke of it.

Consequently her answer was a hesitant one, 'If, and note that I say if, I found someone whom I could trust as well as love, who would not treat me as though I were a child, then I might wish to marry again.'

Russell's face lit up as though she had made him the most splendid present: it was as though he were once again the eager boy he had been and not the blasé dandy which he had become. 'Does that mean that there is hope for me yet?'

It was a measure of how far he had come, both with her and the world, that he could be so abrupt, so sure of himself.

Even when she shook her head and murmured, 'I fear that you are going far too fast for me, Russell,' he was not downcast.

Instead he leaned forward—she was sitting opposite to him—and took her hand, saying, 'I shall not let you escape me so easily this time, my dear. We may be parting soon, but not for long. Eddington is no great distance from your aunt's home and I intend to visit you both.'

He released her hand, partly so as not to seem boorishly importunate and partly because to touch her did dreadful things to him. His smile for her was dazzling, so dazzling that Mary scarcely took in all that he had said. It was only later, alone in her pretty room at Cheyney Court, that she asked herself why he had said, *I shall not let you escape me so easily this time*?

After all, it was he who had abandoned her and not she him. Why should he pretend otherwise? Perhaps he was doing so to win her again? If so, might he not be playing some sort of perverted game

such as seducers often engaged in, gaining his pleasure by betraying her rather than winning her?

Not that he had seduced her the first time. It was
true that he had never breached her innocence, but
was it not a form of seduction to promise her everything—and then leave her without another word until
he had walked into the drawing-room at Markham
Hall?

Mary put her hands over her hot face. Dare she
trust him? Dare she allow the strong attraction which
she still felt for him—no, not attraction, Mary, but
love—to lead her ultimately to confess that love to
him, come what may afterwards? Or should she continue to walk alone as she had done since her husband's death?

And what a barren life that was! No one in her
bed, no child, nothing but the cold figures on paper
which had been her whole life since she had married
Dr Henry Wardour.

Sir Ralph Cheyney had been as good as his word.
He found accommodation for both sets of travellers,
fed them immediately after they had arrived, bellow-
ing at them, 'I have ordered wine to be served instead
of tea, the whole pack of you look quite done up,'
which was truthful, but scarcely tactful, being
Russell's inward gloss on that.

Immediately after he had promised to visit Mary
once they both reached journey's end she had become very quiet. Something told him not to trouble
her further, so instead he sat back and drank in her

charming face. Her beauty was of the rare kind which consists of character and good bones rather than those more blatant traits which society found fashionable. There was nothing showy about her, nothing of the obvious such as Caroline Fawcett and his other women had possessed.

Was that why he had chosen them? To try to blot out the memory of a piquant face, dark eyes, dark hair and sweet mouth, plus the calm self-command which Mary had possessed even as a young girl. To say nothing of her pretty, trim figure and her graceful carriage. More than that, he could talk to her as an equal and discuss matters with her which had bored Caroline and the others whenever he had tried to raise them.

He thought of her remarks about being an MP and the wrongs of the present system of elections and choosing MPs. Oh, yes, there were women in society who knew of such things, but they were few and far between and growing fewer.

If he married Mary, she would be his friend and companion as well as his lover. They would go through life side by side—and he inwardly snorted his derision at the manner in which Henry Wardour had treated his clever and capable wife.

'There,' announced Pickering, who had been helping him to dress while all these new and powerful thoughts were running through his mind. 'You are now fit to go down to dinner, though, if I may say so, m'lord, I wonder whether any of us will have a great appetite for it, Sir Ralph having served us such a sumptuous collation not many hours ago!'

'True,' said Russell, 'but seeing what a kind host he is, I must try to do his dinner justice. You, being in the servants' hall and not under his kind, if eagle eye, may do as you please.'

Pickering bowed his thanks. It was plain that m'lord was still in the happy mood which had taken him over ever since he had met that woman at Markham Hall. Long might it continue. He was a good fellow and had been the slave of the dismals for far too long.

Mary, sitting in the drawing room listening to Sir Ralph's booming voice, with occasional interjections from his widowed sister, Amelia, who was his nominal hostess, although it was plain that Sir Ralph made all the decisions at Cheyney Court, was quite relieved to see Russell enter.

'Ah, there you are,' said Sir Ralph, rising. 'I was just informing Mrs Wardour that she may stay here as long as she pleases. I would not like her to continue her journey until she is quite recovered from today's untoward events.'

It took all Russell's strength not to reply that he had seldom seen Mrs Wardour look more recovered, but he acknowledged Sir Ralph's kindness with a graceful bow and a murmured, 'I'm sure that Mrs Wardour will accept your kind offer should she need further rest. I trust that she does not object to my speaking on her behalf.'

'Not at all,' said Mary immediately. 'Lord Hadleigh has said for me exactly what I would have said for myself.'

'Excellent!' exclaimed Sir Ralph. 'Now we may sit down to dinner with that settled.'

Mary and Russell were later to agree that, while most of his conversation consisted of exclamations and declamations, he was extremely kind-hearted. He also employed an excellent cook and was a good host even if he did spend most of the meal informing his guests that they really must eat a little more of that— that being virtually every cover placed upon the large table.

'And now,' said Sir Ralph, once the ladies had retired and port and cigars had been produced for him and Russell, 'we may further our acquaintance, m'lord. It has been a great grief of mine that although your father and I were bosom friends in youth we have not met for more years than I care to remember. We were both poor young fellows in those days with no notion that we should both inherit great estates— your father's being the greater.

'Oh, we were carefree then, and what a jolly fellow he was—always joking, always ready for a lark. I mind me the japes he played when we were in London. He was a great one for the ladies until he met my younger sister, Serena. After that he sobered down—we all thought that it would be a match. And then his father inherited the earldom of Bretford when his elder brother died and my jolly friend became Lord Hadleigh, the heir.'

He fell silent for a moment, leaving Russell to mull over the remarkable news that his father had been a jolly fellow in his youth, given to practical joking! Anything more unlike the testy and dour man that he had known all his life could not be imagined. He scarcely knew what to say, but Sir Ralph was a great talker and went on with his reminiscences growing freer and franker as most of the bottle of port went down him.

'The next thing I knew was that he was coming to stay at Eddington, which was the home of Margaret Russell, cousin to me and my sisters. Margaret was the Russell heiress—as you doubtless know, she being your mother—and your father had come to offer for her and marry her.

'Married they were. Serena was heartbroken, so much so that my mother packed her off to Brighton to stay with an aunt—the gossip about the wedding would have been too much for her. I wasn't invited, only my elder brother. He died in a boating accident the next summer, so that I inherited everything. What was even odder was that your father never visited Eddington again, not even after it came to him after old Russell died. In fact, he never spoke another word to either Serena or any of our family from the day we last saw him in London at m'father's place in Russell Square.'

He took another giant swig of port and stared across the room at the ornate hearth as though he were seeing the dead past in the flames of its fire.

'Never did know what to make of that,' he came out with at last. Then, apparently inconsequentially, 'Still a jolly fellow, your father?'

'No,' said Russell slowly, not knowing exactly how to answer. 'No, no one would call my father jolly. He's the most serious man I know.'

'Jackie Chancellor, serious! You're bamming me!'

'Indeed not. I have never, in all my life, known my father to tell a joke, or even to laugh at one.'

'Odder and odder,' gloomed Sir Ralph. He leaned forward to give the fire a vigorous poke. 'I expect, since I gather that you're off to Eddington, that he might pay us a belated visit, eh?'

'I doubt that very much, sir.'

Russell wondered for a moment whether he ought to be frank with his father's old friend and inform him that the very mention of the word Eddington to Lord Bretford was always calculated to bring on a fit of the dismals. He decided against it. Mumchance was probably better here.

'Hmm!' exclaimed Sir Ralph, staring even harder at the fire. 'It's time that someone ought to visit Eddington. Don't like some of the gossip I hear about young Shaw. Not that I'm a great one for gossip, no indeed! But his father was not what I would call an efficient man and young Shaw is less than that.

Things have gone from bad to worse since his father died and he took over.'

Young Shaw! Now here was a turn up for the book. So far as Lord Bretford and Russell, himself, knew, old Shaw was still running the Eddington estate; nothing had reached London about his death or about the son succeeding to his father's place.

Russell remembered his own misgivings about the Eddington accounts which had set him off on his northern odyssey and reintroduced him to Mary, but decided against mentioning them to his host. The news that old Shaw was dead and that his death had been concealed from his father made him more determined than ever to press on to Eddington to find out what exactly was going on there.

He might also try to discover something more of his father's past and the reasons why his character had changed so dramatically. If he did, he would remain mumchance about that, too. I'm learning guile from Ritchie, he thought, damn me if I'm not. He was not sure whether that notion pleased or frightened him.

Pleased would be better—he was beginning to believe that he might need all his twin's steel and ingenuity once he reached Eddington. In the meantime there was Mary to look after and to get to know better, so much better that she might change her mind about him...and then, who knew what might happen...

Chapter Six

They stayed at Cheyney Court for two days while Mary's chaise was repaired. Fortunately it had not been greatly damaged and her—and Russell's—remaining journey north was not very long so that the rather tired nags, which were all that the post-house could supply, would be able to manage it.

'I am quite determined to accompany you the rest of the way to your destination,' Russell told Mary firmly on the evening before they set off again. 'If we travel together we are less likely to be attacked by any wandering Luddites, old soldiers or brigands who might frequent these parts.'

Mary did not argue with him. She rather liked this new downright man—so long as he did not overdo things and turn into a bully, that was.

'Furthermore,' he went on, Sir Ralph nodding approvingly the while, 'I would prefer you to travel in my chaise with our servants following in yours. This would have the advantage that my strong right arm and Ritchie's French sporting gun would both be at the ready should any fool still be determined enough to attack us.'

'Quite right,' roared Sir Ralph. 'Very common-sensical of you, eh, Mrs Wardour? M'lord's strong right arm should always be at the disposal of a fair lady—and you are a very fair lady, if I may say so,' and he winked at Mary. He had already privately decided that Russell and Mary would make 'a handy pair' as he put it to himself in his downright way. The sooner the better, too.

'By the by,' he added, 'that rogue you disposed of, m'lord, is being transported to Newcastle Gaol tomorrow, there to await trial and judgement. You might be needed to attend the trial to give evidence so I have forwarded them your address.'

Russell nodded a trifle ruefully. He could not condone what the fellow had tried to do, but he could understand why he had done it. He would plead for mercy for an old soldier fallen on hard times in the hope that the mandatory death sentence might be commuted to transportation to Botany Bay, but the final word would be with the judge.

He had no doubt that if Sir Ralph still possessed the powers of the old English barony he would cheerfully have hanged him before the gates of Cheyney Court as an encouragement to others not to turn high-wayman and murderer. But times were changing a little and the notion that the death sentence was mandatory for all crimes of every kind, including robberies worth more than five pounds, whatever the age of the offender, was coming under attack—particularly now that there was an empty continent in Australia for felons to fill.

He and Mary discussed that, and other serious matters, in the chaise on the way to Ancoates. On the evening before they had left, they had played a game of chess—to the great wonder of Sir Ralph, who had said, most earnestly, 'Surely, m'lord, you will not try a lady's brain too hard by playing such a difficult game with her? I am quite willing to propose myself as your opponent to save her from being overset.'

'Have no fear, sir,' was Russell's reply. 'Mrs Wardour is a mistress of the game and could beat most men of my acquaintance should she care to give them a game. I am reasonably proficient, but I shall need all my concentration when we joust together if I am not to be disgraced.'

The game which followed proved him to be telling the truth. It was a long one and to Sir Ralph's stupefaction it ended in stalemate. He pretended to be reading a local newspaper but every now and then came over to stare at the board and watch a few moves, particularly when it became plain that there was going to be no rapid finish.

'I should not wish to give either of you a game,' he said, melancholy in his voice. 'You had the right of it m'lord, the lady is your equal. Stalemate, eh? Shall you play another game? Stalemate is not a happy ending.'

'On the contrary,' said Mary, smiling at the kind old man. 'It is a very happy one. If no one has won and no one has lost, then honour is equal and no one has bitten the dust.'

She looked across at Russell when she had finished speaking and saw him nodding approvingly. She asked him on the journey whether he really agreed with what she had said, or had nodded merely to make her happy.

'Oh, I agreed, for that game—and also, at the moment, for the game of life, too, in which I am trying to persuade you to think well of me again. Believe me, when that day comes, stalemate will not do. The King must have his Queen—or the Queen must conquer the King. Whichever way one looks at it, there must be an even happier ending—both for the chess game and for us. At the moment, though, stalemate must do.'

'Logic-chopping,' exclaimed Mary joyfully. She seemed to have caught the habit of exclamation from Sir Ralph. 'You are logic-chopping. How pleased my father would have been with you. He always said that you were lacking in that department and what a pity it was that you never exercised your brain enough so that you might excel.'

She coloured. 'I shouldn't have told you that. It was what he said to me, confidentially, in private.'

'Do not reproach yourself, Mary, for breaching his trust, since he often told *me* the same thing in private. I was an idle fellow then, and since. Meeting you

again has done wonders for me. We must arrange to
meet more often and enlarge on these matters. Your
father used to speak to me about trying to invent a
machine which would add, multiply and divide of
itself, thus saving us all a deal of trouble. Did he do
any further work on it before he died?'

'Alas, no. He was struck down when he thought
that he was on the verge of solving some of the problems he encountered in it. I know that he hoped that
my late husband would carry on his work, but unfortunately he thought that my father was chasing a
mirage. Worse than that, he insisted on destroying all
my father's papers which related to it, even though
my father had arranged my marriage to him so that
we could continue it together. So nothing now will
ever come of his dream.'

They sat for a moment in silence. One of the things
which he liked most about Mary was her ability to
sit quietly beside him between their eager bouts of
conversation when they spoke of everything under
the sun. One thing Russell had kept up was his reading—something which his father heavily criticised
him for if he came across him with a book in his
hands.

'What an idler you are, Hadleigh! Have you nothing better to do than waste your time reading—the
latest novel, I suppose?'

He supposed wrongly. Helped by Ritchie, once he
had come back when the wars were over, he had
drawn up a reading list of those books which he

thought might not only improve his general knowledge, but also those which might possibly help him
when he came to inherit.

His father might have been surprised to know that
his despised son was diligently reading the papers
and reports of the Board of Agriculture and was consequently privately critical of the way in which his
father was allowing his lands to be run—even those
which did not surround Eddington and which he visited more often.

Talking to Mary was another thing. It was reviving
his old academic interests and he found himself looking forward to each new day after a fashion which
he had lost many years ago.

They were nearing Ancoates when she asked him,
'Is there any particular reason why you are visiting
Eddington? It is a matter of some wonder to the na-
tives around here, my aunt tells me, that no member
of the family ever visits the place. The Russells rarely
left it, always provided a magistrate, and took a great
interest in the district. The village is very run down,
she says, which is a great change from the past when
the last Russell squire built it, intending it to be a
model for other landowners to follow.'

She was trying not to be critical of Russell's father,
but not only had her aunt deplored what an absentee
landlord had done to the estate, but Sir Ralph had
also dropped in her presence some heavy-handed
hints to the effect that all was not well at Eddington.

Consequently she awaited Russell's reply with some interest.

He was slow in answering her for he was weighing his words with some care, which was yet another change in his habits. He had been impulsive in the past, Ritchie had always complained of it, but the new life on which he had embarked was altering his behaviour day by day, something of which he was not fully aware.

'I have come here of my own volition,' he told her. 'It was my mother's home, and I thought it a shame that neither of her sons has ever visited it. I don't blame Ritchie in the slightest. He inherited a run-down estate from an old uncle of ours and has been busily restoring it for himself and his family. I suppose that watching him at work spurred me on. He made me feel useless—but then, he always did.'

'And you resented him for that?' Mary asked. Since he was being frank with her, she would be frank back. She had already noticed that he rarely spoke of his father. The only time, indeed, that he had done so was when Sir Ralph had been reminiscing about their mutual past.

'No,' said Russell simply. 'I never resented him. I only wished that I were more like him. He is not only clever, but brave and good. I wish...' and he fell silent.

'What do you wish?' Mary made her reply as gentle as possible.

'I wish that I could have gone for a soldier, too. Things might have been different.'

He decided to be honest with her.

'You see, Mary, my father allowed me no other place in life than that I was the heir and would one day inherit—but that day must be far off and I dislike being made to wish that he would die so that I might be free. I can feel deeply how the Prince of Wales must have suffered before his father went mad and he became Regent. He was a clever man and was allowed to do nothing. He was married off, against his will, to an ugly German princess with whom he had nothing in common. I can think of no worse fate. His reply to that was to become totally irresponsible and I do not wish that to happen to me.

'When I reach Eddington I may perhaps find an aim in life, other than being a clotheshorse, going to the races, gambling, attending balls and reviews and talking nonsense to people for whom I don't care and who don't care for me.'

He did not mention Caroline and the other women. He knew that his dear love understood men and the world well enough to know that there must have been women.

Mary was silent again for some time before she said, 'Forgive me if I ask you if one of the things which determined you to visit Eddington was that your father wished you to marry Angelica Markham—someone little suited to be your wife.'

He leaned forward, took her hand again, as he had done the other afternoon, and kissed it. 'I might have guessed that you would have seen that the comparison I drew between myself and the Prince Regent held good there, too. What a wise creature you are.'

'You have shown some wisdom, too,' retorted Mary, a gleam in her eyes. 'At least you have not grown grotesquely fat, taken to the bottle and married someone unsuitable in private. Oh, dear,' she added, teasing him further, 'I am trusting that you have done nothing like that. If you have, pray forgive me, and I will say no more.'

'Witch,' he said, 'to tease me so mercilessly,' and, tempted by her odd mixture of playfulness and cleverness, he leaned forward and kissed her on the lips. He might as well have lit the touch paper of one of the fireworks to celebrate the said Regent's birthday, so strong was their mutual reaction.

'"Where the bee sucks, there suck I,"' muttered Russell, drawing away a little. 'Will Shakespeare was writing about more than bees when he penned that. Let me drink of your divine honey again.'

She had not drawn away from him, rather she was still leaning forward, bemused. Her lips were swollen, her cheeks red and her eyes were bright, glowing at him while he spoke. Her lips did not refuse him when he claimed them again. His hands rose to stroke her neck gently.

Mary gave a little moan. All her resolutions about not allowing him into her life again had flown away.

He had trusted her with the most intimate confidences about himself and his life and, by doing so, had disarmed her. That Russell had not made them with that end in mind was not to the point.

For a moment they clung together as they had done so many years ago, both of them frustrated by the knowledge that, for honour's sake, they must go no further. And, more to another point, to go any further in the closed confines of the chaise would be extremely uncomfortable. On top of that they were rapidly reaching journey's end.

In the end, astonishingly, it was Russell who drew back and released her gently. He had always been gentle, she remembered, despite his liveliness. He raised his hand, the one with which he had been stroking her neck, face and hair, and placed a finger on her lips as though to soothe her.

'No more,' he said, 'not here, but God, how you tempt me.'

'As you tempt me,' she whispered.

'I know. Oh, Mary, how did we come to part? With you by my side I could have faced my father.'

It was such a cry from the heart that Mary was moved beyond words. She put up her own hand and stroked his face. If he had felt like that in their lost past, then why had he left her? She was not to know that Russell, also greatly moved, was thinking the same thing of her.

Mary was certain that sooner, rather than later, they must face their joint past before they could, perhaps, move into a better present. Not now, not in the chaise, rapidly nearing their destination, but at some time and place where they could be alone, with nothing to distract them.

'What an adventure, my dear! And what a blessing that you were with Lord Hadleigh, and that he was able to rescue you so promptly. I am not in the least surprised that Sir Ralph Cheyney offered you hospitality and lodgings—he is an odd fellow, to be sure, but most good-humoured in his brash way.'

Miss Charlotte Beauregard always spoke in a grand rush, without drawing breath, but her kindness, like Sir Ralph's, was undoubted.

They had scarcely arrived at her pretty country house on the outskirts of Ancoates before she was serving them tea and begging Russell to stay overnight before driving on to Eddington.

'I have a particular reason for reaching there as soon as possible,' he told her, 'which, regretfully, makes me refuse your neighbourly offer. What I would ask you is that you allow me to visit you, and Mrs Wardour, as often as possible. The ride from Eddington is not far, and, I was told by Sir Ralph, is through some impressively wild country, quite unimproved. He has, I gather, no time for the likes of Capability Brown and his fellows.'

'Oh, yes, he is a real character,' agreed Miss Beauregard 'Do have more tea, Lord Hadleigh, and of course you may visit my dear Mary as often as you please. The door will always be open for her rescuer. You know, Sir Ralph even disapproves of my garden because he says it is too civilised. I ask you, could anything be too civilised! I told him that he would deplore the disappearance of the wild man of the woods, and he informed me that he did. We do have a real hermit, though—some ancient scholar who lives in a broken-down cottage in the woods between here and Cheyney Court—but he scarcely qualifies to be a wild man.'

It was pleasant sitting in the charming drawing room opposite to Mary and listening to his hostess's diverting prattle. Russell almost wished that he had agreed to stay overnight, but Sir Ralph's cryptic remarks about Eddington had piqued his curiosity.

'A hermit in a cottage,' he said, smiling at Miss Beauregard while she energetically bustled about, making sure that he and Mary were comfortable. 'I thought that they always lived in damp grottoes.'

'Not this one. He does have a long beard and hair down to his waist. He seems to be quite harmless, though the village children throw stones at him on the few occasions when he visits Ancoates. Neither they, not their parents, can be persuaded that the poor creature is harmless. I have never met him—I understand that the villagers call him George.'

'So, superstition is as rife in the country as it is in the town,' said Mary. 'One always thinks of the countryside as a haven of rural bliss.'

'Not at all—and more to the point, country poverty is, in some ways, more harsh than town poverty, and there has been a lot of it about lately.' Miss Beauregard looked hard at Russell before continuing, 'Your agent at Eddington has turned a lot of labourers away recently. Is that why you are paying us a visit? It is many years since any member of your family did the honours here.'

Russell shook his head. 'No, this is the first I have heard of men being turned off. I have come because I was curious enough to wish to visit the only part of my father's estates of which he is an absentee landlord. It is quite unlike him. He takes a great personal interest in all the rest.'

'Odd, that,' said Miss Beauregard, echoing Sir Ralph. 'I remember meeting him as a young man when he was staying with the Cheyneys and he seemed very happy here. If you will forgive a personal remark, you are not in the least like him. You are a male version of your mother, and she was a typical Russell, well built and fair like you. I remember your father as being dark. I was once informed that you have a twin brother. Is he your double?'

'No, indeed. He is dark, but he does not much resemble my father, either. A little more, perhaps, than I do.'

Something in his voice when he had ended his last sentence struck both his hearers. There was an ambiguity about it—almost a touch of regret. If so, it was gone in an instant, and Russell was his usual cheerful self again.

After he and his chaise, now shared with Pickering, had left, Miss Beauregard turned to her niece.

'Now there is a young man of whom I approve. His manners are beautiful and he is obviously taken with you. Are you taken with him? You ought to be, you could scarcely do better. There is more to life, my dear, than being the widow of a dour old man.'

Mary protested, but not as vigorously as she might have wished, 'We are friends only, dear aunt.'

'Now *that* I don't believe. I saw the way in which you were looking at one another, and that was not at all friendly, no, indeed. I know what friendship entails and it is far too tepid a word to describe that which lies between you. I assure you that you have only to say the word and that young man would be on his knees before you, proposing—'

'Aunt,' said Mary, desperately breaking all the rules of etiquette by interrupting the old lady when she was in full flow, 'Lord Hadleigh did propose to me once, years ago, before I married Henry Wardour, and as soon as he had done so, he disappeared out of my life, deserting me completely, never to be seen or heard from again until I met him at Markham Hall last month. I had not meant to tell you this, but I would not like you to believe that any strong feelings are left between us.'

'So you say, my dear, but I am sure that there is something more to your story than you know. I pride myself on my ability to read my fellow men and women and I cannot believe that the man I have just met would betray you after such a dastardly fashion. No, indeed, he is a gentle fellow, not a roué or a rake who would betray a woman in any way. I would say that, if anything, he is too kind for his own good. He's not at all like his father—rather he takes after the Russells.'

Her eyes misted over. 'I was to have married George, the last of the Russells. He was my true love from youth, but he was taken with a fever and died a week before our wedding. That is why I have never married. I never wanted another man after I lost him. Lord Hadleigh looks very like him—and talks like him, too.'

Her eyes were glistening with tears and Mary put an impulsive arm around her aunt and kissed her. She said nothing, but she was hoping that perhaps there was some explanation for Russell's behaviour which would account for his apparent desertion of her.

That night, in the half-life which precedes sleep, she was with him again on their last day together.

It was not long after he had first declared his love for her, and he was about to leave Oxford to spend the long vacation in London.

She had been for a walk and had returned to be told by the butler that m'lord was with her father. He had almost winked at her: she knew that the servants were all aware how much she and Russell had come to feel for one another, but she was not sure how much her father knew.

Later, she remembered, she was walking in the garden at the back of the house when she saw Russell coming towards her, his face eager.

'I'm so pleased to have found you alone,' he told her. 'This may be our last opportunity to be together before I leave for London. Rather naughtily I didn't tell your father that I would come looking for you, since there is something I must ask you, and where better to do so than here, in the place which you love so much.'

Mary knew what was coming and her heart beat so fast that she thought that it would spring out of her chest.

'It is this, my darling. Will you marry me?'

He went down on one knee before her and took her hand and kissed it after he had finished speaking. 'I shall ask my father to approach yours in proper form, but I wanted to tell you myself that I wish to make you my wife without the old men coming between us.'

The look which he gave her when he said this was so mischievous and yet so loving that Mary felt quite light-headed with joy—to say nothing of light-hearted.

'There is no reason why we should not marry soon,' he went on. 'My father will be sure to want an heir since Ritchie and I are the last of this branch

of the Chancellors, and he dislikes ''the other lot'',
as he calls them, intensely. And when we are married
we can play at chess and mathematics to our hearts'
content—as well as enjoy ourselves in others ways.
For example, like this.'

The mischief on Russell's face increased with
every word he uttered and he concluded by taking
her in his arms and kissing her with all the passion
of youth. Mary's response was equally strong. They
stood heart to heart and both believed that there had
never been such fortunate lovers.

'Enough,' he said, breaking away from her and
panting slightly from the force of his desire. 'We can
surely be patient for a little while before I make you
truly mine. It will not be long before everything is
settled. In the meantime we must write to one another.'

'Every day—or nearly so,' laughed Mary, 'however expensive the post is.'

They kissed again—and parted.

Mary watched him walk away from her. When the
path turned to make its way back to the front of the
house and the entrance gates, he swung round and
waved to her, blowing her yet another kiss before he
disappeared.

And that was that.

Mary wrote to him as she had promised, but nothing came back. Her father said nothing of any letter
from Lord Bretford asking for her hand in marriage
on behalf of his son.

The days which had once seemed so bright with promise turned dull and dark, whatever the weather. After a dreadful six weeks had passed without a word from Russell, she spoke to her father of him, saying, 'When Lord Hadleigh returns, shall we go on to study further in Newton's *Principia*, Father?'

Her father looked up. He had just spent several days in London, visiting the British Museum and staying with an old friend in Bloomsbury. His voice icy, he said, as though she had been impertinent in asking such a question, 'Indeed not, my dear. I had a letter from Lord Hadleigh's father but two days ago, saying that his son did not intend to return to Oxford this autumn, but would continue his studies elsewhere.'

Afterwards Mary was to wonder that she had not fainted from shock on hearing this. Numbly, trying to keep her voice both steady and neutral, she asked, 'Did he happen to mention me in his letter, Father?'

Her father looked up from his work again—he had impatiently resumed it as soon as he had finished speaking. 'No, Mary, he did not. Why should he? His relationship was with me, as his son's tutor. I am sorry to lose him—with guidance to help him steady himself he had the makings of a very promising mathematician. Now I really must cease conversing with you—to go on will mean me losing the thread of the argument which I have been developing.'

Even now, so many years later, she could not keep the tears from falling as they had fallen on that evening long ago when she was at last alone. It was shortly after that that her father had told her early one morning before they had begun to work together that he had arranged her marriage with Henry Wardour.

'But he is an old man, Father,' she had exclaimed. 'Do I have to marry him?'

'Dear child,' her father had said gravely, 'he is not so very old, after all. Furthermore, I have to tell you that the physicians have said that I have not long to live. I do not wish to leave you alone in the world. Dr Wardour is a fine mathematician and you can continue with him the work which we have been doing together on the calculating machine. He is a good man and will look after you. You will oblige me by being a dutiful daughter and marrying him—and you will also oblige yourself.'

'And who knows? I might be lucky enough to see my grandchildren before the Good Lord calls me to my last rest. I have arranged for you to visit my brother in London and you will be married from his home: I shall join you there in time for the wedding. I am fearful that my health will not stand up to the planning and other arrangements if we hold it here.'

Mary was helpless before him. She knew that as his daughter he had the right to give her in marriage to whom he pleased. She wanted to say, He is old compared with the one whom I thought was my true love, Russell Hadleigh—but he has left me without a word, has not acknowledged my letters and, by his father writing to mine to say that he will not be returning to Oxford, has destroyed my last hope of becoming his wife.

His supposed love for her had been a sham. He was nothing but a rich young aristocrat enjoying his summer by pretending to love an old scholar's daughter. And so, because nothing else was left for her, she had married Henry Wardour and tried to forget that golden summer when she and Russell Hadleigh had laughed, worked, played and loved together.

The memory of that betrayal could still bring tears to her eyes and cause her to start up from sleep to ask herself why she should let him into her life again—risking the possibility that he might destroy her happiness once more.

And yet, and yet, the mature Mary who had been in his company and rejoiced in it as she had done in her girlhood, thought that somehow, somewhere, there was a false note being struck.

Nothing that Russell had said or done in the last few weeks had shown him as a man who was careless of others. On the contrary, he was invariably kind and thoughtful to all those around him, not only to his equals, but also to servants, officials and other men whom most persons of his rank took for granted. As her aunt had said that afternoon, he was almost too kind.

Now that she had brought herself to try to remember that lost past, and not forget it, there was another puzzle to be solved also—and that was the speed with which her father had arranged her marriage to Henry Wardour.

He had said subsequently that he had always intended her to marry him so that his work might be continued after his death, but he had never spoken of it to her before that fatal Long Vacation during which Russell had abandoned her.

Mary sat up and peered restlessly into the darkness. Was she imagining things? Was there more to Russell's disappearance from her life than she had at first thought? Was she starting at phantoms, trying to find excuses for him? More than ever she wished to talk to him about why he had left her after promising her so much.

Yes, she would talk to him, and soon. Matters could not be left as they were.

After that she could sleep.

By a coincidence, which was no coincidence at all, but something entirely to be expected since they had recently spent so many days together working, talking and laughing together as they had done at Oxford, Russell was also revisiting his lost past that night. It was not, however, until after he had been brought up short by the truth of the brutal present.

Once he had found himself on his father's land he was shocked at how derelict it was. Eddington village was particularly run-down with signs of neglect in all directions. Tumble-down cottages with leaking roofs housed a population of ragged and resentful beings. One scrawny fellow spat at the chaise when it rolled along the one main street, another shook his fist at it. It was quite unlike the rural idyll which he had imagined it to be before he had set out from London.

On impulse he stopped the chaise outside the village's one ale house: a place which had obviously seen better days. A battered sign, on which the Chancellor arms could just be made out, hung on a pole over the main doorway.

Pickering said doubtfully, 'You'll surely not be wanting to venture in there, m'lord, it looks none too clean to me.'

'I could do with a pint of ale,' returned Russell, short for once. 'You may stay in the chaise, or come with me, as you please.'

He was not really thirsty, but the day had been a long one and, for some reason he could not explain, he was desirous of finding out how the labourers on Chancellor lands lived when not at work. A group of villagers standing before the doorway watched him climb out of the chaise and walk by them. One man said something beneath his breath and the rest snickered.

Russell ignored him. He was not sure whether it was his splendid turn-out or the Chancellor arms on the chaise door which was the more responsible for arousing the glares which he was receiving. He pushed the door open and found himself in the most miserable caricature of a village inn which he had ever encountered.

Behind a dirty counter a middle-aged man watched him in silence as did the room's few patrons. One old gaffer sat before a hearth in which a minimal fire burned. Conversation had died at his entry and every eye on him was resentful as though he were some enemy to be faced down.

'A pint of your best ale, landlord,' he said, as cheerfully as he could.

'I have no best ale, young sir,' grunted the man.

'Then your worst will have to do,' returned Russell cheerfully.

The old gaffer snickered. 'Best you don't try it, sir,' he advised. 'Bart, here, used to brew a good tipple, but them days are long gone, more's the pity.'

'He asked for the worst and so he shall have it,' groused the landlord.

Russell offered him his most dazzling smile when he was handed a grimy pewter tankard. He swallowed his distaste at its appearance before managing to swallow the tasteless stuff as well—to the amusement of the old gaffer and the indifference of everyone else.

He waved his tankard at him, saying, 'You seem to be a man of parts, my friend. Perhaps you might be able to tell me what state the by-way to the big house is in. Would my chaise be able to manage it?'

'Just about,' the old man cackled. 'Been right neglected, so it has, since young Shaw took over. Better in summer than in winter when t'mud takes over, too. Visiting him, are you?'

Russell put down his empty tankard. 'You might say so. He's not expecting me, though.'

The old man's gaze on him was suddenly shrewd. 'You've a right look of the Russells about you and no mistake. Some sort of relative of them, are you?'

'Yes,' said Russell, amused by the old man's lack of respect for the gentleman he obviously was.

'Well, don't expect much comfort when you get there. The place has never been the same since the new man took over and that's the truth.' He began to laugh gently to himself.

The new man? thought Russell. Who can he mean? Enlightenment suddenly dawned. I suppose he is speaking of my father who inherited Eddington when the old gaffer must have been in his prime.

He was about to question the old fellow further when the door opened and a burly man, as ragged as the rest of the inn's patrons, burst in.

'So help me Gawd, there's a chaise outside with the Chancellor arms on it—and who the devil can be inside is what I want to know, because if it's one of them I'll be sure to give him a piece of my mind.'

He suddenly saw Russell standing at the bar and began to stutter. 'I meant no offence, sir, no offence at all.'

'I trust not,' said Russell coolly. 'You said a moment ago that you would give one of them a piece of your mind. I am Russell Chancellor, Lord

Hadleigh, and you may give me as many pieces of your mind as you may care to offer.'

The old gaffer cackled again. 'That's Josh Whateley, m'lord. Noisy when the gentry ain't about, as quiet as a mouse when they are.'

'I meant no offence, m'lord, none at all,' blustered Josh.

'And none taken, but I would dearly love to know what you might have said—had you a mind to.'

'Nothing, nothing at all,' raved Josh, turning and running out of the door.

The old gaffer cackled again but a dour, burly fellow who had been sitting in one corner nursing an empty tankard which had once held ale, stood up and said, 'If Josh won't say it, I will. The fancy clothes on your back, m'lord, are paid for by the men Mester Arthur Shaw's laid off and who will starve this winter or end up in the workus. Shame on you and the man who owns Eddington and don't care a damn about it. I'd say more except that I'll not risk prison, but I won't stay in the same room as the man who lives off my back.' He brushed past Russell and strode out of the room, slamming the door behind him.

Every fearful eye was on Russell. He scarcely knew what to say when confronted with such shameful poverty. Fellows in London talked cheerfully abut the agricultural depression, but here, in the north, far from London's salons, he was seeing the stark reality of it.

'It's a free country,' he said gently, 'and a man has the right to speak his mind. Until I reach Eddington I shall not know the truth of this matter, but be sure that when I do I will discover it. In the meantime I will bid you all good evening.'

He left a noisy room behind him, but his determination to discover what was going on at Eddington House had been strengthened even more by what he had seen and heard in its village.

Chapter Seven

The drive to Eddington House was through yet more uncared-for land. A few sheep grazed in its park, but nothing like as many as might have been expected. The day had been a dark one and some lights could already be seen in the manor's windows. It was also a bad omen that he had driven through open gates where there was no sign that the lodge beside them was inhabited.

The drive led up to a sweep before an Elizabethan family home which had had been partly improved in the middle of the last century. To its detriment, Russell decided, when he stepped down from the chaise after handing Pickering his dispatch case to carry. The door to the stable-yard was closed and locked and there was no sign of any grooms or out-side workers.

Pickering, annoyed by the delay, walked up to the big oak door and hammered on it. Nothing happened. He hammered again, this time with all his strength, but still nothing. Russell, standing beside him, said, trying not to sound too exasperated, 'Why don't you push at the door and see what happens?'

Pickering nodded and obeyed.

To the surprise of them both, for Russell had not really expected the door to be unlocked, it opened, and they walked in. Immediately the sound of singing could be heard coming from somewhere not far away. There was a big Chinese gong in the dirty entrance hall and Pickering hammered on that with the stick which hung beside it.

Still nothing. The noise the singers were making had presumably been too loud for the gong to be heard. Master and man looked at one another. Pickering said, 'Shall I go exploring, m'lord?'

Russell made up his mind. He would start as he meant to go on. 'No,' he replied. 'This is my home and I mean to find out what is amiss here. The noise seems to be coming from that direction,' and he pointed to the double doors which had faced them when they entered. 'You may wait for me here—and don't let the dispatch case out of your hands.'

He strode to the doors, flung them open and found himself in a huge room with a hammer-beamed wooden ceiling. In the centre of it was a long oak table whose top was being enthusiastically banged by pewter tankards wielded by half-cut singing men and a few half-dressed women. The man seated on his own at the far end of the table, and who was leading his guests in a drunken rendering of 'Do ye ken John Peel', was obviously the host.

He, and his guests, were so intent on their song that they failed to notice that they had a visitor. Russell walked slowly forward until he arrived in the line of sight of the lone man.

'Good evening,' he said in his most pleasant voice. 'Am I interrupting something important?'

The heads of everyone at the table turned to stare at him. The host, putting down his glass—he was the only man there who boasted one—exclaimed in a voice meant to dominate and to cow, 'What the devil are you doing here—and who the devil are you?'

Russell offered him his sweetest smile, the one which charmed everyone he met, but which did not charm this fellow, and retorted with, 'More to the point, what the devil are you doing here? And who the devil are you?'

Arthur Shaw, for Russell was certain that he was the man playing host, turned to a battered old retainer who was standing just behind him, 'Briggs,' he bellowed, 'see this fellow out before I send for the constable to remove him. And you, young man, oblige me by leaving quietly. I've no wish to set the dogs, or the law, on you.'

At the mention of the word 'dogs', a large wolfhound suddenly rose from beneath the table and rushed at Russell, barking madly. He held his ground, saying as commandingly as he could, 'Sit, sir, sit!' before giving its owner another smile when the dog, surprised, obeyed him.

'Oh, I really wouldn't set the law or the dogs on me, Mr Arthur Shaw—for I believe that to be your name—for you would have a deal of explaining to do to the authorities as to why you tried to turn the son of the owner of Eddington House out of his own home. I am Russell, Lord Hadleigh, the Earl of Bretford's son and heir.'

The company, which had been buzzing gently while Russell and Arthur Shaw exchanged words, fell suddenly silent. Shaw himself was nothing daunted.

'That's an extreme claim to make, young fellow. How do I know that you are who you say you are?'

Russell moved forward. 'A good question that. Send Briggs for my man, Pickering, who is waiting in the entrance hall for me, and all shall be revealed.'

'Off with you, Briggs,' snarled Shaw, 'and bring in anyone waiting there so that we may clear this matter up once and for all. By the by, sir—or m'lord, if that is who you are—you may do me the goodness of informing me of how you managed to enter the Manor.'

'With pleasure,' drawled Russell, now in total command of himself and the room. Indeed, he noticed that one or two of the revellers had risen from their seats and were trying to make an unobtrusive exit through the far doors. 'I am not a housebreaker, nor a burglar, I merely walked in by the front door which you had carelessly left open—something which will not make my father happy with your conduct here when I inform him of it.'

This was deceitful of him, since his father had no knowledge of his visit to Eddington and he had no intention of allowing him to learn where he was. In any case, Pickering's arrival, looking highly offended, and holding the ancient retainer by his right ear, cut this dialogue short.

Before saying anything, Pickering handed Russell the dispatch case. 'What is it, m'lord?' he began. 'This man...' and he flung the retainer from him '...has been most offensive, demanding that I prove that you are Lord Hadleigh. Of course you are Lord Hadleigh, who else could you be? There are the Chancellor arms on your chaise and in that case which I have just handed to you are letters and papers which will act as further confirmation of your identity. It also contains a draft from Coutts, a draft which allows you to draw money from most country banks. I can fetch further evidence from the chaise, m'lord, if this insolent fellow is not satisfied by what we already have to offer.'

He waved a lordly hand at Arthur Shaw, who was beginning to look as though he had eaten something which disagreed with him.

Russell's admiration for Pickering grew—why, he was behaving as haughtily as though he were the accused aristocrat!

'Oh, I think that it might be wise if you brought in further proof,' he said, still at his most charming, 'and while you are doing so, Mr Shaw would be wise if he were to dismiss this unseemly mob who are busy ruining a rather fine table. I see that several of the roisterers are vomiting on the floor—one of the kitchen staff present might be good enough to mop it up.'

Arthur Shaw, having taken the dispatch case from Russell and examined it, sullenly conceded that he accepted that Russell was who he said he was even before Pickering returned.

'Peg,' he ordered the half-dressed woman nearest to him, 'go to the kitchens and do as m'lord asks. The rest of you go to the servants quarters, except for my personal guests who will be staying the night here.'

Peg, thrusting her ample bosoms back into her bodice, rushed off in her bare feet, to return a little later with a frightened-looking little maid, two buckets and two mops. By then all of the revellers had disappeared, save for Arthur Shaw, and Pickering had reappeared with further proofs of Russell's identity.

'Now,' said Russell, seating himself in the high chair which Shaw had vacated, having motioned him to remain standing, 'you may inform me of what the devil is going on at Eddington. The Manor appears to be a giant pigsty, the village and the lands are in ruins and you are conducting a saturnalia in the Great Hall with the Manor's servants and the cronies whom you call friends. You are sending accounts to my father which purport to show that you are making a vast profit while at the same time fields lie fallow, sheep are few and you are laying off labourers.'

'Oh, I think that you are mistaken, m'lord,' whined Shaw. 'I don't think those who live down south know how bad times are up here. I have had to lay off labourers to make up for the loss in income caused by last year's bad harvest—and I have still managed to increase your father's revenues. Not a bad thing, surely.'

'Bad times up here, are they?' enquired Russell, leaning back in his chair. 'You looked as though you were having a jolly good time when I came in. I suppose those bottles of port, wine and ale all came from my father's cellars. Will their use be featured in your next set of accounts or are they what I believe are called perquisites of office—or perks for short?'

'Oh, yes, m'lord,' babbled Shaw. 'Seeing that I had made a profit on the year and since your most noble father has repeatedly told me that he has no intention of visiting us, I thought that he would not object if I rewarded my servants and friends with a little sup of something now and then.'

'In this case,' said Russell, examining the contents of the table, 'I would describe it as rather a large sup. Never mind, I will pass no judgement on this until I have examined your accounts and estate papers myself.'

'In the morning, m'lord, I take it,' said Shaw eagerly. 'It grows late and I assume that you have had a long journey today.'

'Then you assume wrongly. I have had a short, and pleasurable, one. And no, I don't wish you to bring me the accounts and papers in the morning, I order you, in fact, to bring them to me now. Or rather, I will accompany you to the estate office and there you may hand them over, immediately.'

'Indeed, m'lord, if that is what you wish,' croaked Shaw desperately. He had hoped to do more than a little doctoring of them, but no matter, the idle young aristocrat before him would find dealing with them rather difficult and a little flim-flam might mend all. 'I shall be happy to explain them to you, now if you wish, although morning would be better.'

'My thanks to you,' drawled Russell, standing up. 'But I have no need of your advice. I would prefer to examine them on my own. Now, lead me to your office.'

Arthur Shaw looked wildly round the room. 'But, m'lord, you will not be used to figuring—'

He stopped because Russell was gently shaking his head at him. 'As you wish, m'lord, but I don't use the estate office to work in. During your father's long absence, my father and predecessor, who died three years ago, thought fit to use the study attached to the library—the office was too draughty for an old man, you understand. Besides, you couldn't carry all the papers away, too many...'

He was babbling and knew it, and it wasn't helping him at all. M'lord was looking at him as though he were some species of insect and when he spoke his voice and manner had changed completely.

'I don't think that you understand me, Shaw. Without further ado lead me to wherever your accounts and the estate's papers are kept and hand them over to me at once. If there are too many for me to carry, I assume that you have a few footmen about who aren't too drunk to assist me to carry them. If not, you may have the honour.'

It was hopeless. Shaw's surrender was abject.

'Very well, m'lord. As you wish, m'lord.'

'Oh, I do wish, Shaw. You and your father may have been the masters here for the last thirty years, but no longer; whether or not you remain as my agent is dependent on what I might discover from your accounts and on your behaviour while I am here. Not only that, but I would like an explanation as to why your father's death and your succession were never reported to my father.'

Russell had never in his life spoken to anyone after the fashion in which he was speaking to Shaw. He was discovering in himself a will of iron, a will which he had never been required to use before he had come to Eddington. Here, however, on his own, against his father's wishes, but with a sudden determination to put right—if he could—what was so patently going wrong at Eddington, he was beginning to realise that he was more like his twin than he had thought.

Exhilaration ran through him when he followed Shaw into the study. He had acquired an aim in life, and given luck he might try to act as Ritchie had recommended before his father had the chance to find out what he was up to—and stop him.

Later that night he was not feeling so sanguine. He had been examining all the estates papers—such as they were. From them it was difficult to make out what exactly the financial state of Eddington was—other than that it was not what it was supposed to be. It was obvious to him that the accounts Shaw had sent in were a total invention. He had succeeded in bamboozling his father because he was sure that the old fool—for that was how he was uncharitably beginning to think of him—had, after a cursory examination, thrown them over to his secretary, Graves, as passed.

It was not unreasonable to suppose that, at some point, either his father, or Graves, ought to have realised that what had been paid in to the local bank and what the accounts reported did not match. Apparently the nearest bank was at Ancoates. He grinned a little when he found that out. Here was a splendid opportunity to kill two birds with one stone. It would make it easier for him to visit Mary.

That Shaw had been systematically plundering Eddington for years—embezzling being the more proper term—was quite plain and now he would be able to prove it. Russell laughed out loud. It amused him that the first real use of his mathematical talents, nurtured by Dr Beauregard and Mary, would be to solve the problem of the looting of one of his father's estates.

Before that, however, he must sleep and in the morning he would decide on a plan of action. He yawned. He had been hard at work for several hours and it was now after midnight. His bed was a damp and uncomfortable affair, even in summer, and had scarcely been warmed by the dirty brass warming pan the frightened little maid had brought up after being bullied by Pickering.

Worse, his head was buzzing with figures, making it difficult for him to sleep. In desperation he tried to banish Eddington, Arthur Shaw and the account books from his mind and think of Mary. Not only of the love they had shared, but of what had happened after he had left Oxford and gone to tell his father of his love for her and his wish to marry her...

Like Mary, Russell was not certain whether he re-visited the past or was dreaming it. He remembered that last day with her in the garden. He could see her lovely, piquant face which had charmed him pre-cisely because she was so different from all the smooth society beauties he had seen since his father had become Earl.

He had gone down from Oxford in a dream of love. He remembered, wincing, how he had been so stupidly sure that his father would approve of his choice of wife. The Beauregards were an old family, even older than the Chancellors—their origins dated back to Norman William. They were comfortable, not rich, but surely, he had told himself, the Bretford Earldom was such a wealthy one that there was no necessity for its heir to marry a rich heiress—a moderately rich one would do.

His father's greeting of him on his return was so cold that Russell thought that it might be wise not to raise the matter immediately. Give the old man time to adjust to the fact that he was going to be about for the next few weeks, being his considered judgement.

Alas, his father grew no warmer towards him, so, not wishing for further delay, he asked if he might speak to him of an important matter. He had not yet received a letter from Mary. He had sent her three since he had arrived home, but he assumed that it might be some days before she received them.

'Now what important matter can that be, Hadleigh?' his father enquired nastily.

'It is this, sir,' he began, his manner hesitant. 'I have met a young lady at Oxford. She is the daughter of Dr Beauregard, the celebrated mathematician and one-time astronomer of whom you may have heard—'

'Yes, yes,' his father said testily. 'I have heard of Dr Beauregard. I recently attended a lecture he gave at the Royal Society.'

'Excellent.' Russell beamed in his naïve folly, as he later glumly recalled. 'Then you will not be surprised to learn that his daughter is both beautiful and well informed.' He did not say clever—he thought that his father might not approve of cleverness in a woman. 'And I have decided that—with your permission, sir, which I now ask—I wish to marry her.'

'Marry her!' his father snorted. 'What nonsense! I have higher ambitions than that for you, Hadleigh. There are, at present, few on the marriage market who are good enough in terms of wealth and station for the future Earl of Bretford, but I have no doubt that, if we wait for you to be of a suitable age to marry, there will be plenty to choose from. Why, you are barely out of childhood's frocks and already prating of marrying a nobody of little fortune.'

'The Beauregards are not poor!' exclaimed Russell desperately.

'As I—and my kind—count poor,' said his father, 'poor is what they are. No, no, forget this youthful folly. See the world and other women before you babble of marriage to me.'

The words flew out of Russell's mouth before he could stop them. 'I shall not change my mind, sir. Mary is everything which I could want in a wife. She is good and clever, as well as being beautiful. I can talk to her as I have been able to talk to no other woman.'

His father began to laugh. 'Go to, Hadleigh! Don't prate to me from the depths of your lack of experience of the world about what is desirable in the wife of the future Earl of Bretford. This is the last I have to say on the matter, except that I think it better for you not to return to Oxford. I am disappointed to learn that Dr Beauregard has allowed matters between you and his daughter to go so far as for you to discuss marriage with her. I had thought that you attended Dr Beauregard's home to further your small talent in mathematics, not in the arts of illicit courtship.'

He paused, stared hard at his son and said, 'As my heir, dependent on me, I expect you to do as I wish. You may leave me now, Hadleigh. I shall not change my mind.'

'Nor I mine,' had retorted Russell mutinously. So mutinously that he told himself savagely that his father had not ordered him to stop writing to Mary, and write to her he would. After that—well, after that he would decide what action to take to try to make his father change his mind. If he could be persuaded to meet Mary, that might do the trick. He surely could not behave so harshly once he knew what a treasure she was and what a splendid future Countess she might make.

He ran downstairs to find that the post had arrived and, despite Graves's annoyance, demanded to go through it first to see whether a letter from her was waiting for him. It was not, neither on that day nor on any other.

Shocked and distressed, he wrote to her daily, begging her to write to him—but nothing came back. In the end, damn what his father might say if he knew, he made a clandestine visit to Oxford to try to see her, and to ask why she was not replying to his letters after everything which had happened between them.

It was a wet summer's day when he arrived at the Beauregards' home. He asked the butler if he might speak to Miss Beauregard. The butler looked at him strangely and showed him into the drawing room where he waited eagerly to see her.

Instead, it was Dr Beauregard who walked in. He wore his sternest academic's face. 'I am surprised to see you here,' he said, without further preamble. 'I understood that you had left Oxford for good.'

So his father had already written to the College authorities, telling them that he would not return! Nothing daunted, he said, 'I came to visit Miss Beauregard, sir. I trust that she is well?'

'Of course, she is well. Why should she be otherwise? She is staying with her mother's sister while she prepares for her wedding.'

'Her wedding,' Russell remembered stammering. 'Her wedding! Is she getting married, then?' He knew that he sounded stupid, but the shock of what Dr Beauregard was telling him had sent his senses reeling. Whoever she was marrying, it was not Russell Hadleigh.

'That is the usual reason for a wedding, m'lord. It has long been planned. Her husband-to-be is my friend and colleague, Dr Henry Wardour. She will make him a most suitable wife since she shares his interests and will be able to assist him in his work—and, incidentally, carry mine on when I am gone.'

'But he is an old man,' Russell burst out, 'and I love her.'

Did she love him, though? Was their heavenly summer together just a light flirtation undertaken to pass the time pleasantly before she settled down for life? Was that the reason why she had not answered his letters?—those letters in which he had poured out his love?

His face must have betrayed the agitation which he felt, the sense of betrayal, but it did not move Dr Beauregard for, pulling out his watch, he said impatiently, 'Come, m'lord, come, m'lord, this is childish nonsense after a summer's play which you are engaging in. You are by no means ready to marry, nor would I approve of her marrying you. Nor does she, I may safely say, wish to marry you.

'I have some friends arriving for luncheon. I think that there is nothing further to be said between us. I bid you goodday and wish you well.'

On looking back, now, in the middle of the dark night, Russell was asking himself whether there was not more to this sad story than he was being told. At the time—and ever since—he had taken Dr Beauregard's words at their face value. Now he began to wonder whether he and Mary might not have been manipulated in some way by a pair of fathers who had very different ideas for their children's future than the one which their children had planned for themselves.

Somehow that hopeful thought sent him to sleep. It was hopeful because, if he were to speak to Mary of their past, he would tell her that after he had received no letters from her he had visited Oxford and had had an interview with her father. He had gone there to speak to him of his wish to marry her and that, to his great surprise, her father had told him of her coming marriage. Worse than that, he had said quite plainly that she had no wish to marry him. In no way had he ever betrayed her as she seemed to think.

Was it also conceivably possible that she had not betrayed him?

Mary did not fret when Russell did not immediately pay his promised call on her, but after a week had passed she began to wonder whether he was about to abandon her again.

She said something of this to her aunt, who replied robustly, 'Nonsense, my dear child. Depend upon it, he has probably found that matters at Eddington needed seeing to if all the rumours I have recently heard have any truth in them. Give the poor fellow a few more days and I'm sure that we shall see him again.'

A week later Mary was seated in the garden, trying to decide whether to read Miss Jane Austen's *Persuasion* or to go again through the calculations which she and Russell had made at Markham Hall. Somehow the day seemed too charmingly sultry for her to engage in either and she was falling into a happy doze when she heard footsteps coming, those of her aunt and another person.

Her aunt was talking to a man, and when he replied to her she recognised him as Russell! Sleep flew away. She sat up so sharply that the first volume of Miss Austen's novel and her own papers tumbled from her lap.

'Here he is,' exclaimed her aunt triumphantly. 'I told you that he would come. He informs me that he was sadly delayed by reason of his need to mend matters at Eddington, but has come to apologise for not calling on us sooner.'

Mary, who had risen and was standing in a little sea of scattered papers, said breathlessly, 'No need for apologies. I am sure that Lord Hadleigh was only doing his duty.'

'Alas, yes,' he said. He was standing before her in all his glory, and what glory it was. He had obviously, as he had promised, ridden over from Eddington, and the clothes he was wearing showed off to perfection his athletic body. 'I knew that you would both forgive me if I offered that as an excuse.'

'No excuse,' said Miss Beauregard gaily, 'if what I and half of the neighbourhood have heard of is true. Now, sit down and tell Mary all about it while I go and order tea and Sally Lunns. I fear that, given the weather, ices would be better, but, alas, I have no ice-house. I am informed, though, that the Chinese drink tea in hot weather in order to keep cool, so perhaps we can try a little experiment of our own.'

'I like your aunt,' Russell said, sitting down and stretching his legs before him—which had Mary admiring his boots' high polish and wondering whether it had been achieved by the application of champagne. 'She has a true appreciation of the vital things of life: food, erudition, gossip—and a delightful sense of tact, by which I mean leaving us alone to converse privately.'

Mary smiled back at him. One of his charms was his easiness of manner, plus a sense that he was giving his whole attention to the person he was with. 'Yes, I have been very happy here. Until I undertook this journey north I had not realised how lonely I was in Oxford.'

She blushed after she had come out with this. She had not meant to say anything quite so personal and revealing. His tact was shown by his gravely nodding his head and saying, 'I was sorry that I could not visit you earlier, but things were in a worse way at Eddington than I had supposed, and I felt it my duty to try to begin to clean the Augean stables before I engaged in the kind of pleasure which visiting you would bring me. I can only hope that you approve of my decision.'

'Very much so,' replied Mary energetically, 'although I have to say that you don't look a bit like Hercules, who was the first to undertake that task. All the statues which I have seen of him make him look most wild and ferocious—quite unlike yourself.'

Russell laughed. 'I suppose I ought to take that as a compliment. On the other hand, you have not seen me during the last fortnight when I believe that with the best will in the world I did look rather wild and ferocious at times. It was very lonely, though,' he added, his smile disappearing.

'Would you like to talk to me about it?' Mary asked. 'A problem shared is a problem halved, my father used to say.'

'Yes, I think I would, but on the other hand it is not exactly what I thought that we might talk about when we met again.' He looked down at the papers which Mary had hastily lumped together and said, 'I rather thought that we might talk about that—among others things.' The look he gave her was a meaningful one and Mary blushed again.

'There will be other times when we can talk of those,' she said, 'and since I have experienced loneliness I know that to speak to others of the matters which concern us most is a healing thing, so, if you can bring yourself to tell me a little of your problems at Eddington, pray do so.'

This was a stiff way of speaking, she knew, particularly when what she really wanted was to throw her arms around him—or feel his around her—but with Aunt Beauregard about to return at any moment this was definitely taboo.

'My lady commands,' he said, giving her a low bow without exactly getting out of his basket chair, and he began to tell her of his early days at Eddington and of how he had been trying to mend matters.

'With some little success,' he ended with a sigh. 'After all, I believe that matters were never very good under the long years when Shaw's father was the agent, and since he inherited the post they have gone downhill rapidly. Incidentally, my father is quite unaware that old Mr Shaw had died. The younger one, having the same name, presumably took over without informing him, or Graves, my father's secretary.'

Mary's face was a picture. 'But how could that have happened?'

'Alas, for some reason my father has no interest in anything to do with Eddington, more's the pity.'

'So he sent you here?'

Russell could not lie directly to her, any more than he had done to Shaw, who obviously believed that he was his father's emissary. He had not seen fit to enlighten him because Shaw, being the kind of fellow he was, would probably have written to London and that was the last thing which Russell wanted. He could not imagine his father's reaction if he were to be informed, either by Shaw, or through local gossip, that his son and heir had gone to Eddington and proceeded to turn everything upside down! Even if by doing so he hoped to restore the estate's prosperity.

'Well,' he said, smiling, 'I am the heir,' which was no answer at all. The rapidly growing empathy between him and Mary had her wondering exactly what his answer had meant when a simple yes or no would have done. She said nothing, however. There was something about Russell which was beginning to intrigue her: a hint that he was a sterner, harder man than he had been, and if restoring Eddington was doing that to him then it was all to the good.

'Have you turned Shaw away?' she said. 'Aunt Beauregard said yesterday that the rumour was that you had either dismissed him already or were on the point of it.'

Russell shook his head. 'No—but only on condition that he works with me to remedy matters. You see, I also have to say that if my father had managed his estates as he ought then the Shaws would not have been able to cheat him so easily—if at all. I am certain that Shaw has stolen from us, but it would be damned difficult to prove and would rebound badly on the family name. Absentee landlords are in general not much liked.'

He did not say that, when riding around the estate and through Eddington village and the other hamlets, many men and women had come up to him to try to shake his hand and thank him for coming to save them from the Shaws' exploitation.

'We always knew,' said one old gaffer, 'that some day a member of the family would come up here to put things right. They tell me, young man, that your name is Russell, and it is like having them back again. They were always good to the tenants and labourers. My granddaughter is dressing her third babby in the shawl which the last Mrs Russell gave to my wife when our first child was born.'

Russell did not feel particularly virtuous, rather that in learning how to manage the estate he had found something which he could do, and do well.

'It's odd,' he said, after a short silence in which he had been musing upon the change in his life, 'what started me off on this venture was quite accidental. I was looking at the Eddington quarterly accounts and by using my mathematical skills I realised that there was something odd about them. And then I met you again, and thus not only have I found myself using them at Eddington, but also employing them to help you with your work. I hate to think of all the years I have wasted in empty pleasure when I could have been doing something useful—and being more like Ritchie.'

Mary could not stop herself from leaning forward and putting a hand on his muscular thigh. 'You love, hate and envy him, don't you? But you need not now. What you are trying to accomplish at Eddington is fast becoming the talk of the neighbourhood. I have a confession to make. When you first delayed your visit I began to think that you had deserted me again, but later, when Aunt told me of what was happening there, I knew that I was wronging you.'

Russell picked up the loving hand and kissed it. 'It was the memory of you that inspired me and kept me going at Eddington when things proved difficult. Besides that, there is something else I ought to tell you. I have been thinking of that last summer of ours at Oxford and I believe that we ought to forget our self-denying ordnance and speak of it. There is a false note there, I am sure. I have the strangest feeling that a great wrong was done to us and if we were to speak of what we each thought had happened we might be able to uncover it.

'Not today, though, and not here. In a few days' time I would like to ride with you into the woods. They say there is an ancient cairn there, not far from where the hermit has his cottage. We could take a picnic with us, sit beside it, look out over the quarry, and talk in private, away from prying ears.'

Mary began to laugh. 'Oh, yes. I would like that because my memories are beginning to worry me, too. As for prying ears, I think that we might encounter a few prying eyes if we were to ride out alone—but what of that? I have been a prisoner of convention for far too long and would wish to kick over the traces for a change!'

In her sparkling merriment she was almost the young girl he had once known, and if time had left its marks on them, then it had also given them certain strengths which might have passed them by if they had led too easy a life. Absent-mindedly Russell kissed not only the hand he held, but the pulse-point of her wrist and her arm up to the elbow. They were gentle kisses, but Mary could feel the suppressed passion beneath them.

'It is taking your aunt a devil of a long time to assemble three cups of tea and a plate of crumpets,' he whispered into her ear when his kisses reached the ruffled hem of her short sleeve. 'I mentioned tact earlier—I'm sure that she's practising it, but I must stop where I am lest she find us in what is known as ''a compromising position'', something which varies between being found kissing on the lips to criminal conversation itself!'

Mary knew that criminal conversation was a polite description of the act of love itself, but she could not object to Russell's indirect reference to it. After all, had she not expressed a wish to kick over the traces? On the other hand she had no wish to kick over the carriage itself! At least, she amended hastily, until after they had had their long-delayed discussion about what exactly had happened—and why—thirteen years ago. In any case here, at last, came Aunt Beauregard with a footman behind her carrying the promised tea and crumpets.

'I do trust,' she said, smiling at her two protégés who were now chastely sitting well apart from one another, 'that you have found plenty to talk about. There were a few problems with the kitchen range, but all is now well. I do hope that you like crumpets, m'lord.'

'Hadleigh will do,' he said, giving her his brilliant smile, 'or Russell, which I think that I would prefer you both to use. And yes, I do like tea and crumpets very much. I'm rather afraid, though, that you are going to find me a constant visitor if you continue to feed me like this.'

'Oh, that won't trouble us at all, will it, Mary? As for Cook, she is constantly complaining that I don't have enough visitors for her to show off her culinary skills—so come as often as you can and make us all happy.'

'Be very sure,' he said, smiling and raising his tea cup to offer them a teetotal toast, 'that I shall certainly accept your kind offer with great pleasure.'

Chapter Eight

'He is coming over this afternoon,' almost carolled Mary, several days later, waving a note at Aunt Beauregard. 'He will be bringing a picnic and we shall make our promised ride to the cairn in the woods. Would you think me very fast if we do not take an attendant with us? I am sure that I shall be quite safe in Lord Hadleigh's company. He has a very strong sense of honour.'

'So do you, my dear,' said her aunt, 'and, after all, you are a widow. Widows are allowed more freedom than single women. When you return he will perhaps stay a little longer—I believe that he will be happy to give you the game of chess which I am too ignorant to offer you.'

Had Mary not, in the past, resolutely refused to consider remarriage, her match-making aunt would not have been so eager to throw her in the way of such an eligible young man as Russell Hadleigh. Particularly when that young man had looked at her so fondly.

*   *   *

He was doing it again when he arrived with an attendant groom who helped Mary on to her horse before being told to enjoy himself in the kitchen at Ancoates. Mary looked particularly splendid in a deep blue riding dress and a little black top hat. Russell, of course, was as debonair as usual. The promised picnic was being carried by a pack horse.

Aunt Beauregard, waving them a fond goodbye from the front of the house, thought sentimentally what a handsome pair they made. Someone ought to paint them—preferably that fellow Lawrence who was all the rage these days; and if Russell thought that Mary looked splendid, she was returning the compliment by thinking the same of him.

The ride to the cairn was not a long one and the path, though rough, was not so difficult that it troubled their horses. It was made in absolute silence— the characteristic of all true woods, Russell remarked to Mary—so much so that conversation and chatter seemed to profane the almost holy quiet. The cairn, when they reached it, was a relic of the Iron Age, standing near a settlement in a small clearing on ground a little higher than its attendant stream, one of the tributaries of the Tyne.

After tethering their horses, Russell lifted down from the pack horse a blanket and the stout knapsack which held the picnic. He spread the blanket on the ground and invited Mary to sit on it.

Mary gazed around her. 'I wonder what they were like,' she said, 'the people who lived near the cairn so long ago.'

'Like us, with different clothing and a different language.'

'Really,' said Mary, 'but their lives must have been so different. Fancy living inside those stones in winter.'

Russell, who was busy unpacking a sumptuous little repast, said, 'You must remember that that is what they were used to.'

'Perhaps people didn't live there at all,' she suggested. 'It might have been a tomb.'

'The locals think not,' Russell said, handing her a pewter plate. 'Apparently the hermit, before he became quite such a recluse, told them that the men who lived here built the cairn because it was isolated, in the shelter of the wood and near a supply of water, oh, and a quarry from which they took the stones to build the cairn and the settlement.

'Here are some sandwiches, madam, with some excellent beef. The cook has suddenly remembered most of her old skills, forgotten since matters at Eddington grew so dire. She has packed us some little cakes which the locals like as well as home-brewed ale and pewter mugs in which to drink it.'

'How are things progressing at Eddington?' Mary asked.

'Slowly,' he replied. 'You must understand that the people living in the house have grown used to an idle life and don't like to be made to live a busy one. On the other hand, I am extremely popular with the tenants and the labourers because they can see that I am beginning to improve matters. Shaw is dragging his feet a little, but I don't like to dismiss him because his local knowledge can be helpful. I have hired some carpenters and builders to repair the structure of the house itself, and begin to paint the outside. Some of the local women have also been drafted in to clean the rooms and make them fit for civilised beings to live in.'

He hesitated a minute, and offered Mary one of the little cakes before going on. 'I know it's an imposition and the place is abominably dirty, but I wondered if you might like to help me to examine what has been stored in the attics.

'For some reason nearly all of the paintings and most of the furniture have been moved there—in order to save the trouble of looking after them, one supposes. I'd like to restore them to their proper places again. I think that a woman's touch might be helpful here. My sister Margaret spends a lot of time buying furniture and rearranging her husband's old home, which had been horribly neglected by his grandfather in his old age.'

'Of course I would, and Aunt Beauregard, too, I suspect. You have only to say the word.'

The eager face which she offered him set Russell all of a-twitch. He had only to look at her these days to desire her. He hadn't felt like this in a woman's mere presence since he was a very young man—since he had last been in Mary's company before their parting, in fact. He told his body to behave itself, but it seemed to have a mind of its own, or rather, to be truthful, no mind at all!

'Very well, then. We shall arrange it before I leave. Now, drink up your ale, it's supposed to be good for you and there is no one here to tell you that young ladies should not drink such a common thing—although your female ancestors did.'

He handed her the pewter mug and, in doing so, their hands met. The wave of passion which passed between them was so strong that for a moment time stopped and they sat there, transfixed, before time began again.

'Now,' said Russell, looking away from his loved one, 'I know why the rule that unmarried men and women should never be alone together was made. I hope that I do not distress you if I tell you that simply to be alone with you has the strongest effect on me—but I shall try to behave myself, although, God knows, it will be even more difficult than it was when we were girl and boy together at Oxford.'

Mary looked away from him and drank some of her ale before saying, 'I think that I ought to tell you that being with you has the same powerful effect on me as it did all those years ago. That being so, I also think that we ought to discuss why you deserted me then, if what you now say is true.'

Russell sat up sharply. '*I* deserted *you*? No, indeed, forgive me for saying so, but you deserted me to marry old Wardour without so much as a letter from you to tell me so.'

The effect of this speech on Mary was so powerful that Russell thought that she was about to faint.

'Dare I believe that you are speaking the truth?' she finally faltered, her face ashen.

Russell, who had been lying stretched out, on one elbow after he had passed her the ale, stood up before falling on to his knees before her.

'Believe that I am telling you the truth. A terrible truth which I have had to live with ever since for, so far as I was concerned, our love was a true and deep one, not that of a boy and girl playing with it for the first time. Why did you desert me, Mary, why? Or ought I to ask you whether you did desert me—for I am beginning to think that we were both tricked. Tell me, did you receive my letters?'

'No,' she replied, her face still white, her whole body trembling. 'No, I received nothing from you, nothing at all. The first news which I had of you came weeks later when my father informed me that you were not returning to Oxford in the autumn. I cannot tell you how strongly that affected me. Even now I have difficulty in holding back my tears.'

The face she showed him told him that she was not lying. Two tears were slowly falling down her pale cheeks.

Russell leaned forward and took her by the shoulders. 'Nothing? You received nothing? And Henry Wardour—how did you come to marry him?'

'My father called me into his study one day to say that he had arranged my marriage to him. He said that it was a most suitable one, and that he expected me to fall in with his wishes. I was left with no choice. Had I received any letters from you I might have argued with him—but because of that I believed that you had deserted me. Now you tell me that you hadn't.'

She fell silent. Russell, still holding her, said passionately, 'Mary, believe me. I told my father that I wished to marry you and he refused to give me his permission. I didn't allow that to deter me. I came at once to Oxford to see you, but you were not there. You were with your mother's sister, your father told me, arranging your marriage to Dr Wardour. Can you imagine what a blow that was to me? Particularly when he said that the marriage was also your wish.

'So, what is the explanation of these strange events? It now seems that we were writing to one another—but neither of us received any letters. It was the old men, was it not, who tricked us? Your father and mine. For their own reasons they did not wish us to marry, so they intercepted our letters and destroyed them. My father wrote to Oxford saying that I would not be returning there in the autumn. He also told me that I must marry a woman he would choose as soon as a suitable one could be found. Your father married you to Henry Wardour—and consequently we each thought that it was the other who was faithless, and have believed so ever since.'

Still holding her, he kissed her gently on the brow. 'I am not lying, and nor are you, so my understanding of the matter must hold good. Do you believe me now? Do you believe that we were tricked and manipulated?'

'Yes, yes, yes,' Mary said passionately. 'Of course I believe you—look how cunningly they kept us apart.'

The knowledge of the wasted years which they had spent apart, the regret, the unhappiness, the sense of betrayal and the misery which they had each suffered, caused Mary to shiver violently. She was cold, oh, so cold, and he, the man she loved who, after all, had never betrayed her, was now tenderly holding her in his arms. He was kissing her, and stroking her hands for it was plain that she was so shocked that she was on the verge of unconsciousness.

She had been so brave, as he had been. They had come to terms with life—but at what a price. Slowly Russell lowered her down beside him, so that she lay in his arms, beneath the tender blue of the summer sky. He was murmuring something to her in a low voice but what he might be saying did not matter to her—what mattered was that *he* was saying it.

Mary wished that she could remain like this for ever, lost in time, with no demands being made on her while she came to terms with what their fathers had done to them. She was almost comatose, her eyes closed, her breathing light, but Russell was very much alive, aware of what holding his beloved so closely to him was doing to his self-control, particularly since in the state she was in he ought to say and do nothing which might distress her.

Time passed. So alone were they that they might, Russell thought, have been a pair of Iron Age lovers out to enjoy themselves in the time-honoured way under the summer's sun. If only he could do the same, but a thousand things kept him still and silent while Mary fell at last into a deep sleep.

He heard footsteps, light ones which seemed to be coming nearer and nearer. Dare he, for the sake of Mary's reputation, allow them to be found like this? Before he could answer that question the owner of the footsteps came through the trees to stop, silent, before them.

It must be, it was, the so-called hermit, the wild man of the woods with his long hair, his long beard and his unkempt clothes.

He made no attempt to speak, to walk nearer to them. Moved by some unknown instinct, Russell put the first finger of his left hand to his lips to indicate that the visitor must remain silent. The man nodded his hairy head, and sat down on the stump of a tree, obviously determined to remain where he was.

The magic of the place held all three of them— until Mary awoke and struggled to sit up. Russell disengaged himself, the wild man rose and bowed to her where she sat, bewildered, half-asleep, not sure where she was.

The hermit—his accent was that of an educated man—said in a deep, rusty voice, rusty perhaps through lack of using it, 'I, and the cairn, Mrs Wardour, are at your service—and Lord Hadleigh, too.'

Russell rose and bowed, motioning Mary to remain seated. 'You know who we are, then?'

The hermit's laugh was as rusty as his voice. 'Indeed, there are so few strangers to these parts and you, Lord Hadleigh, are already notorious, Mrs Wardour less so.'

For some reason this answer amused Russell. He threw his head back and laughed. 'Because of my reforms at Eddington?'

'Exactly, m'lord. Dare I ask you both to do the honour of taking tea with me? I see that you have already eaten your nuncheon and the tea-board usually follows it—although I have no board, only tea. My cottage is not far away.'

Mary looked her assent at Russell.

'Assuredly,' he said, bowing again. 'With two provisos: that you offer me your name and that you allow me to pack up the remnants of our al fresco meal before we follow you.'

'By all means. I am George Russell—a relative of yours on the wrong side of the blanket,' and he threw a comical look at the one which Russell was folding up. 'I was once a scholar and a friend of Mrs

Wardour's father and her late husband. I also knew your father, Jackie Chancellor, when we were both young men, so you see that we are not really strangers. You may bring your horses with you—after you have allowed them a drink from the stream.' It was the first time that he had ever offered his surname to anyone local but, after all, Russell Hadleigh *was* a relative of his, the first he had seen for many years and the words had flown out before he could stop them.

Mary, who had resumed her top hat and was untethering her horse, whispered to Russell, 'Do you really believe all that—and by the by, whatever must he have thought when he found me lying in your arms?'

'What a lucky dog I was, I should think,' he whispered back, and when she blushed scarlet, murmured, 'I shouldn't have teased you—but I thought that as "by the bys" went, yours was a bit of a masterpiece. Besides, since we were behaving innocently—to Hades with whatever anyone else might think!'

Their unlikely new friend had walked ahead of them already and could scarcely have heard this byplay. He led them along a narrow track before they came to another clearing where a thatched cottage stood, smoke rising from its one chimney.

'My home is rough but clean,' he told them, 'which also applies to my person. The brook is my bath and serves to wash my clothing,' and he waved them forward into the cottage's one main room.

It was, as he had said, clean if roughly furnished. It was also filled with books. A table, on which were paper, ledgers, an ink well and a quill pen, stood beneath a window, a bed stood beneath another and a fire blazed in the hearth. A kettle stood on the hob. A door opened on to a kitchen and an open store-room. Beside the fire stood a small side-table on which was a chess board, with a game in progress on it.

The hermit waved them towards two kitchen chairs before seating himself at the one before the table.

'I see that the kettle has almost boiled. I timed my walk quite accurately so that we should return before it did. Having no clock has made me create my own in my head as our ancestors must have done. In these days we gather a great deal of unnecessary para-phernalia about ourselves—but you do not wish to hear of that, I am sure. You do not resemble your father, young man, but I suppose that you have heard that before—you take after the Russells, I think. If I shaved off my beard and hair, you would see a re-semblance between us. I gather that you have a twin brother—does he take after your father?'

'No, nor does he look like the Russells. He is dark, intense-looking and wiry.'

'Is he, indeed? Interesting that,' but the hermit did not explain wherein the interest lay. Instead he rose and, carrying the kettle to the kitchen, made the tea, returning after a few minutes carrying three china mugs without handles. A battered tin teapot and a small brown jug of milk arrived after yet another journey.

'I've no sugar,' he announced brusquely, 'nasty stuff. Spoils the taste of everything.' He poured tea and milk into the china mugs and handed them to Russell and Mary, who were both intrigued by the man, his fashion of speech and his way of life. Mary could not resist shooting a few glances at the chessboard. Her chair was next to its table.

The hermit, who seemed to miss nothing, did not miss her interest. 'Play chess, do you, Mrs Mary? And you, Hadleigh?'

Russell was amused to notice that now they were in his own home the hermit was addressing them familiarly. 'Both of us play. Years ago it was our joint passion, but then I gave it up. My passion for it has been revived recently: Mrs Wardour has always retained her interest in it.'

'So I understand. You are continuing your father's work, I believe, Mary.'

Startled, Mary looked across at him. 'You knew of my father's work, sir?'

'Indeed, and that you and Hadleigh here were deeply involved in it years ago. You have renewed that work, I hope, Hadleigh. A pity to waste a gift like yours in unrewarding idleness. I, too, am engaged in working on a noble theory with which I shall not trouble you for you must both resume working on your own when Hadleigh has reformed

Eddington. I came here to concentrate on mine in a place where I could forget the world's distractions.

'I would, however, be grateful if you would both look at Black's position and try to discover whether there is any way in which he could avoid what appears to be an inevitable defeat.'

They both rose and strolled over to the table. Mary was the first to speak, looking at Russell before she did so. 'I think, no, I am sure, that Black has a way out. Do you agree with me, Lord Hadleigh?'

She was being formal to try to erase from the hermit's mind his memory of finding her in Russell's arms.

'Yes,' he replied, 'and this is it,' and he moved an apparently innocent pawn.

Mary nodded agreement. The hermit clapped his hands together in praise and she sketched him a curtsy. 'It was not really very clever of us,' she told him. 'We have been experimenting recently in the hope that one day we might build a clockwork machine which would be able to play chess. This is one of the positions we have studied.'

The hermit clapped his hands again. 'As I thought. You are undoubtedly a pair of prodigies, and you, Hadleigh, are wasting your time playing a reforming agent on behalf of your father, who, I dare swear, knows nothing of what you are doing and probably won't be grateful for it. You should be nurturing your rare talent.'

On hearing this, both heads swung round, Russell's to stare at the hermit and Mary's to stare at Russell. Now, how the devil does he know that? was Russell's furious thought, and, Can it really be true that Russell is here without his father's knowledge—and why? was Mary's response.

'Enough,' said the hermit abruptly. 'It is time that you left. Be sure that I will keep watch for you, Hadleigh. Do not underestimate the hatred which young Shaw must nourish for you. You have stopped his little gallop and no mistake—but take care that, in revenge, he does not stop yours after a fashion which you would not like.'

Russell said coolly, 'I thank you for that warning, sir, and am grateful for your interest in my affairs. May we visit you again?'

'When I send for you,' was the hermit's answer, 'and not before. Now go.'

'Was what the hermit was saying true, Russell?' Mary asked while they walked to where their horses were tethered.

'About what?' he returned stiffly—but he knew quite well to what she was referring.

'That your father does not know that you are here.'

'I am afraid so, yes.'

The very brevity of his reply piqued Mary. She considered her words carefully before continuing. 'Would you care to speak to me of it? It seems such an odd thing to be happening—particularly when you have allowed everyone to believe that you are your father's emissary.'

They had reached their horses. Instead of beginning to untether his, Russell decided on total frankness. After all, he had been deceiving Mary as well as everyone else and she must be finding that hurtful.

'Before we ride back,' he said, 'let us take a short walk. I will be as honest with you as I have previously been dishonest about my reason for being here. When I have finished I hope that you will forgive me. I promise that, in future, I shall have no secrets from you.'

'Very well.'

Russell had never admired her more. The calm way in which she was accepting what she must see as a breach of trust was directly opposite to that in which he knew most women of his acquaintance would have reacted. No reproaches, no sad looks, but the same kind of rational response which she would have given to a problem in mathematics.

As a reward for her he decided on the most complete frankness, beginning with the confession that his relationship with his father had always been a poor one. Slowly he told her everything, ending with the occasion when he had, quite accidentally, come across Shaw's reports and had found them wanting.

'I raised the matter with my father, and he dismissed what I had to say as ignorant meddling. He had absolute trust in old Shaw, he said, and did not wish me to interfere. Needless to say he had no notion that old Shaw had died three years ago and that his dissolute son had taken over.'

'That was very wrong of him, Russell, to ignore your wishes completely. After all, you are his heir.'

'Quite so, but he has always resented me for being the older twin. He has made it quite plain that he would have preferred Ritchie to succeed. Which makes his desire to see me married to some half-witted heiress quite bizarre.'

'No, Russell. He wished to control you, that is quite plain from all that you have said. Why, then, did you secretly defy him by coming north to find out what was going on?'

'Oh, that was Ritchie. I made the mistake of complaining about my useless life to him and he read me the Riot Act and said that only I could remedy my sad situation. He hinted that I ought to defy Father over Eddington and follow my star. You see, he has no wish to be Earl. He has told me more than once that it is not his sort of thing at all and I believe that to be true.'

'I should like to meet him,' said Mary approvingly. 'He seems a man of sound common sense.'

'Unlike me?' But Russell's tone told Mary that he was joking.

'Not at all. From all I hear, you are making a great fist of turning Eddington round. Be sure that I shall not give you away, but I am sorry that you did not tell me the truth earlier.'

'Not as sorry as I am,' Russell said earnestly. 'I think...no, I know that I am still somewhat unsure of myself, but I think that I am improving in that department every day. Mostly because of your influence on me. You inspire me and give me courage because your own is so great.

'Now I am afraid that I must take you home. Aunt Beauregard will be thinking that we have drowned ourselves in the stream.'

Mary began to laugh. 'Not at all. She is a cunning match-maker and the longer we are alone together the happier she is since it means that we are more likely to come to an accommodation.'

They had reached their horses again. Russell turned to her, saying, 'Have we reached an accommodation, Mary? Years ago I asked you to marry me and you answered yes. If I ask you again, will your answer be the same? Even if, because of the peculiar position I am in vis-à-vis my father, it means that we shall have to delay the actual ceremony?

'Since I have just said that you have given me the courage which I was previously lacking I also have to tell you that if he refuses to sanction our marriage and disinherits me for going against his wishes as he has previously threatened, then I shall still marry you and look for work elsewhere. I met Lord Chard for the first time a few days ago. He visited Eddington and began to admire what I have already done. His own land agent is growing old, he said, and he will soon be needing a new one. He joked that it was a pity that I was not looking for work. If I were, he would gladly offer me the position.'

'Should you like that?'

'It would be much better than being Bretford's idle and unconsidered heir. He has forfeited my affection and my obedience by his behaviour to me. Nor can I forgive him for the cruel fashion in which he cheated us both. Now let us leave that. For the present I am here and he is there. That being so, when do *you* propose to give me an answer to *my* proposal?'

'Now, immediately! And, of course, the answer is yes.'

Her reward was a quick kiss on her cheek, which was all that Russell dare offer her, but his heart was so full of joy he felt that he was about to burst.

'Splendid,' he managed at last, 'and when will you feel able to visit Eddington's attics and explore them with me?'

'In two days' time.'

Russell groaned. 'I'm not sure that I can wait as long as that to see you again. Before we untether our steeds, do you think that you could allow me a kiss to tide me over until then? I promise to behave myself.'

Mary offered him a subtle smile. 'Suppose I said that I don't wish you to behave yourself? What then?'

Russell gave another groan. 'Don't tempt me. I haven't the patience of a saint, even if I have improved in other ways. What makes matters worse is that we cannot soon be married and in the meantime we must both burn. Are you burning, Mary?'

Of course she was burning! The fact that he had lowered his last defences of all by telling her the truth about his father and himself had made her love him more, not less. That she had been married was not saving her from desiring him more and more each time they met. On the contrary, the supposed passion which she had shared with Henry Wardour was daily being exposed for the tepid thing it was.

'I am not to have my kiss, then,' she said, her eyes teasing him.

Did she know of the terrible effect she was having on him? Of course she did. Mary was no fool and, as a once-married woman, was not a complete innocent. Her pretty mouth had curled up at one corner and her dark eyes were dancing—oh, yes, she was well aware what a temptation she was to him. She was no longer the untried girl of their lost youth.

Russell gave yet another groan and gathered her into his arms. She fitted there as sweetly as though she had been made for that purpose alone. His mouth was as hungry as the rest of him and when hers opened itself to him he teased and played with it as only a man long starved of true love and genuine affection could.

This was heaven, was it not? To taste and savour the loved one, mouth to mouth, heart to heart, body to body, particularly when Russell's, clad as it was in fashionably tight breeches, was telling her of the power of his desire. Her own was revealed by the way she clung to him, by her hands which reached up to stroke the loved face, by the little cries she was making when his hands caressed her back, then her shoulders and finally stole round to fondle her breasts...

Without warning, Russell shuddered and stepped back from her. He had been on the verge of lowering her to the ground in order to consummate finally what had begun so long ago and whose inevitable climax had then been denied them.

'No,' he managed, as Mary tried to pull him back. 'No, for both our sakes we must behave ourselves. Were we able to marry soon then we might continue but, things being as they are, that is not possible. We must be patient, and I, as the man, must be the most patient of all, for it is your reputation and your honour that are at stake here. A man is allowed to be a rake, but a woman, never.'

'I don't care about that,' cried Mary passionately, 'not at all.'

But Russell would have none of it. 'You may not now, but think, later it would be different. I have seen what scandal and gossip have done to women and I would not expose you to them. We must have a new self-denying ordnance and trust that it may not be too long.'

He saw that there were tears in Mary's eyes, and each small pearl reproached him. He should not have touched her, begun to make love to her...but it was stupid for him to repine. He had taken her in his arms and the passion between them, so long lost, had been revived again. It was even more powerful because now they were a mature man and woman, not inexperienced children.

'Come,' he said, not daring to touch her again lest he reignite the spark which had passed between them and which might create a fire which, this time, they could not put out. 'Our horses will be growing tired and I have a mind to enjoy Miss Beauregard's excellent tea and cakes.'

This down-to-earth remark set Mary smiling ruefully. She dried her tears. 'Tea, the universal cure-all,' she said, mounting her horse and turning it towards home. 'I wonder what we should do without it!'

Universal cure or not, it was not tea which was occupying Miss Beauregard when they finally walked into the drawing. Oh, the tea was there, set out and waiting for them with a plate of Sally Lunns which Russell had gravely informed her were his favourites.

No, it was the letter which she was holding which was exciting her. 'Oh, my dears,' she exclaimed. 'Such news as you would never believe. I collect that you both stayed at the Markhams' place in the late spring. I have just received a letter from the General's wife: we were at Miss Pinkerton's Academy together and I think I ought to read it to you. But only after you have sat down and I have poured you both a cup of tea—you must be dying for one after such a long afternoon's ride.'

She waved them to two armchairs—luxurious ones, quite unlike those in which the hermit had already served them tea. Neither Russell nor Mary informed her aunt of that, but after all, he had not served them Sally Lunns, which Russell was eyeing wistfully.

'Now, my dears,' she began, 'listen to this.'

Dear Charlotte,
I have dreadful news for you. We had arranged a splendid marriage between our daughter Angelica and the Marquess of Horsham. They were to be married from the Hall a week ago and a large number of the best-known figures of the *ton* had been invited to be present at the ceremony. The wedding presents were of the greatest magnificence. There was even a splendid one from the Regent who had been a great friend of Horsham's in the days when he was the Prince of Wales.

Judge then, of our horror, when on the morning before the wedding, Angelica's maid had no more common sense than to rush into the breakfast room and inform us, and the assembled visitors, that Angelica was not in her bed, nor was she to be found anywhere, either in her suite of rooms or in the house. Her bed had not been slept in. She had, however, left us a note on her pillow, which the stupid maid had dislodged when she had first realised that Angelica was missing, and it was the next morning when one of the under-servants found it under the bed.

It informed us that she had no wish to marry Horsham, whom she described as an ugly old man, and consequently was eloping with the Honourable Thomas Bertram whose old aunt had died and had left him enough for them to live on. He was bound and determined to marry her, so we were not to try to trace them. The real tragedy was that, due to the idiocy of her maid, we could not hush the matter up. The only good thing about the whole wretched business was that she did not leave Horsham waiting at the church.

I have been ill in bed ever since and the General has been so enraged that the doctors feared an apoplexy. To make matters worse, if possible, Perry had lost a great deal of money at cards to Horsham, and now Horsham is threatening to have Peregrine sent to a debtors' prison if he does not repay it. He had agreed to cancel Perry's debts once his marriage to Angelica had been arranged.

If you hear anything of my poor child's whereabouts, pray inform me. She could be at Gretna, or in Scotland, or, if the wretch has obtained a special licence, they could already have been married in a church—anywhere!

Miss Beauregard ended this sad narrative with a rueful shake of her head. To her surprise both Russell and Mary began to laugh. It was Russell who recovered first.

'And to think that my father wished me to marry the bolting Angelica,' he choked. 'What an escape for me! I might have been the unfortunate fool left at the altar. She and the Honourable Thomas were casting sheeps' eyes at one another all the way through my stay there. Fortunately, her charms held no attraction for me, or I might have obliged my father by offering for her.'

'This sad story does not surprise you, then?'

'Not in the least. I wasn't aware that if I failed to come up to scratch that Horsham would be the next candidate for her hand. I doubt that the Markhams knew that he was up to his ears in debt—but I suppose turning their daughter into a Marchioness was a great attraction for them, even if he is old enough to be her papa. I wonder where the runaways are.'

Mary said, wiping her eyes, 'Angelica told me that she had a *tendre* for Thomas Bertram, but that her parents were determined to marry her to either money, or a title, or both.'

She looked wickedly at Russell. 'Don't tell me that she held no attraction for you at all. Most of the men at Markham Hall were under her spell.'

'Well, I wasn't. The only woman at Markham whose spell I was under was someone not five yards away from me at the moment—as you well know.'

Mary's smile grew more mischievous than ever. 'Yes, indeed. I have to inform you, Aunt, that Lord Hadleigh has offered me marriage, and that I have accepted. For some good and sufficient reasons we have to delay the ceremony—principally because Russell wishes to see Eddington in better shape before he takes on his marital duties. As a result, this is a private announcement for your ears only.'

She and Russell had agreed on this on the way home. They did not wish to deceive Miss Beauregard while Mary was living with her.

'Oh, congratulations to you both,' exclaimed her aunt. 'I knew the moment that I saw you together that marriage was inevitable. I shall be completely mum, you may be sure, and shall not be writing poor Mrs Markham a letter long enough to surpass her own.'

'That would be difficult, to say the least,' Mary said. 'Would you think me heartless if I told you that I have not a great deal of sympathy for either her, or the General?'

'No, indeed, not now that you have explained matters to me. I collect that you visited the cairn this afternoon. Did you see aught of the hermit? He lives quite near.'

'Surprisingly enough,' said Mary, 'we did. He even invited us into the cottage and gave us tea.'

'And vile stuff it was, if we are to be truthful,' Russell added with a grin. 'Not like your best leaf from China.'

Miss Beauregard looked thoughtful. 'How strange. He has never before asked anyone into his home— rather he has driven them away. Did he offer you any reason as to why you were so honoured?'

'Only that he had the same name as myself. He claimed to be a Russell, George Russell to be exact, born on the wrong side of the blanket. He seemed to know a great deal of what is going on in the district.'

For some reason Miss Beauregard looked quite stricken.

'George Russell,' she said at last. 'I only knew one George Russell and he died long ago. I was to have married him.'

It was Mary's turn to look stricken. 'Dear aunt,' she said. 'We would not have told you of him, but I forgot about your long-ago engagement.'

'No need for you to start repining now,' said her aunt. 'I did all my weeping then. Think nothing of it. I would not like my past sorrow to spoil your splendid news. You must come to dinner soon, m'lord, so that we at least may celebrate it in proper style.'

'Not m'lord,' said Russell, bowing to her. 'Now that we are to be related you must bring yourself to call me by my Christian name—as I believe that I asked you once before. So few people do that I am in danger of forgetting it.'

'Now that,' said the old lady, 'would give me the greatest pleasure, seeing that you will shortly become my nephew-in-law and such a familiarity would become quite proper. It will be particularly so since all my memories of the Russells are fond ones.' She frowned, 'That is why I find it strange that I cannot remember a George Russell other than my own. Of course, it is possible that his existence was kept secret.'

Both her hearers nodded. Most families had such secrets and preferred them to remain so.

'By the by,' Russell said to Miss Beauregard before leaving, 'I have asked Mary to join me in sorting through the jumble in the attics at Eddington, and she informed me that you might like to help me as well. Would it be an imposition if I asked you to visit Eddington for that purpose in two days' time?'

'Not at all. I had heard that for some reason young Shaw had consigned all the paintings and much of the furniture to the attics when he dismissed most of the staff who were looking after the place when his father died. I take it that you intend to restore the house to its original pride.'

'If I can. I have already had most of the rooms which I occupy cleaned for the first time in years and I shan't rest until the entire house is spick and span once again. I think that I might like to settle here. I haven't enjoyed myself so much in years as I have done since I started to try to restore Eddington, the house and the estate to its former glory.'

He came out with this in such a heartfelt manner that Miss Beauregard grew thoughtful. She said nothing until he had gone, when she asked Mary a question.

'I have the impression that Russell was not particularly happy before he came north. Is that true—or am I being fanciful?'

'Not fanciful at all. Without betraying any confidence he has made me, I gather that he has long felt that he has had no serious interest in his life—and now, running Eddington, he has found one.'

'The talk is that he has already done wonders. The parson only said to me yesterday that it was a great pity that Lord Bretford had not sent him here to mend matters before.'

Sadly, Mary knew that she must deceive her aunt by inference in remaining silent and not telling her that Russell's father had not sent him, but that he had come as a consequence of his own worries about what was happening at Eddington.

'On top of that,' went on Miss Beauregard, 'the whole district is exceedingly happy that a descendant of the Russells has not forgotten us. I only wish that he had made a clean sweep and turned Shaw away—I fear that he may be being too kind-hearted to be wise. I hope that I am wrong.'

Chapter Nine

Russell was not feeling too kind-hearted when he returned to Eddington. It was plain that Shaw had used his afternoon's visit to Ancoates to invite a few cronies over for a drinking party. They were still hard at it when he walked in.

He waited until he had changed into the informal clothing he had taken to wearing at Eddington before he sent for the visibly fuddled agent.

'I believe,' he said coldly, 'that I have already told you that I didn't want Eddington House to be turned into the village taproom either when I am present or when I am absent. By behaving as you have done this afternoon, you are straining my patience, Shaw. I should by rights have turned you away when I discovered your misbehaviour, which I believe to have been criminal, but I wished to give you a chance to redeem yourself by helping me to turn this place round. One more piece of folly like this afternoon's and I shall dismiss you on the instant. Do you understand me, sir?'

Shaw's reaction was to begin to grovel, although beneath his apparent penitence the hate which he had begun to feel for this jumped-up London dandy who had arrived to spoil his little game was slowly turning murderous.

'Yes, m'lord,' he whined. 'I hear you, m'lord. I thought that I might celebrate Jonty Jordan's birthday, but we perhaps overdid things a little.'

'You mean that you were so fuddled that you forgot the time? It might, perhaps, be advisable for you never to strain my patience again by such behaviour.'

'Yes, m'lord, of course, m'lord. Point taken, m'lord.'

'You may go, Shaw. You could better have spent your time in correcting last month's accounts as I directed you yesterday. Your arithmetic was, to say the least, a little faulty. See that they are on my desk by noon tomorrow.'

Russell was well aware that Shaw was beginning to feel a seething hate for him. When the man had left him, cringing and promising to do better on the morrow, he thought of what Miss Beauregard had said, and wondered if it might not have been wiser to dismiss him. To have done so, however, would have left him working in the dark for the wretch did possess a fund of knowledge about local matters which Russell had already found useful. He did rather think, though, that his more ruthless twin would have disposed of Shaw on the spot—but then, he was not yet quite Ritchie's equal in hard determination, although well on the way.

He shrugged his shoulders. He had meant what he had said about dismissing the man and hoped that it might bring him to his senses—if he had any, that was.

In the agent's office, where many of the staff were assembled, Shaw was rapidly proving his master was right. He was busy complaining to Briggs and anyone else who would listen to him about m'lord's dictatorial ways. Some of his hearers were loudly sympathetic; others, like the cook and housekeeper who liked what Russell was accomplishing at Eddington, kept their counsel.

'If it might not make matters worse, I'd write to his pa, that I would,' whined Shaw privately to Briggs, his major ally, 'but...' and it was his turn to shrug his shoulders.

Briggs knew what he meant: that the Earl was still under the illusion that it was Shaw's father who was running the estate—and that all was well.

He was in the middle of another tirade about insolent popinjays when the door opened and Russell put his head in. 'Incidentally, Shaw, Mrs Wardour and Miss Beauregard will be coming the day after tomorrow to rummage through the attics with me. I have ordered the housekeeper to have the drawing and dining rooms made presentable and Cook has been warned to be ready with a cold collation around mid-day. The wine which I have ordered from the vintners at Newcastle should arrive tomorrow. See that it is stored in the far cellar, the one which the workmen have already cleared and cleaned.'

'Yes, m'lord, indeed, m'lord.' Shaw was so servile that his servility was almost insolent. 'As you wish, m'lord.'

Russell ignored his agent's parody of an obedient servant, but mentally noted it down as another black mark against him.

'Do this, Shaw, do that, Shaw? Does he never stop issuing orders?' grumbled Shaw when Russell had gone.

'He does work hard himself, though,' said a bold under-footman. 'You have to grant him that.'

'I don't grant him anything. I wish to God he'd stayed down south and the sooner he leaves us the better. We were all happy before he came.'

The under-footman, a man in training, one of those Russell had employed to help to clean and refurbish the house and gardens, opened his mouth to argue with him, but a well-aimed kick in the calf from his neighbour silenced him.

'What'd you do that for, wor Jackie?' he said when Shaw, still fulminating against fate, had left them.

'He's a nasty piece of work is Shaw, best not end up on the wrong side of him while he's still here. I've a feeling young master might get rid of him if he doesn't mend his ways, and then you'll be able to speak your mind freely. Until that happy day, keep

mum, and out of his way. He might do you a mischief, else.'

'Still and all—' began the footman.

'Still and all,' mocked his friend, the farrier, also
newly employed. 'Besides, who's to know that young
master might not grow bored and disappear as suddenly as he came. Least said, soonest mended.'

The older heads nodded wisely at this piece of folk
wisdom before making their way to the servants' hall
for their evening meal—except for those who were
carrying Russell's to the dining room where he sat in
lonely, if still somewhat dingy, state.

Mary and Miss Beauregard were alike eager to discover whether all the rumours about what Russell
was doing at Eddington House were true. They rode
over in Miss Beauregard's modest chaise, clad only
in their most down-to-earth and practical clothing.
Miss Beauregard had even packed two large brown
holland aprons to protect them the more.

'Even in the best-kept houses,' she proclaimed, 'attics are dirty places. One trembles to think what those
at Eddington must look like after nearly thirty years
of neglect!'

Mary was more exercised about meeting Russell
again than about the condition of his attics. She had
spent the previous day working on the problems
raised by the chess game which they had started at
Markham Hall and, even if she could not discuss
them during the visit, she would leave a careful copy

of her work with him. It was as though she wished to make up for the years they had spent apart by seeing him as often as possible, never mind that to do so had her all of a quiver—one of Miss Beauregard's favourite phrases.

Their carriage had scarcely had time to arrive on the gravel sweep before the entrance when he was with them. A dirty boy ran up to open the chaise door for them and there was Russell, greeting them as enthusiastically as though it had been weeks since he had seen them, and not a mere forty-eight hours.

He was wearing rough countryman's clothing—as starkly practical as their own, and it suited him, Mary thought, equally as well as, if not more than, the dandy outfits which he had worn at the Markhams.

'What a splendid day you have brought with you,' he exclaimed, giving Miss Beauregard his arm. 'A pity, perhaps, that we have to spend it frowsting in the attics, but alas, duty calls. I gather that there might be treasures to be found there, as well as dust and cobwebs. So, before we start, I have ordered Cook to provide us with tea and my favourite Sally Lunns.'

Mary remembered that, in the past, Russell had always had the power to make even the dullest day interesting and he had certainly not lost that talent. He swept them by a sullen Shaw who had spent the previous afternoon working twice as hard as he had done before Russell's arrival.

'It's rather amusing if a little sad,' Russell told his guests over tea, 'but my valet, Pickering, disapproves mightily of my transformation into Eddington's agent—for that is what I really am now. He was particularly annoyed this morning when I insisted on putting on what he persists in calling ''subfusc fancy dress, sir, which is not at all the thing in which to entertain ladies''. My efforts to assure him that what I am wearing these days is suitable country clothing and that subfusc refers to a dark or grey costume, nothing like my daily garments, didn't satisfy him at all. He is pining for the streets of Mayfair and Vauxhall Gardens, not the scenic delights of the north country.'

Mary said, 'Papa would have approved of subfusc. He said it was the only proper wear for a gentleman. He was very pleased when Beau Brummell introduced the fashion of wearing black—particularly in the evening. Papa, of course, wore it all the time.'

'Well, he *was* a reverend gentleman, my dear,' explained her aunt.

'Russell isn't, though, and contrary to what Pickering might think, I like you in country clothes, sir.'

He bowed in her direction. 'But you approve of my working and Pickering does not.' He pulled out his hunter, consulted it and said, 'Much though I am enjoying our conversation, I think that we ought to begin work in the attics soon.'

'True,' said Mary, 'and I, for one, am eager to explore them. Who knows what treasures we might find?'

'I have arranged for one maid-servant to be present to assist the ladies and two of the stronger estate workers to be waiting for us should we need to do any heavy lifting,' Russell said as they walked up several flights of backstairs.

Half of the attic space was given over to the servants' quarters, although only a third of that was in use because Russell had not yet completely filled all the vacancies which Shaw had created. The other half was entered through a door usually kept locked. Daylight came through several windows set in the sloping roof which Russell had recently caused to be cleansed of the grime of the ages. Furniture, china, statuettes, chests and paintings were huddled about higgledy-piggledy. There was barely space to walk between the objects.

Mary and Aunt Beauregard had put on their aprons. The servant girl had brought up dusters, a bowl of water and some clean cloths. The menservants were lifting a tallboy away from the wall for them to inspect. Dusty and uncared for as it was, it was still a magnificent specimen of the furniture maker's art. All three of them stood back the better to admire it.

'Have you any notion why this was banished to the attics?' Russell asked the foremost man of the

two whose judgement he had already come to respect.

'Why, m'lord, I believe that Mr Shaw wished to
be rid of the furniture so that he might be able to
dismiss most of the staff who looked after the house,
seeing that empty rooms need no caring for.'

'Well, it can go downstairs again,' said Russell
firmly. Mary and Aunt Beauregard were nodding
their heads in agreement. 'Move it over to the far
wall and we'll arrange for it to be taken there. Have
you any notion where it used to stand?'

The second, smaller man said, 'I was the under-
butler before I was dismissed. I remember it being in
the entrance hall. A black marble bust used to stand
on it.'

Russell turned to Mary. 'You and Aunt Beauregard
might find it useful to pick out the china and the
bibelots which are lying around under the dust. Those
you think worthwhile could stand on the tallboy for
the present.'

Aunt Beauregard nodded agreement and added,
'Later I would rather like to identify the paintings,
most of which seemed to be leaning against the far
wall, behind the furniture. I remember that there used
to be a lot of portraits and conversation pieces of the
Russell family and I think that I could identify them.
There were some beautiful landscapes by Richard
Wilson, too.'

They all set to work with a will, growing increasingly dirty in the process. Mary and the little maid

washed the fine china which stood in every nook and cranny between the larger pieces of furniture. Aunt Beauregard turned her attention to the little tables, painted armoires, lacquered cabinets and fire-screens on poles—all covered in grime.

It soon became plain that most of the attics' contents were fine enough to return to their original homes—the former under-butler was helpful here. Russell had taken some paper and a pencil up with him and in the intervals of helping to heave furniture about was busy recording where it was to go and any repairs which might be needed.

'And this is only one of the attic rooms where furniture is stored,' Russell exclaimed. 'When it is all back in its proper place Eddington House will be one of the most beautiful in the county. Only Chard's place will be better.'

They worked their way across the room towards the paintings, all of them too excited by the treasures they were uncovering to feel tired. The larger workman had gone to collect a troop of men to carry the selected furniture and objects into the rooms which had been cleaned since Russell arrived. Bedroom furniture they left behind to be moved later since only Russell's, Pickering's and the indoor servants' rooms had been dealt with.

Finally they reached the paintings. Russell directed the smaller workman, Stubbs by name, to turn them round one by one so that they might all inspect them together.

Aunt Beauregard had been right. There were some splendid landscapes including a small Gainsborough, and two by Wright of Derby. The cream of the collection were, as she had said, the landscapes of Richard Wilson. Finally he began to uncover the portraits. The early ones dated back to the seventeenth century, brown, undistinguished things, but the distinctive face of the Russell family was already present in them, and it rapidly became plain that Russell took after them.

'You have the Russell nose,' Mary whispered to him when a late eighteenth-century grandee had been shown to them. 'To say nothing of the hair. I wonder if the hermit looks like this under all *his* hair!'

So far all the portraits had been those of men, but now a hidden cache of women appeared. These, too, had been carefully stored in chronological order so that it was not until almost at the end when they were presented with a young blonde girl with a pretty eager face.

'Why, I do believe that that is your mother, Margaret Russell, done by Romney, as she was when I was a girl,' said Aunt Beauregard. 'I had thought that that had long gone south with your father. It was a pity that she died so young. I told you that you are very like her, Russell, and that painting proves me right.'

So it did. Mary looked from the pretty girl on the canvas to Russell, and allowed that the likeness was remarkable, even given the difference between their sex.

'Downstairs, at once,' said Russell, his voice cracking with emotion. 'It must go on show immediately. I have never seen a portrait of my mother before. One of my cousins told me that I was very like her, particularly when I was younger, but I could not have guessed how great the resemblance is.'

He wondered why it had been left behind and not taken south—although he was now beginning to recognise that nothing had been taken from Eddington which might remind his father of the family into which he had married.

It was the next painting, though, which was the real surprise. Turned around, it showed a girl who was as dark as Margaret Russell had been fair. She had a thin clever face and glossy black hair dressed in the fashion of the late 1780s. It was another Romney and in many ways was superior to the previous one as though the painter had fallen in love with his subject.

Its effect on Russell, Mary saw, was immediate and surprising. He turned white, his mouth thinned and he said nothing, although previously he had been free with his comments. It was left to Aunt Beauregard to speak.

'So that's where that painting ended up. I wondered what had happened to it. The painter did it as a favour to Serena Cheyney and her brother Ralph. They were as poor as church mice at that time and couldn't afford to pay him. They were Margaret Russell's cousins, but took after their father, not their mother. I remember that your father, Russell, was very taken with her. We thought that they might make a match of it, but when he came back, a year later, it was to marry your mother.

'Of course, by then your mother was the Russell heiress. Serena married Courtney Lascelles a year later. This was after her brother, Ralph, suddenly inherited. Lascelles died when quite young. She never had any children and lives not far from here.'

Russell's face had recovered its normal colour. 'Is this portrait as good a likeness as the one of my mother?' he asked, apparently casually, but Mary could see that something about it had disturbed him.

'Very like.'

Russell said, trying not to sound too moved, although what he was seeing, had affected him powerfully.

'I asked you that because, although I resemble my mother, Ritchie, my twin, by some freak, is a male version of Serena Cheyney when young. We are, after all, blood relatives of hers, but it is still an odd thing that my twin should take after our second cousin, even if we are not identical ones.'

He turned to Aunt Beauregard. 'I hope that this question does not offend you, madam, but was it really true that my father loved Serena Cheyney?'

'Yes, it was really true. In fact, when he returned north we all thought that it was to propose to Serena, but after a few months it was Margaret whom he asked to be his wife. By then, of course, his father had become the Earl of Bretford and your father was no longer poor as he was when we were all young together. It was an odd coincidence that both your father and Ralph Cheyney should suddenly inherit titles and wealth.

'My George Russell was one of our little group of friends: it was because of his death, shortly before your father returned, that Margaret became the Russell heiress and the Eddington estate passed to the Chancellors by her marriage to him.'

She did not add that she had been unfortunate and lost, not only her own true love, but the chance of becoming the mistress of Eddington House. Russell, for his part, was privately beginning to suspect that his father had lost his true love when he became the heir to the Bretford Earldom. Mary, who had been listening carefully to this interchange, was thinking the same thing. Russell was also beginning to see the reason why his father had always favoured Ritchie, the son who looked like his lost love.

They continued to clear the attics, finding one room full of books from the dismantled library and another where fine copper pans, covered with verdigris, lay quite abandoned among the large kitchen furniture. All three of them were pondering on the mysterious workings of fate which had brought Eddington House down to near ruin, as well as the strange behaviour of its owner whose carelessness had allowed it to reach this sorry pass.

'I never thought I should enjoy myself so much,' Mary confessed. 'I'm not sure whether it was finding that fine Meissen porcelain which excited me the most or that lacquered cabinet from Japan. It will be quite wonderful to see them restored to where they can be freely admired when you have finished transforming the house.'

'Which might be some time yet,' lamented Russell. 'But never fear, I intend that, in time, everything will be restored to its proper place—we cannot let such treasures rot beneath the leads.'

'Talking of leads,' remarked Aunt Beauregard, 'when the Russells owned Eddington they used to give tea-parties on the leads—there is a staircase up on to the roof near the servants' quarters. The view from it is magnificent.'

'Excellent,' exclaimed Russell. 'As soon as we have finished all the improvements we shall christen them by inviting half the neighbourhood to one, eh, Mary?'

'What a splendid notion,' she exclaimed, her face rosy with pleasure.

'Agreed, then,' he said, taking her hand and bowing over it, 'and now let us go downstairs and find out whether my cook can rival Aunt Beauregard's in the tea-and-crumpets line!'

Their excursion to the attics set the tone for their whole happy summer. Never mind that it was one of the wettest in recent history—Russell and Mary's burgeoning love cast a golden glow over it. There were only two flies in the ointment: one was that the rain ruined the harvest, but fortunately Russell had spent most of the estate's surplus from its rents in buying sheep on Lord Chard's advice; and the second was Pickering's desertion.

Russell knew that Pickering was unhappy in the north, 'so far from civilisation' as he once glumly put it, but all the same it came as a surprise when one morning, after laying out Russell's country clothes for the day, he said, his face grave, 'I would have a serious word with you, m'lord.'

Russell, tying a large cream-coloured handkerchief around his neck, riposted idly, 'I thought that you were always serious, Pickering. It is one of your many virtues.'

'Even more serious than usual, then,' said Pickering who liked to bandy words with his master. 'It is this, m'lord. I would ask you to release me from my contract of service with you before quarter-day to allow me to return to London as soon as possible.'

M'lord was so surprised that he dropped his handkerchief. Pickering lifted it from the floor and handed it to him with a bow.

'Really, Pickering, you really wish to leave me? Why?'

'Truth to tell, m'lord, I am not happy here. My home has always been in London and I miss it very much. All my family and friends are there, and besides, you do not need me any more. You live and work in country clothing and the services I have always done for you are not required. I have been privately training one of the under-footmen to do for you all the necessaries of your new life, for, forgive me for saying so, I think that you intend to remain here—which is why I am asking you to allow me to leave.

'I have always been happy to work for you—as, indeed, have all the servants here and in London. We could not have a kinder or more considerate master, but the city lights beckon, if you will allow me to be poetic.'

'I will allow you anything—even to leave before quarter-day arrives, for I could not have had a more efficient or faithful valet. You will require me to write a reference for you, I suppose, and I shall do so gladly—although I do not gladly lose you. When would you like to leave?'

'By the end of next week, if that is suitable to you, m'lord.'

'Of course it's not suitable, but if you must, you must. I shall miss you greatly, but all the same, I wish you well in the future.'

'Thank you, m'lord, I knew that I could trust you to be kind.'

Kind! thought Russell when Pickering had gone. Ritchie would be sure to say I was too kind in letting Shaw stay on and in allowing Pickering to go when he pleases and not work out his time. The devil of it is, though, the fellow is right: he needs some fine gentleman to look after, not a country fellow dressed in flyaway clothing. For someone London born and bred, the country must seem a dull place.

He was not to know that Pickering's going would make the countryside seem far less dull, if not positively dangerous.

'Leaving us, Mr Pickering, are you?' commented Shaw that night when the valet broke the news to him. 'Can't say that I'm surprised—you're a right regular cockney, aren't you, if you don't mind me saying so. We'll give you a good send-off, though, be sure of that.'

The send-off took place two days before Pickering was due to leave. Privately Shaw had always thought that Pickering acted as though he were superior to them all because he served m'lord directly: to make him drunk thus became a kind of revenge. It also provided for Shaw a bonus which he didn't expect.

They were seated in the servants' hall, the debris of revelry about them. Most of the servants, other than Shaw's crony, Briggs, had already retired. Shaw had rightly judged that m'lord would not object to his faithful valet being given a right royal send-off. Pickering was already halfway to being maudlin when once he and Briggs were alone with him, Shaw began to question him about his life with Russell in London and out of it.

'Bet you were a bit surprised when the Earl sent him up here,' commented Shaw. It was an idle remark with no hidden meaning in it, other than to set Pickering talking in the hope that he might give something damaging away about his master.

Pickering, his senses awry, looked earnestly at his interrogator. 'That's just it,' he said, the drink making him careless—indeed, come morning he had no memory of what his loose tongue had given away. 'The Earl didn't send him here. The talk was that when m'lord asked his father if he could visit Eddington he was expressly told that he would never give him permission to do any such thing. It was the first time m'lord ever disobeyed his dad. The Earl don't know that he's here—my master just came.'

Shaw's jaw dropped. He almost asked Pickering to say all that again so that he was sure that he had not misheard, but Pickering was already near to *point non plus* so far as consciousness was concerned.

'That right?' he managed.

'Jus' said so, din' I? The Earl's no idea he's here, no idea at all.'

Rage consumed Shaw, who had been careful not to drink level with Pickering while he pumped him. So, the damned upstart had no business to be present, had not been sent by the Earl, but had come to Eddington to make trouble for them all on his own initiative. What's more, the bastard had always spoken as though he were his father's emissary!

Shaw's busy and devious brain, honed by a life-time of dishonesty, was beginning to grasp that he might be able to make use of what Pickering had just told him so that he could regain his one-time virtual lordship here.

'Any idea why he came?' he ventured.

'The gossip in the servants' hall was that he thought that there might be something going wrong here.'

'Such as?' was Shaw's next venture—but he was too late, Pickering slipped sideways from his chair, dead to the world, with no notion that he had be-trayed his master and had given his enemy a means of revenge on the man who had spoiled his little gal-lop at Eddington.

Shaw looked across at Briggs. 'Help me to get him to bed, Briggs, and then you and I will have a little talk.'

They lifted the unconscious Pickering so that he hung between them.

'What did you make of all that about m'lord being here, unknown and against his father's wishes?' asked Briggs once they had deposited Pickering on his bed and had returned to the scene of his recent downfall.

'Hush!' said Shaw, putting his finger beside his nose. 'That's for you and me to know, and not the rest of the fools around Eddington. I've got a right handy notion that we might be able to make good use of Pickering's loose tongue, but the less that oth-

ers might know about it, the better. If you keep quiet
we might both be made for life—best avoid drinking
too much from now on or you could give away any
little game you and me might care to play when the
time is right.'

Briggs nodded agreement and put down his tankard, the ale in it half-drunk. 'Anything you say,
Arthur, anything you say, you always did right for
us both before that popinjay arrived and spoiled
things.'

'Not for much longer,' said Shaw, laughing, 'not
for much longer.'

Chapter Ten

September had arrived. Around Eddington and Ancoates the countryside was turning golden and scarlet—when it wasn't raining, that was. In London the Earl of Bretford sat in his study, fuming. It was well over three months since he had heard anything from his son and heir.

He had learned, to his great annoyance, that Angelica Markham had first been betrothed to old Horsham and had then run off with young Tom Bertram. All of which went to show that Hadleigh had disobeyed him once again by not making an offer for the silly chit. It was natural that she didn't want to tie herself to that old roué Horsham, but if she had to run off with someone why couldn't it have been Russell Hadleigh? Not that she would have needed to run anywhere if Hadleigh had had the sense to propose to her.

None of this was worth worrying about while Hadleigh was still missing. What was he doing for money and where was he spending it? Had he been set on by robbers and been done away with? Who was harbouring him? Was he travelling from one country house to another?

The only thing the Earl could be sure of was that Hadleigh was disobeying him. He should have returned to London, after his failed attempt with Angelica Markham, so that he might be told which suitable heiress to propose to next. A more unsatisfactory son and heir than Hadleigh he could not imagine.

He chose for a moment to think of his more satisfactory son, Richard—or Ritchie, as he preferred to be called. Richard, who had already provided the family with an heir if Hadleigh failed, as usual, to do his duty. It was a great pity that he was not the older twin, then he would not be sitting here worrying about what Hadleigh was up to.

An idea struck him. Was it not possible that Richard knew where Hadleigh was? If he did, a visit to him at Liscombe might save a deal of time and worry about the wretch. Besides, it would be pleasant to see young Pandora again and his grandson: better to do that than sit here fretting about Hadleigh.

Ritchie Chancellor was sitting in his study going over his last month's accounts which his bailiff had left on his desk earlier that day when the door opened and his wife, Pandora, burst in. Pandora was given to bursting in: it was one of the things which he loved about her since it contrasted so well with his own complete calm.

'Yes, my love,' he said, smiling. 'What is it this time?'

'It's your father. He's just arrived. Why? How very odd that he should not write to us to inform us that he proposed a visit. He's always so punctilious about such matters. Can anything be wrong?'

Another thing about Pandora which Ritchie liked was her total common sense beneath her apparently flighty exterior. She was also able to detect the false notes in people's behaviour and certainly his father's completely unexpected and unannounced appearance was very odd.

'Perhaps,' he said, hedging his bets as usual. Pandora was to think later that it was one of the things for which she loved him. 'I take it that his unexpected arrival will not strain our hospitality overmuch.'

'Oh, no. I always have the spare room ready for use and plenty of food and the stables are—' She stopped. 'Ritchie, you are bamming me, are you not?'

'True,' he told her with a grin. 'I know what a splendid housekeeper you are. Now add to your splendour by going to greet Father and put him in a good humour by showing him Will while I finish these books.'

'Done,' she exclaimed and bounced out.

She must have exercised her charms on the Earl with great success, Ritchie thought later, since his father looked very much at ease both that afternoon and later during and after dinner. Particularly since it soon became apparent to him that his father must have had some important purpose behind this impromptu visit. Important because impromptu was usually the last word to apply to any of his father's actions.

Pandora gone, he pushed the bottle of port over to him, saying, 'Now, sir, perhaps you will do me the goodness to explain why you have come here in this ramshackle fashion without giving us warning and in as little state as possible.'

His father laughed and then grunted, 'You should go to Greenwich Fair, Richard, and set up as a mind-reader—much easier than toiling here turning this place into a money spinner.'

'True,' said his son, 'but you haven't answered my question which, I admit, wasn't really one.'

The Earl took a great swig of port, set his glass down carefully and said, 'It's Hadleigh. I haven't heard a word from him since early spring—it's as though he's vanished off the face of the earth. I know he visited you about that time—have you any notion where he might be? If you have, I should be greatly pleased if you would inform me of it.'

'Suppose I told you that he might not wish me to inform you of his whereabouts, what then?'

'Why ever not? And may I remind you it's your duty, as my son, to honour my wishes, and to tell me the truth.'

'Ah, but we have a conflict of interest here, sir. Between father and brother, where does my honour lie?' He lay negligently back in his chair, having said this, his half-drunk glass of port in his hand, and his eyes hard on his father.

'I would say to me. Besides, Hadleigh owes me a duty and you should assist him to honour it, not conceal anything which might enable me to learn what the devil he thinks he is doing. What do you say to that, sir?'

'That I am a free spirit who, for almost twenty years, has not depended on you for support, either financial or otherwise. I admit that I owe you some consideration because you are my father, but that consideration does not extend to my betraying my brother's confidence. If I tell you that I am not sure that I know exactly where he is, but that I could give a good guess, that is as far as I am prepared to go.'

The Earl brought his fist down on the dining table so hard that all the glasses and the remaining cutlery on it rattled alarmingly, and roared, 'Do I take it that you are in a conspiracy with him? A conspiracy to defy me.'

The worst thing about Ritchie Chancellor, everyone was agreed, was that it was impossible to wrongfoot, shake him, or make him lose his temper.

He said, his voice quite agreeable, 'To some extent, yes. I also think that you have kept him on leading strings for far too many years and I am surprised that it has taken him so long to defy you. Russell is no fool, as you would soon find out if you took the care to speak sensibly to him, but he has never been given a chance to exercise his intellect. If he has chosen to do that while he has defied you by disappearing, then you might ask yourself why you have driven him to this pass.'

His father stared at him, his face purpling, 'Why, sir, you are insolent—'

He came to a sudden halt when he saw that Ritchie remained unshaken and was saying, still calm, 'Yes, but truthful, Father. Would you have me lie to you? I am not lying when I say that I know where he might be, nor when I tell you why he might have disappeared. I also believe that he will at some time return, although not, perhaps, quite as the son you have always known, and whom you have consistently bullied and demeaned. That you have favoured me over him does not make me happy.'

His father rose to his feet. 'Enough, sir. I will leave on the instant. I will not stay to be insulted.'

Ritchie said, 'Pray do not, sir. You will distress Pandora, Will and myself. I blame myself that I have never been truthful with you before. Do me the honour of believing that I have no wish to hurt you unnecessarily, but at the beginning of our conversation you begged me to be truthful, and so I have been. I believe that if you stopped to think you might even know where Russell is, and I ask you to do that.'

He saw that his father was struggling with what he hoped was his better self. After a moment the Earl sat down again and said heavily, 'I know you to be an honest man and a brave soldier. That you defend your brother—whose mere existence means that you are denied the title which he now holds and the one which he will one day hold—proves what an excellent fellow you are. No, do not argue with me. I own that I have been hard on him, but there are reasons...reasons which you do not know—'

He stopped and Ritchie saw that his father, surprisingly, was on the verge of breaking down. He said nothing, but allowed him to recover.

'Enough of that. I see that you have, in your own fashion, done your duty to me. Of course I will not leave tonight, nor tomorrow, but I may not stay long because I must find out what in the world Hadleigh has been doing.'

He held out his glass. 'And now, if you will allow, let us drink a final toast together to show that there are no hard feelings between us.'

'Agreed, sir,' and Ritchie picked up the bottle of port to do as his father had asked.

Unaware of his father's worries and Ritchie's defence of him, Russell, with Mary by his side, was surveying the results of his summer's work. The interior of the house was starting to look almost as it had done before the Shaws had virtually dismantled it. The outside was also beginning to show the results of months of work and, if the harvest was proving meagre, the extra sheep, given that they survived the winter, would be bringing in a useful profit by spring.

Eddington village had begun to look more spruce than it had done on the first day when Russell had driven through it, although to rehabilitate them further, the house, the land and the village would all need a great deal more work done on them, and that would cost money.

'The pity of it is,' Russell was telling Mary on one of mid-September's few fine days, 'that my father has enough surplus cash from his other, better-run, estates and his investments to enable me to finish the work I have begun this year. Alas, things being as they are, it is impossible for me to ask him yet. I want to have set things so much to rights by next summer that I may be able to go to him with the consciousness of work well done and ask him to allow me to stay here as Eddington's master.

'Of course, when—and if—I inherit, that might have to end, but I am not looking so far into the future as that.'

Aunt Beauregard and Mary both agreed that he had done wonders and told him so.

He waved a hand at them, smiling. 'It is far from being all my work, you know. I have had so many willing helpers—including your good selves. Even Shaw, since Pickering went, has been ready and willing to fall in with whatever I have asked. It has been such a transformation that it quite justifies me in keeping him on.'

*   *   *

Aunt Beauregard was not mollified. 'I dislike that man, I really do,' she told Mary while Russell went to the stables to solve a problem which had arisen while they had been working in the library, restoring books to its shelves, even polishing the big desk which had been one of the last things brought from the attic. A fine chess table had been restored to its place by the fire and a battered chess set had been laid out on it. Mary and Russell had already been playing and working there.

'I don't like him much, either,' said Mary, 'but it is true that lately he seems to be quite reformed. Russell says that he could not have done so much without his active help.'

'That's as may be,' her aunt replied tartly, but fell silent when Russell returned and suggested a stroll in the gardens. They had not been improved quite so much as he had hoped—the weather had been too poor—but compared with their condition when he had arrived they were in splendid shape.

'You two young things go,' she said. 'I would like a nice doze in the comfortable armchair Russell has had brought out for me.'

Neither Mary nor Russell argued with her and set off through the herb gardens and on to the much-neglected lawn which one of the gardeners had been scything preparatory to digging the poor thing up and starting again, he had said.

'The trouble is,' Russell began, after they had crossed the lawn and found a broken stone bench to sit on from whence they could see the algae-covered lake whose water was supplied by a tributary of the Tyne, 'I have no wish to wait until next summer before we marry. I really think that to carry on as we are doing would be a drain on my health and sanity! Not only that, I wish to start a family before we both fall into "the sere and yellow leaf", as Shakespeare has it. Am I right in believing that you feel the same?'

Mary nodded. Lately to be with him had become sweet torture. 'Exactly the same. Have you considered what we might do about it?'

'Well, we could get married at any time that we liked, so far as a church service is concerned. The local rector would be only too happy to call the banns. He virtually told me so the other day! The problem there is that a man of my rank and a lady of yours are expected to be married only after the most astonishing legal arrangements are gone through regarding both our finances. That would inevitably mean that my father would have to take a hand in the game since I have no income of my own, other than the allowance which he makes me because the Russells allowed him full access to my mother's money instead of settling anything on her and then, at twenty-one, on me, as is common.

'That is why I have been using the income from the Eddington lands to pay for their improvement and my living costs. Before I ran away, for that is what I have done, he told me that he would cut off my allowance unless I married a woman of his choice before three months were up. The three months have come and gone and I have no notion what he might say if I were to tell him that I have found you again and still wish to marry you. Particularly since I have defied him by coming here at all.'

Mary offered him a wry smile. '"Oh, what a tangled web we weave when first we practise to deceive."'

'Exactly. You see my dilemma—which is yours, too.'

'No,' said Mary. 'I love you and trust you. If we married without all the legal piff-paff, I know that you would not cheat me over my money. What troubles me is not that, but that our deceit of everyone among whom we live—other than Aunt Beauregard, that is—would go even further than it already has done.'

Russell took her in his arms and kissed her. 'I am happy beyond belief that you trust me not to exploit you. But not only would the world think that I was a fortune hunter by marrying you if my father cast me off, but I have no wish to live on your money. If it were not my hope that my father and I might somehow become reconciled, I would go at once to Lord Chard and take up his offer to be his land agent so that I might bring something to our marriage.'

Secure in his arms, Mary looked up at his beloved face. It was not her imagination, she was sure, which led her to believe that, since he had arrived in the north and begun to run Eddington, his face had become sterner, stronger and more mature.

He kissed her gently on the forehead—a caress which was almost impersonal, but neither of them wished to go too far since passion was starting to hold them in its thrall and once certain boundaries were passed who knew what might happen?

'Would you marry me if I were only Chard's land agent, Mary?' he asked, bestowing another butterfly kiss on her.

'You know that I would. I would throw away my fortune if I thought that it kept me from you. I would marry you tomorrow without a settlement if that is your wish. I would come to you in rags, or in style if you were in rags, I cannot say fairer than that.'

'Brave girl,' he whispered. 'The time is not yet. If we are still in no-man's land by the time that winter arrives, then we shall think again. We never know what the morrow might bring and it is even possible that our problems might be solved for us, after a fashion which we could not have imagined.'

Later, he was to think wryly that he had spoken truer than he knew, but at the time his words flew away and, lost in a dream of love, perhaps the more powerful for not yet being fulfilled, they sat side by side enjoying one of the few sunny days of that disastrous year.

Shaw told Briggs of his scheme to be rid of Russell Hadleigh—to Briggs's horror, at first, but the more often Shaw spoke of it the less horrific it began to seem. He had involved Briggs because he needed an ally who was respectable and who could lie as convincingly as himself.

'We couldn't do it if Pickering hadn't left for London,' he said, 'or if the Earl had really sent Hadleigh to check our goings-on. As it is, I can't see any problems for us. We make him disappear'—he never used the words 'kill', or 'dispose of him', in respect for Briggs's more delicate feelings—'and then you drive his chaise, filled with his belongings, into the woods and hide it, telling everyone he's grown bored with playing about at Eddington and has gone back to London.'

'I don't know,' Briggs said. 'I don't like it, too risky.'

'Oh, damn that for a tale,' exclaimed Shaw. 'Think of all the lovely loot we shall get back again. There's another reason we ought to do it soon. I have a suspicion that he's been checking where the money went before he arrived here, so the sooner we're rid of him the better.'

'But what about his woman at Ancoates?' asked Briggs desperately. 'Won't she think it's odd if he takes off for London without her—*and* without telling her he's going?'

'Now, Briggs, you know better than that. His sort takes up and drops women as often as we change our clothes. No, if we do what I suggest then there's no need to worry. We can even give it out beforehand that he's growing bored and talking about going back to the bright lights before winter comes. Who's to contradict us, eh?'

It was probably more the thought of hanging or transportation if m'lord found out, and could prove, that he and Shaw had been on the take which convinced Briggs that he ought to join Shaw in his reckless scheme to make m'lord disappear. Besides, the more he thought about it, the more foolproof the scheme began to seem.

Of course, those locals whom m'lord had recruited or had given their previous posts back would have to be laid off again and would doubtless be noisy about it. As Shaw pointed out, however, all they had to do was blame m'lord for raising their hopes and then leaving them to starve again after he had driven off to the fleshpots of the idle south.

Shaw particularly liked the word fleshpots. He was already practising what he would say when m'lord's departure became general knowledge. Yes, all his troubles would soon be over—and m'lord's too, if it came to that.

Shaw had been right to worry about Russell's investigations into his goings-on before he had arrived at Eddington. Geoffrey Norman, who ran the country bank at Ancoates, had said something which had roused his suspicions about what Shaw had done with the money he had saved by dismissing most of the house and estate workers. That, and Aunt Beauregard's constant moaning about his simple-minded trust of a proven cheat like Shaw, had set him watching the man and listening carefully to what he said and did.

Russell was, as Shaw had suspected, on the verge of being able to tell the authorities of his embezzlement and thus bring about his arrest. In fact, on a fine early October day he saddled his horse to ride over to Ancoates to see, not the banker, but the local solicitor and discuss the matter with him. He had debated with himself whether to drive over to Loudwater and see his new friend, Lord Chard, who was the Lord Lieutenant of the county, but had decided that he would do that after consulting the solicitor.

On his way there, he would, as he had promised her, visit Mary. He had a splendid and elegant new solution to their latest chess problem in his pocket and he wanted to see her face when she read it.

He was travelling down the rutted by-way to Ancoates when he heard the sound of two horses being ridden hard behind him. He turned round in his saddle to see that it was Shaw and Briggs who were following him.

Russell stopped his own horse and waited for them to reach him. Shaw promptly rode ahead of him while Briggs stayed behind so that he was caught between the two of them.

'Might I enquire, m'lord,' asked Shaw swinging his mount around to face him, 'where you are off to this afternoon?'

'To Ancoates,' he replied shortly, 'although it is no concern of yours where I choose to ride.'

'Ah, but if I think it might be,' said Shaw, leaning forward in his saddle, 'what then?'

There was nothing of his usual greasy deference in the way he answered Russell and the expression on his face was a mocking one.

'I have no need to explain myself to you,' Russell replied, and he had never sounded more like Ritchie, 'and you will do me the goodness of removing yourself from out of my way.'

'Now, that,' said Shaw, 'I will not. I am sick of doing you any goodness and I have a mind to put an end to it here and now. Briggs, do as I asked you earlier.'

Behind him Russell heard Briggs give a great gulp before quavering, 'I have a pistol trained on your back, m'lord, and it will stay there until you dismount.'

'For goodness' sake,' said Russell impatiently, without turning his head to look at Briggs, 'the pair of you had better stop play-acting at once. I am a busy man these days and have no time for this. Put your pistol down, Briggs, before you do someone a mischief with it.'

Shaw grinned evilly at him. 'Oh, we mean to do a mischief, both of us...' and he had produced his own pistol to wave at Russell '...so do as you're told, my haughty lordship, and get down at once.'

So, it was mutiny or worse and Russell was blindingly aware that his life was in the balance.

'Very well,' he said, apparently meekly, but secretly determined to do something of which his brother might approve so he dismounted, but the moment he reached the ground he slapped his horse hard on its haunches with the crop which, like Ritchie, he rarely used.

It gave an enraged whinny and bolted—straight at Shaw, who was thrown from his own horse, losing his pistol in the process. Briggs, also taken by surprise, fired his pistol, but hit nothing. Unfortunately for him his own horse took fright at the noise and threw him.

In the confusion Russell ran rapidly through the trees away from the pair of villains whom he now knew intended to murder him. He also knew that he were not far from the hermit's cottage which, if he could reach it and the recluse was there, would mean salvation.

Briggs, the lesser of the pair, at first made no effort to rise, but Shaw, whose determination equalled his cunning, scrabbled around until he found his pistol before running past the prostrate Briggs, roaring, 'Get up, man, go after him, or we'll both hang.'

He then plunged into the woods after the unarmed Russell, who by now had reached the cottage—to find it locked. Desperately looking round him, he decided to run back towards Eddington, taking the short cut home by the quarry in the hope that he could outpace his pursuers.

Behind him Shaw and Briggs panted on, now terrified that if they did not catch their prey it was their lives which would be at stake. The few moments which Russell had spent trying the hermit's cottage door had enabled them to gain on him. Not only that, it had also shortened the distance between them so that he was now in the range of Shaw's pistol if he cared to use it—which he did, although he would have preferred Russell's body to be found without a bullet hole in it.

Russell ignored Shaw's repeated calls for him to stop and ploughed on, widening the distance between himself and his pursuers again until, in his haste, he stumbled over a fallen tree branch concealed by the autumn leaves which were heaped everywhere. Worse than that, he caught his head as he fell and lay there, dazed, in his turn.

'Splendid,' gasped Shaw when they reached their prey as he struggled to rise, not quite certain where he was or what he was doing. 'There's no need to waste a bullet on him after all. Let's knock him on the head and heave him into the quarry. Come on, you lazy devil, we can't afford to let him go now. It's him or us,' he roared at Briggs, who now that the fatal moment had arrived was beginning to regret having become involved in this wretched business at all.

Briggs stumbled forward. Shaw clubbed the struggling Russell with his pistol, caught him under the arms and began to drag him to the edge of quarry. 'Take him by the legs, Briggs,' he howled, 'and be quick about it. We don't want that damned hermit finding us.'

Galvanised both by fear of Shaw and by fear of hanging, Briggs did as he was bid. Together they heaved Russell over the edge and watched him tumble down, to be trapped by some bushes halfway down to the quarry's floor.

Shaw dusted his hands together.

'Home now, Briggs. Remember—he went off to London this afternoon.'

'But there's them as knows he didn't, and what will they think?'

'Nothing, Briggs, nothing. I've sent the groom who brought his horse round for him today over to the farm Hadleigh way as soon as he'd mounted m'lord. They wanted another labourer there. He grumbled a bit, but I told him it's his duty to go where I send him. That leaves only the pair of us to give evidence of his whereabouts—and who's going to put their living at risk by questioning anything we might say. Besides, by the time m'lord's been gone forty-eight hours they'll have forgotten that he was ever here.'

Privately Briggs doubted that, but Shaw seemed so certain that all would be well that he kept his own counsel. After a short search they found Russell's horse contentedly cropping at some sparse grass and led him back to Eddington House, fortunately meeting no one on the way back.

Unknown to them both, they had been watched by the hermit who had heard Briggs's accidental firing of his pistol and wondered what was up. He had walked towards his cottage in order to avoid trouble, only to stop in the trees, hidden by them but near enough to hear Shaw and Briggs talking before they had heaved Russell's unconscious body into the quarry. He was fearful that if he interrupted them at their deadly business they would make short work of him, too.

Once they had gone he walked over to the quarry and looked down. He gave a short exclamation: m'lord was stirring and was like to fall to the quarry floor at any moment and so finish himself off for good. The question was, how to rescue him? He pondered this for a little, went back to his cottage and found some rope. Had he still the strength he had once possessed which would enable him to tie the rope to a tree, lower himself down and bring the half-conscious man back up to safety?

George Russell had spent the last thirty years avoiding his fellow men and doing nothing for them. He never knew what stirred him to try to rescue Russell Hadleigh. Perhaps it was some dim memory of happy days long ago with Jackie Chancellor, the imperilled young man's father, which caused him to set about his near-impossible task.

Mary had looked forward to Russell's visit that morning. He had seen her two days ago and had promised to look in on them after he had consulted the solicitor at Ancoates. He had told them nothing about the visit itself: he thought the less said about his decision to cast off Shaw before he had taken legal advice, the better.

At first she was not surprised that he was late, but as the day wore on and he never appeared she began to worry a little. On a previous occasion when he had had to cry off at short notice he had sent her a message by a groom with his apologies and his promise to call on the morrow. She knew that as the acting manager of the Eddington lands he was occasionally confronted with crises which required him to act immediately.

Her worries, and to a lesser extent, Aunt Beauregard's, grew stronger the next day when she still received no message from him.

'He's probably busy, dear,' her aunt said. 'I expect he'll come tomorrow.'

But he didn't and Mary began to grow a little frantic. She remembered only too well how she had felt all those years ago when he had deserted her the first time. Had he simply invented a convincing explanation to account for his earlier desertion and now that he had grown tired of his duties in the north, and of her, had he deserted her again?

She did not want to think so, but the burned child fears the fire, as she told Aunt Beauregard on the fourth day.

'Come, come,' said her aunt. 'This is foolish. The sensible thing would be to take Payne and ride over to Eddington. He might be ill—or Chard has called on him to carry out some of his new plans for the county. Best to find out what might be going on.'

Mary with Payne, the groom, riding behind her, set out for Eddington House early the next day. She arrived on the gravel sweep before its main doors with her heart in her mouth. She asked Briggs, who answered her determined knocking, if Lord Hadleigh was in.

She thought that Briggs looked at her oddly before he said, 'Please allow me to escort you to the drawing room, madam. I had better fetch Mr Shaw to speak to you.'

Shaw came in almost immediately. 'Ah, Mrs Wardour, Briggs said that you were asking to speak to Lord Hadleigh. Did he not inform you that he was returning to London? He set out at dawn three days ago.'

Her face white, Mary said as calmly as she could, 'Did he not leave any message for me, Mr Shaw?'

He shook a regretful head. 'I'm afraid not. I never thought to ask him if I were to send you one. I assumed, seeing as you were such friends, that you were already aware that he was returning south.'

How she rose to her feet without falling over, Mary never knew. Russell had done it again. He had left her without a word after all his protestations of eternal love. If she had been shattered by his previous desertion, it was as nothing to the effect of this one.

Twice! He had deceived her twice! What a fool she had been—and Aunt Beauregard, too, who had been so sure of his integrity.

Were all men lying traitors? And he the worst of them all?

'Thank you, Mr Shaw,' she managed. 'I expect that I shall be hearing from him when he reaches London.'

'Possibly so, madam, possibly so.'

He bowed her out. To return to Ancoates and her aunt, not to cry, not to revile him for his treachery, but to tell her as simply as she could that he had deserted her again and this time possibly for good. What a fool she had been to believe him when he had told her that they must have been tricked. Trickery there had been but it had been his.

Her tears were threatening to fall, but she would not cry, she would not. She would get on with her life and try to forget him.

If she could: it was going to be difficult.

Chapter Eleven

At the end of the first week when Briggs and Shaw were congratulating themselves that their murderous plot had succeeded, Mary went for a ride in the woods on her own. She had refused Payne's offer to go with her. She said that she needed to be alone.

When she had returned from Eddington with her sad news, even Aunt Beauregard had been compelled to agree with her and admit that she had been mistaken about Lord Hadleigh.

'I would never have thought it of him, never,' she was constantly saying, 'but, there it is, history seems to be repeating itself. The only thing that I can say to comfort you is, that given everything, you are well rid of him.'

This, of course, was no comfort at all. Nor did the passing days bring any kind of peace to Mary—rather the contrary. Instead of trying to forget him, her wretched memory insisted on going over and over again the events of the past summer and the love they had seemed to share. Somehow this second desertion without a word of warning seemed worse than the first. It indicated a callousness which she would never have dreamed he possessed.

Had all her time with him been an illusion?

One afternoon she was picking flowers in the garden when Payne, the groom who had accompanied her to Eddington, came up to her and asked for permission to speak to her.

'Of course,' she told him. 'What is it you wish to say to me?'

'Only this, Mrs Wardour, I know that it is no business of mine, but one of the servants at Eddington told me yesterday that he thought that there was something odd about m'lord's going. I thought that I ought to tell you of it—you and him being so friendly, like.'

'Something odd,' she repeated numbly. 'What kind of odd?' She did not tell him that it did not seem odd to her since history had simply repeated itself.

'Just that he left some of his clothes behind, and a rifle which he treasured. He went very suddenly, too, without saying a word about his going back to London at such short notice to anyone but Mr Shaw. All the servants at Eddington think that it was very unlike him: he had always been a most kind and considerate master. They would have expected to have had a few words in farewell from him—particularly since he had arranged for most of the books and furniture to be taken down to the library the following day. Most eager about it he was.'

'Is that all?' she said. 'There's probably a simple reason for his behaviour—that he was desperate to return to London.'

'Perhaps so, madam,' he said and bowed. 'But I thought you ought to know.'

She could not take comfort from anything as tenuous as that, but would behave with the same stoicism which had supported her before, although every time that she looked at her chess set in the window and remembered him sitting there opposite to her, and smiling, the treacherous tears threatened to fall.

That night Mary awoke in the small hours—she had been sleeping badly—but this time the memory of her dreams brought her neither pain nor anguish.

For some reason in one of them she had been with him again on their trip to the cairn, before the hermit had surprised them. They had been discovering how they had been tricked by their parents and she had been so overwhelmed that, afterwards, she had fallen asleep in his arms. And he had made no attempt to seduce her but had just comforted her. Surely, a true villain, a villain who would have deserted her, would have cold-bloodedly exploited her vulnerability, not repressed his own desires, but attempted to fulfil them.

She would not have resisted him then, and he must have known that. There was more to puzzle her— Shaw and Briggs's behaviour when she had called at Eddington House, and now, this afternoon, Payne telling her how out of character his desertion of the folk at Eddington had seemed to them.

Russell had mentioned the word trust to her on several occasions and now Mary asked herself, as the dawn light grew stronger and stronger in her bedroom, Had she been wrong not to trust him?

No, she told herself firmly, I cannot believe that the man I have come to know this summer would ever betray me. If I believe that to be true, as a consequence, I must then believe that he has never left for London and therefore has not deserted me.

This, however, presented another problem for her to solve. She had to admit that his departure seemed plausible enough, but if, as she now believed, he had not left for London, then where was he? More than that, Shaw and Briggs must have been lying, not only to her, but to everyone else.

Mary's logical mind, trained by her father and then her husband, had her asking herself who might stand to gain by his disappearance and the answer was the pair who were lying to her. Russell had stopped their looting of Eddington, but they had probably been unable to plot against him because they had believed that he was his father's agent.

But supposing that they had discovered that he was not. What then?

Which raised the fearful possibility that he might be already dead.

No, she would not believe that, she would not. She would have known. In any case, there must be something she could do to discover the truth, and, if Russell had truly deserted her, then she must let him go and try to build her life anew.

She could not tell Aunt Beauregard of any of this. Much though she loved her, Mary recognised that she was the prisoner of her emotions. No, the best thing, perhaps, was to visit Lord Chard at Loudwater and tell him of her suspicions. He was the Lord Lieutenant of the county and she knew that she could depend upon his judgement.

After deciding this she fell asleep at once, but not before deciding that she would rethink this whole wretched business in the daylight away from her aunt, away from everyone and then map out a plan of action. She would go to the cairn where she had been so happy, sure of only one thing: that Russell had not betrayed her after all.

'Go riding on your own? Is that wise?' her aunt exclaimed.

'I must be out of the house,' said Mary, as calmly as she could, 'and try to work out what I shall now do with my life.'

This was no lie, but it was an evasion of the truth which her aunt had to accept. In the event she was never to reach the cairn. Before she did so, she had to pass the hermit's cottage. For once, he was outside in the little garden at the back where he grew a few herbs and simples and, at the right time of the year, potatoes. The moment he saw her he waved at her urgently. She waved back, but continued on her way, respecting what she had come to know was his wish for solitude.

This time, however, she was mistaken. He ran after her, calling her name so urgently that she stopped.

'Yes, Mr Russell, what is it you wish of me?'

He had reached her and put out a hand to grasp her horse's reins, so determined was he that she must stay and speak with him.

'I am most happy to meet you, Mrs Wardour. You have saved me a visit to Miss Beauregard, a visit which I did not wish to make because it might have caused gossip.'

He paused for breath as though the effort of speech had been too much for him. Mary said, surprised by his continuing urgency, 'Well, I am here now and you may speak to me. I can always give Miss Beauregard a message from you.'

'No! no!' he exclaimed, more urgent than ever. 'It is you to whom I must speak, not your aunt. And not in the open where we might be seen or heard—too dangerous. Pray come to my cottage as you did once before where we may speak in private. I promise you that you will not regret it.'

Well, here was a thing! What could the poor man mean? Had solitude driven him mad? He was pulling on the reins now, and lest he frighten her horse which was beginning to grow restive Mary decided to brave all and do as he wished.

'Very well,' she said, once down. 'I'll come with you.'

'Good, excellent,' he said, 'allow me to lead your horse. A gentleman should always make a lady's life as easy as possible. You see that I have not lost all my manners.'

The way back to his cottage was not far, but Mary was already starting to regret that she had agreed to accompany him, but he kept such a firm hold of her horse, tying it carefully to the fence, before taking her arm and leading the way into his humble home as he described it when he opened the door, that she had no option but to obey him.

Inside it was as dark as Mary remembered it to have been, but much tidier. The hermit still held on to her arm, saying, 'Come with me, I have something to show you,' and then led her across the room to his rude bed in the corner.

For one ghastly moment Mary thought that he was about to assault her, but then she saw that the bed was occupied by a man whose head was turned away from her and who seemed to be sleeping.

Why have you brought me here? she started to ask, but only managed to get out the word 'Why' when the hermit, releasing her arm at last, bent over the bed, and shook the man by the shoulder, whispering, 'I have brought her to see you—as I promised.'

The man gave a short exclamation, sat up and turned his face towards Mary—and it was, of all people, Russell, her Russell! She would have recognised him anywhere, even if he was greatly changed with his bruised face and a week's growth of beard.

Her head whirling, she stared at him and of all things was only able to say, mindlessly, and in the circumstances, stupidly, even as she fell on her knees by the bed, 'But you have not gone to London after all!'

Russell smiled at this, and it was his special smile for her. 'So that is what they told you. I prayed, and have been praying since George brought me back to life, that you would not think that I had deserted you again, if that was their explanation for my disappearance.'

He tried to raise himself more, but fell back on his pillow, too weak to do so, his eyes closing.

Mary, the tears beginning to fall, bent down to kiss his cheek.

He opened his eyes and said, 'Are you truly here? George said that he would fetch you soon, but he did not wish to leave me alone while I was so weak in case my would-be murderers by some sad chance found me and finished me off this time.'

'Shaw,' Mary choked out, 'and Briggs, too, I suppose. I knew that there was something odd about Briggs's manner to me when I called at Eddington House to find out why you had failed to visit us, as you had promised. And Payne, my groom, told me some of the servants there thought your desertion of them—for so they thought it—peculiar. God forgive me, at first I thought that they were wool-gathering, but then, when I began to think of our happy time together this summer, and the vows which you had made to me, I knew that there was something wrong, that you would never betray me by leaving without a word. I was going to visit Lord Chard this afternoon and ask him for his advice.'

Russell was struggling to sit up again. 'Oh, my darling, you have made me so happy that in the end you ceased to doubt me. What else could I think, though, when I could think again, which was only three days ago, but that you would certainly believe me traitor? I worried more about that than how soon it would be before I recovered enough to be able to confront those who have tried to kill me.

'They were Shaw and Briggs, as you rightly suspected. They waylaid me not far from here, knocked me unconscious and threw me into the quarry. By the grace of God, George found me there and got me out, the good lord knows how, and then nursed me back to near life—as you see. I am most eternally grateful to him.'

He sank back, exhausted, on to his pillow again. The hermit said gruffly, 'I couldn't let Jackie Chancellor's son die without trying to save him. Now that you have seen him, Mrs Wardour, I will leave you alone with him for a time. I believe that your presence will be as good a restorative as medicine for my poor patient.'

After he had left them, Mary sat on the stool beside the bed. Her relief was tempered with shame that she had ever doubted him—even for a short time. She leaned over to stroke his forehead, which was as cold as ice. He opened his eyes and smiled at her, 'You have no notion how pleased I am to see you again.'

'And I you,' she said. 'I began to fear that you might be dead. I was riding to the cairn to work out in peace what I should say to Lord Chard.'

'That's my clever darling,' he said, and began to shiver. He gave her a rueful smile. 'Ever since George brought me round I have been unable to get warm. Ritchie told me once that soldiers injured in battle often suffer in this way. I suppose that the attack on me has had the same effect.'

To Mary's shock his lips were turning blue.

Oh, he must not die now, not now that she had found him again! She would not let him. She would warm him and to the devil with all the constraints which society put on women's behaviour. Later she was even to wonder whether the hermit had intended this when he had left them alone.

She leaned down, pulled off her boots and with one swift movement she threw back the covers, slipped into the bed beside him, drew the covers over them and put her arms around him.

'Come,' she said. 'I will warm you. It is the least that I can do after failing to trust you when you disappeared. Remember how you warmed me on the day when we worked out how our parents had deceived us.'

It was true that he was cold, so cold, but she was warm, and she was Mary his love, and after a little time he ceased to shiver and then put his arms around her and she felt him drift off into sleep. She was not to know that it was the first peaceful sleep he had had since the hermit had brought him back to consciousness again.

And as he became warm and slept, Mary, too, held so innocently in the arms of the man she loved, also slept. And there the hermit found them, chaste in each other's arms, the man on his way to recovery and the woman doing sweet penance for ever having doubted him for a moment.

On the evening of the day on which Shaw and Briggs had pitched Russell into the quarry m'lord the Earl of Bretford was still fuming over the fact that October had arrived and he had still heard nothing from his wayward son.

Despite Ritchie having told him that if he thought hard enough he would be able to guess where his brother was, he still had no notion of where he might be. That morning he had snarled first at his valet, then at Graves and finally at the butler. While never a very even-tempered man, he had always been reasonably considerate of those who served him and his own loss of control vexed him nearly as much as it did them.

In the evening he went to a reception given by Lord Sidmouth, preparing to be horribly bored, which he was. Until, while walking from one overcrowded room to another, he was accosted by someone whom he had not seen for years.

'Damn me,' announced a cheerfully rotund gentleman, 'if it isn't my old friend, Jackie Chancellor, after all these years. I have to say you've worn better than me and no mistake.'

The Earl put up his quizzing glass and said in a tone of deadly indifference, 'Do I know you, sir?'

'Well, I'm aware that I've changed, but I hadn't thought I'd changed so much that you wouldn't recognise me,' the fat man said, no whit flustered by m'lord's arrogant dismissal of him, 'but surely you're the Jackie Chancellor who let a bear loose into the Fellow's common-room at Oxford as I'm still the Ralph Cheyney who helped you.'

The Earl lowered his quizzing glass. 'Yes, you are Ralph Cheyney, I see that now, and, by God, you *have* changed, sir.'

'Sir Ralph now, too, not plain Mister. Like you I came into what I hadn't expected. But if I've changed in looks I'm still a bit of the merry-andrew I always was while you've turned into the sort of solemn chap we used to avoid like the plague. Never mind that, let's find a corner where we can talk about old times,' and Sir Ralph, without waiting for an answer, set off through the double doors to do exactly that.

Resignedly the Earl followed him until they arrived at a quiet ante-room away from the crowd, where Sir Ralph sank gratefully into an armchair and invited the Earl to do the same in another.

'By the by,' he began, 'before we begin reminiscing I ought to tell you that I met your son and heir, Hadleigh, last spring. Sterling fellow, isn't he? With a bottom of sound common sense. I hope he marries the pretty little mathematician who was travelling north with him.

'Added to that, I've heard nothing but good of what he's been doing at Eddington. You should be proud of him and for having the common sense to send him there to mend matters. Ever since old Shaw died a few years ago that wastrel son of his has been ruining the place. Let the House go to rack and ruin, turned staff away and let the lands go to rot as well. I wondered what he was doing with the rents. But I suppose that's why you sent Hadleigh there. He's done marvels in a jolly short time, they say. You wouldn't recognise the place. He put the locals back to work, improved everything beyond belief, Chard told me just before I came south. Chard was most impressed by him and he isn't impressed by many or by much.'

The Earl stared at the gossiping fool, rendered almost dizzy by this cascading mixture of idle joviality and unbelievable information. Sir Ralph looked keenly at him.

'I say, old friend, are you feeling quite the thing? I thought that you were going to have a funny turn there for a moment.'

'No, no,' said the Earl hurriedly. 'I'm a little tired, perhaps, that's all.'

Not for a moment would he betray to the half-wit before him that he had not had the slightest notion either that Hadleigh had gone to Eddington or, that he had, improbably, transformed the place. Old Shaw dead! When had that happened? Why had he not been informed? What had young Shaw been doing to the place?

Later, when he had shaken off Sir Ralph who had talked steadily at him about everything and everybody for the last half hour, the Earl remembered something which Ritchie had said to him. That if he thought hard enough he would know exactly where Hadleigh had gone.

Now how the devil could he be expected to know that he had gone north to Eddington, the one place on earth which the Earl detested most of all? Something at the back of his mind pricked him sufficiently for him to shake his head and remember that Hadleigh had made a fuss to him and Graves about the accounts which old Shaw—no, young Shaw—had sent down from Eddington. Hadleigh had even, he remembered now, asked if he might go there to find out what was happening.

Of course, he had refused to allow him to do any such thing.

So! The disobedient swine had set off on his own initiative! Oh, he would have a word with Graves about this in the morning and then, damn him if he would not set off for Eddington himself as soon as maybe and send Hadleigh packing for good and all.

He stopped for a moment—on the other hand, Chard thought highly of him, and Chard was no fool.

No matter, it was not Hadleigh's business to defy his father by meddling with the Eddington estates. Besides, there was another thing. What was all that talk of a pretty female mathematician and some nonsense about Hadleigh marrying her?

Well, he'd soon put a stop to that!

The following morning, after speaking to a friend of Cheyney's who lived not far from Eddington and was also at the Reception, the Earl discovered that matters might be even more serious there than Cheyney had suggested. The Earl walked rapidly into Graves's office. His agent and secretary sat there, working as usual.

He rose. 'M'lord?'

'Graves, I have just discovered that Hadleigh has, against my express wishes, gone north to Eddington and is meddling in things there without my knowledge or my permission. I have a mind to go up north myself and put a stop to it. Order the stables to prepare everything for my journey there tomorrow.'

Had the Earl not been so determined to punish his son he might have noticed the fleeting expression of alarm which passed over Graves's face.

'Is that wise, m'lord? To make the differences between you and Lord Hadleigh so plain to the world? Think of the gossip which might ensue.'

The Earl, who had already begun to turn away, swung on his heel. 'I don't give a damn for gossip. Besides, someone ought to go there. Were you aware that old Shaw died some years ago and that, without informing me and asking for authority to do so, his son took over from him, pretending that his father was still alive?'

Graves put on a shocked expression. 'Indeed not, m'lord. The signatures on the accounts seemed to be in order—as did the accounts.'

'Well, something damned odd has been happening at Eddington if my informants are to be believed. Sounds as though Shaw has been looting the house and grounds. My fault, not yours. I hate the damned place and only Hadleigh's running off to it and this news about old Shaw's death and his son's misbehaviour would take me there.

'Oh, and Mr Richard and his family were due to visit me in a sennight. Write to them explaining that I have been called north on an urgent mission and will entertain them on another date as soon as I return.'

'Of course, m'lord. Certainly, m'lord, as soon as possible.'

'Excellent. I knew that I could depend on you.'

The moment the door had closed behind the Earl, Graves swore a great oath which damned young Shaw and his overdone greed to hell for the devil to deal with him there. He then sat down and began to write a frantic letter to his fellow conspirator, warning him of the Earl's intention to visit Eddington in the somewhat vain hope that the letter might reach him before the Earl did.

Who would have thought that the old man would suddenly throw off the habit of a lifetime in order to travel to a place which he had so often told Graves he would never visit again? Damn Hadleigh and his meddling! Who could have guessed that he was clever enough at figuring to be able to detect something strange about Eddington's accounts and then would decide to drive off and check them on the spot!

If the worst came to the worst his own best plan would be to pack his bags and make off as quickly as possible with his share of the loot from Bretford's northern estates before the Runners arrived to arrest him.

Mary and Russell were playing cards. From the moment of Mary's first arrival he had recovered rapidly, and was almost his old self again. Several days of eating good food had restored the roses to his cheeks. Mary had been smuggling it from Aunt Beauregard's kitchen on the pretext that she was taking it to the poor of Ancoates—making sure that some of it reached them on her journey to the hermit's cottage.

He was sitting in the hermit's Windsor chair, dressed in his own clothing which the hermit had, after a fashion, washed. The hermit had not only shaved Russell's face for him, but he had also cut his own beard and hair and had then shaved himself. The man who had emerged from this shearing had proved to be one who had carried his youthful good looks into old age.

For his part, Russell had never looked less like the London dandy he had once been, but even so his recent experiences, far from destroying his attraction for Mary, had enhanced it by strengthening his face even further. Once his first debilitating weakness had passed, he had had only one idea in his head and that was to bring Shaw and Briggs to justice. Particularly Shaw, because he had repaid the charity and mercy shown to him by trying to murder the man who had offered it.

Unknown to Mary, for the first time he looked like his twin a little. It was more in his expression than in his overall facial structure and colouring where the resemblance lay. Russell now shared the appearance of hard determination which was Ritchie's hallmark. When playing cards with her his face softened a little since their game, played as it was between two such mathematical tricksters, resulted, to the hermit's amusement, in a great deal of mutual teasing.

The game over, they ate the pikelets and biscuits which had come from Aunt Beauregard's kitchen and began to talk strategy. The hermit proved surprisingly strong in this. It was he who had suggested, from the first, that no one should be told of Russell's where-abouts, or of how he came to be thrown into the quarry when all the world thought him back in London.

He was reiterating it now.

'Yes,' said Russell, who had been a narrow winner at piquet, an excellent card game for two sharpers like himself and Mary. 'Giving Shaw false confidence that he has succeeded in his villainy is an excellent notion. By now he will be confident that I am gone for good. Besides, if by some mischance he knew where I was hiding, he would most likely come after me again. In the meantime, as soon as I have recovered, we must all three secretly inform Chard by some means of the plot to murder me. Doubtless he, too, thinks I have tired of reforming Eddington and by now will have been back in London for some time. As Lord Lieutenant he will be best placed to summon up the power and the majesty of the law to deal with them.

'Our biggest advantage will be that of surprise when I reappear again with that law at my shoulder. I trust, sir, that you will form one of our party, for were it not for you I should not be sitting here with my dear Mary, enjoying beating her at cards and eating Aunt Beauregard's excellent provender.'

'May I remind you, m'lord,' replied Mary demurely, 'that since we agreed to play the best of three games, and so far we have only played two and each of us has won one, that last statement of yours was somewhat inaccurate, to say the least.'

'Mere nit-picking,' returned Russell easily. 'I shall of course, win the last one in a canter. Speaking of canter, I can't wait to get on a horse again. All this sitting about is more tiring than I would have thought.'

'When you are quite better,' she told him, 'you may ride again. For the present, concentrate on a complete recovery so that you may be fit enough to travel to Loudwater where you may persuade Lord Chard that you are not, as report has it, enjoying yourself in London.'

Russell leaned over the table and kissed her on the nose. 'Dear, dear, I see that you are determined to nag me even before marriage. What in the world shall I have to endure when you have finally carried me off into unpeaceful domesticity?'

'Nothing, sir, if you behave yourself. As it is, shuffle, cut the cards and deal again.'

'Willingly,' he laughed and his eyes promised her in some near future more than the chaste kiss he had just bestowed on her. Like many men who have narrowly escaped death, Russell was enjoying life more than ever now that it had been given back to him. The best thing of all was that Mary was enjoying it with him.

Dominic Hastings, Lord Chard, one of the great magnates who ruled in the north of England, had just joined his wife and baby son, Henry, in a mid-day meal before retiring to his office to go over the returns from the coal pits and the iron ore reserves which, together with his farming interests, formed the basis of his wealth.

Since inheriting he had, by his own efforts, transformed the Loudwater estates from a position of near bankruptcy to one of great prosperity. His latest venture had been to join with Sir Thomas Liddell in backing the locomotive which George Stephenson, Liddell's engine-wright, had been developing on Liddell's land.

He had been delighted to discover that young Hadleigh, whom rumour had always said was a lightweight, was nothing of the kind. Instead he was doing for Eddington what Chard himself had done for Loudwater. In fact, he had been on the point of visiting him to ask him to join the cartel which Liddell and he had set up when the news had reached him that Hadleigh had returned to London.

He was, alas, probably bored with life in the north, so far from the bright lights of London, one supposed.

Chard had scarcely sat down when there was a knock on the door. He sighed, put down his pen and called, 'Come in.' He prided himself on always being available to his staff.

'Beg pardon for interrupting you, m'lord,' said his butler, 'but a Mr George Russell has called and has asked to see you. He says it is a matter of some urgency.'

He paused, began to speak again, but stopped.

'Well, what is it? Did this Mr Russell give any explanation of his reasons for urgency?'

'No, m'lord,' he hesitated. 'It is not for me to put forward an opinion, but a stranger trio I have seldom seen. By the dress and general appearance of the two men, one would have supposed that the servants' entrance would have been their proper place. The lady with them, however, is dressed in the most impeccable style. Mr Russell is, however, very well spoken. To cap all that, the other gentleman would not give his name.'

His master rose, looking amused. 'Now you have intrigued me. Send them in, by all means. Life has grown a little dull lately.'

'Very well, m'lord.'

Chard walked to the window and looked out across the park where, on this mid-October day, his little family, well wrapped up against the cold, were walking. A moment later, the butler showed in his visitors.

As he had said, the men's clothing was minimally genteel, to say the least. The lady he immediately recognised as that most respectable gentlewoman, Mrs Wardour, and it was difficult to understand what she was doing in the company of two almost ragamuffins!

What was even more surprising, however, was that, after a brief moment when recognition failed him—largely because of his shabby appearance—he knew that 'the gentleman who had refused to give his name' was, in fact, none other than his new neighbour, Russell Chancellor, Viscount Hadleigh!

Of all stupid things he found himself saying, 'Hadleigh! What the devil are you doing here, and in that get-up? I thought that you were in London!'

Russell broke into a delighted grin. How many more times was he to hear that remark before this unlikely adventure of his was over?

'So pleased to see that you can recognise me,' he murmured. 'I had wondered a little whether I was still recognisable! And, no, I am not in London, I am in your study and with the help of my friend and saviour here, Mr George Russell and of Mrs Wardour, I will tell you how I come to be so.'

Dominic Chard began to laugh. 'It had better be a good explanation, but before you begin to satisfy my curiosity, pray sit down, and allow me to ring for some really splendid port. You both look as though a jorum of it would do you the world of good—Mrs Wardour would, I think, prefer an excellent Madeira. You, Hadleigh, look to weigh quite a bit less than you did when I last saw you, so perhaps I had better order you some more solid refreshment when you have finished telling me why you are dressed like one of your lesser servants.'

'Delighted,' said Russell, as they all did as they were bid, 'although I have been doing rather too much sitting about lately. I warn you that my story is somewhat lengthy and very improbable, and that to complete it you will be called upon to exercise your powers as Lord Lieutenant of this county.'

'Now you intrigue me more than ever,' said Chard, assuming his seat behind his desk. 'Pray continue.'

Which Russell did, detailing everything that had happened to him since he had left Eddington on that fatal day. He gave George Russell full credit for saving his life and then revealed Mary's share in helping to hide him from his enemies as well as nursing him so devotedly that he was restored to health sooner than might have been expected.

'You know, Hadleigh, and Mrs Wardour, too,' Chard remarked drily after hearing this, 'women are supposed not to be able to keep a secret, but from the evidence of my life, and now of yours, that is a most thundering lie. As to my own part in this—we must consider it carefully. I think, that for the present, for your own safety, you and Mr Russell must remain here—incommunicado—while we work out our plan of action. Mrs Wardour, I believe that you may be safe at home.'

'Oh, indeed, m'lord. My going innocently about my own business will surely rouse no suspicion—to be busybodying about might seem odd.'

'Exactly,' said m'lord, bowing in her direction. 'Now I agree with you, Hadleigh, that the less Shaw and Briggs know of your resurrection before we move against them, the better. You have explained Mrs Wardour's role in this, and I agree that she must be one of the party which to give evidence against the villains. The more credible witnesses that we have, the better.'

Russell nodded. As he had expected, Dominic Chard had proved, once again, that he was a man of sterling common sense.

'The only thing about accepting your hospitality,' he said, 'is that one of your staff might, without meaning to, give us away.'

Chard began to laugh. 'Not at all. You will be an old friend of mine down on your luck and an invalid who is travelling with another friend who is a doctor. You have appealed to me for help and I am offering you shelter. Your illness means that you will be confined to your room, where Mr Russell here will nurse you as devotedly as Mrs Wardour has done for the few days that we shall need to prepare to spring our trap.'

'More sitting about for me, I see,' moaned Russell, 'but I must congratulate you, Chard—a more ingenious pack of lies I have seldom heard. You even surpass my brother in that department, which is something of a miracle.'

On that cheerful note, and the arrival of an excellent nuncheon and some first-class port for the two gentlemen, who had not recently enjoyed a good meal, and some Madeira for the lady, the serious part of the interview ended.

Chapter Twelve

'I have had another letter from my old friend, Lady Markham,' Aunt Beauregard informed Mary over the breakfast table. 'It seems that her daughter and her husband are still missing. From something that Thomas Bertram said to Perry before he ran off with Angelica, Perry thought that they might call either on me, or at Eddington House. She again asks me to let her know at once if we hear anything of her.'

'Hardly likely that they would visit either place,' said Mary, 'but one never knows. People do the oddest things.'

'They must be somewhere,' said her aunt. 'It makes me almost happy that I never had children. Was there anything interesting in your letters today, my love?'

'Oh, yes. It seems that Lord Chard is about to pay a flying visit to Eddington House and would be grateful if the pair of us would arrange to meet him there for nuncheon on the day after tomorrow. I think, from what he says, that he is unaware that Lord Hadleigh has left for London. Unfortunately, there is no way in which I can inform him of that since he will be calling at Eddington House on the way from Newcastle. He says that he will have a pair of friends with him whom he thinks that we would like to meet, as well as several other important persons in his train.'

Now all of this was in Chard's letter, which had been written after such a fashion as to enlighten Mary as to the true state of affairs without revealing anything to anyone else should it be intercepted. Not unnaturally Aunt Beauregard put quite a different interpretation on it.

'Two friends whom we would like us to meet. What is the betting that Chard is match-making for you?' she exclaimed.

'Most probably,' agreed Mary, her face solemn. Which was not an untruth, since she already knew that Chard's two friends were Russell and the hermit, because she had left them at Loudwater several days earlier and that Lord Chard would be present in his capacity as the legal head of the county.

'You know,' said Aunt Beauregard thoughtfully, 'these great persons never seem to be aware how expensive it is for the people who are expected to give them, and all their attendants, instant hospitality.'

'Oh, I don't think that Lord Hadleigh would mind any expense Lord Chard might engage him in so far as this visit is concerned,' replied Mary—again employing a double meaning.

'One has to hope so. I'm not sure that I wish that Mr and Mrs Thomas Bertram might turn up here—even if it meant that I would be able to set her mother's mind at rest about her whereabouts.'

'And read her the riot act for upsetting all her family so much,' offered Mary with a grin.

'That also,' agreed Aunt Beauregard. 'Meantime, we must decide on our *toilettes* for the day after to-morrow and thank providence that I am not bearing the expense of entertaining Lord Chard!'

Privately Mary thought that Lord Chard might be the one providing the entertainment—but did not say so!

'What the devil does Chard mean by visiting us at such short notice?' grumbled Shaw to Briggs early in the morning of Chard's visit. 'And for what? Some nonsense about employing extra constables to help to keep the peace in these times when riot is becoming commonplace. We have had no rioting—'

Briggs interrupted him. 'There was that fracas at Eddington village, though, when we laid off so many labourers.'

'Maybe, but since that popinjay arrived here and employed most of them again everything has been quiet. I don't like Chard. He thinks that he's better than the likes of us. Oh, well, we must be on our best behaviour and hope that he won't stay too long—or ask too many questions about young

Hadleigh. If he does you know what to say—that he should have reached London by now.'

He had barely finished speaking when the under-butler entered in a hideous state of fluster.

'Oh, Mr Shaw, you'd never believe it but a grand coach has just arrived and it's not Lord Chard's. When Thomas, the groom on duty, asked him if he were, the gentleman said that he wasn't, but that he needed to see Mr Shaw immediately. He wouldn't give us his name.'

'Not Chard and needs to see me immediately! Now, who the devil can that be? You go and attend to him, Briggs, and bring him in as soon as he con-sents to give his name—if he doesn't send him off with a flea in his ear.'

Briggs bustled off, and alas the flea was to alight in Shaw's ear and not the visitor's, for Briggs re-turned a few minutes later, not in front of, but behind a splendidly dressed large man, whom Shaw had never seen before.

'Your flunkey is insolent, Shaw,' growled the large man, 'for that is who I take you to be. I am Bretford, your employer. I have come here to find out what the deuce is going on at Eddington, but before that I demand to see my son at once. By the by, I find your butler singularly lacking in manners—I hope the rest of your staff are not equally boorish.'

Shaw, disconcerted beyond belief by the sight of the man whom he believed to be permanently and safely settled in London, stammered, 'Oh, m'lord, had he known that it was you he would, I am sure, have accorded you all the honour due to your station.'

'Damn that,' said Bretford pleasantly. 'You should teach him to be polite to every caller, regardless of their station. But this is dilly dally; send for my son at once, I have rather a lot to say to him.'

Shaw gave his employer a melancholy smile, 'Alas, m'lord, I fear that you have arrived too late. Lord Hadleigh left for London well over a fortnight ago and should have arrived there by now—possibly after you left. I fear that he grew tired of country living.'

'Did he, indeed? I suppose that it is most likely that he would. Very unsatisfactory of him. Did he give you any explanation of why he came here at all?'

'Only that he had come as your agent to oversee how Eddington was being run, you not having been here for so many years.'

The Earl stared at him. 'He said that, did he?' He did not inform Shaw that Hadleigh had arrived at Eddington without his father's knowledge or permission, but went on to pick another bone with the agent.

'Leave Hadleigh to me. I'll deal with him when I see him in London. What I do wish to know now is how it came about that you never informed me of your father's death.'

Shaw gulped. In for a penny, in for a pound. 'Oh, but I am sure that I did, m'lord. I distinctly remember that I wrote a despatch to your secretary, Mr Graves, telling him of my father's sudden and sad end. Hearing nothing, I took it upon myself to act as agent, seeing that I had been my father's assistant in his last and fatal illness.'

'Your father never told me of that, either,' said the Earl severely.

Salvation from this extremely damaging inquisition came from an unexpected quarter in the arrival of Lord Chard and his attendant secretary. From not wishing to entertain him at all, Shaw was now unimaginably grateful for his timely appearance. When the under-butler came in, Briggs having remained with Shaw and the Earl, to announce the Right Honourable, the Earl of Chard, Shaw rushed forward to greet him, all greasy servility again.

His welcome over, he begged both Earls to take a seat. 'Not before you have introduced me to Lord Chard,' said Lord Bretford glacially, 'and him to me. Your manners, sir, are sadly wanting.'

Shaw nearly bent double in doing the honours.

'Delighted to make your acquaintance at last, Bretford,' said Lord Chard. 'And on your home ground, too. You must visit Loudwater before you leave.'

'I should be honoured to do so,' said Bretford, smiling for the first time. Chard was certainly living up to his reputation as a handsome man with a great deal of presence and abilities out of the ordinary where running an estate was concerned.

He told him so.

Chard smiled. 'I am particularly pleased to meet you after having met your son, Lord Hadleigh. I was most impressed by him and the work he has done here, both on the estate and in the house. Eddington has been quite transformed, has it not, Shaw? I believe that your father had allowed both parts of Lord Bretford's property to become neglected. You, Shaw, must have been most pleased by Lord Hadleigh's arrival, particularly when he proved to be such an able improver of what needed improving. You must also be proud of him, sir,' he said directly to his fellow peer.

If Shaw's mind was not now totally fuddled by Lord Bretford's unannounced arrival, he might have grasped that Lord Chard was subtly baiting him. Instead he muttered 'quite so, quite so', at suitable intervals. Lord Bretford, equally surprised, merely rose and bowed his acknowledgement of the compliment paid to his son.

'From your letter to me arranging this meeting, m'lord,' said Shaw once they were all seated except, of course, for Briggs, who was standing by the double doors, 'I believe that you have come expressly to discuss the rising level of unrest in the county and the necessity for more constables. We have had no unrest or rioting lately at Eddington, but I understand your natural concern over the general position.'

'Indeed,' said Chard, leaning back in his chair, 'but it is not simply rioting and Luddism which perturbs me, but also the rising levels of other kinds of crime—attacks on decent persons, highway robbery and, I am less than happy to say, murder and attempted murder. These, too, must be dealt with—and ruthlessly—as I am sure you will agree.'

'Quite so, m'lord, of course, m'lord,' gabbled Shaw again, the weight of his own guilt heavy on his shoulders.

'But before we discuss these matters, you will allow me a word with my secretary. John,' he said, pulling out his hunter and inspecting it, 'I think that in about ten minutes or so you may leave to fetch the other persons whom I have brought with me to help in our efforts to rid the county of misdoing.'

'So noted, m'lord,' said the secretary, bowing and resuming his seat a little behind his lordship's.

If Shaw was being baffled by Lord Chard's manoeuvres, the Earl was even more so. What the devil is going on here? was his inward comment.

'Excellent,' said Chard, putting his hunter away. 'Now, where were we?'

Before Shaw could answer him there was a rap on the double doors. Briggs opened them to reveal the under-butler who announced, 'Lord Chard's other guests have arrived—do I show the ladies in here?'

'Ah,' said Chard. 'They must be Mrs Wardour and Miss Beauregard. I believe that I mentioned inviting them in my letter to you, Shaw. I particularly wished to meet Mrs Wardour again. She is, as you may already know, an extremely gifted mathematician and, as such, being a female, is a rarity with whom I had great pleasure in conversing. I think that you will agree with me, Shaw that this was not an opportunity to be missed.'

'Quite so, m'lord,' gabbled Shaw again. 'Show them in at once,' he bade the under-butler, who fled before he could commit any further gaucheries.

Lord Bretford, who was no fool, was beginning to wonder even more what the devil Chard was up to and why Shaw was so obviously in an advanced state of nervous excitement.

He was soon to find out.

Mary, after she had dressed herself in a toilette suitable for a day to be spent with Lord Chard, was wondering what exactly she would find when she arrived at Eddington, and what would happen when she reached there. She hoped to meet Russell and the hermit, of course, but she had no notion of what Lord Chard had planned for this impromptu meeting.

Aunt Beauregard, quite unaware of all the dangerous currents swirling beneath the surface of her normal orderly and somewhat boring life, was all of a-twitter at the notion of meeting Lord Chard. She had heard of him, had, indeed, seen him, having been part of a crowd which had watched him lay the foundation stone of a new Grammar School for Ancoates, but she had never spoken to him.

He was an extraordinarily handsome man, even more so than Russell Hadleigh, but Russell, until he had deserted them, had possessed the common touch while Chard had the reputation of being a little aloof. So both ladies were a little worried about their visit to Eddington, but for quite different reasons.

What neither of them had expected was what they found.

Mary was disappointed to find that Russell was not already there. She wondered where he was. Aunt Beauregard, on the other hand, was surprised to see Lord Bretford rising to greet her when they entered. She knew him immediately, despite all the changes which the passing years had wrought.

She exclaimed, defying all the forms of politeness by doing so before introductions had been made, 'Jackie Chancellor, by all that's holy! What are you doing here?'

Lord Chard, giving the lie to the rumour of his aloofness, began to laugh, before saying, 'I see that you are as surprised as I am to meet the Earl of Bretford in Northumberland. We all thought him wedded to the south of England. He came, I understand, to see his son who, most unfortunately, had left for London before his father arrived. You, I take it, madam, are Miss Beauregard of Ancoates and this charming young lady must be the celebrated Mrs Wardour. Since you already know Lord Bretford, I must do the honours of introducing Mrs Wardour to him. She is, of course, the daughter of the eminent mathematician Dr Beauregard, Miss Beauregard's late brother, and the widow of Dr Henry Wardour.'

Now it was Lord Bretford's turn to fall into a state of nervous excitement when Lord Chard had finished his introduction. Mary, also, was strangely moved to see him. This, then, was Russell's father, who with her own had destroyed their chance of happiness together all those years ago.

She bowed and offered the Earl no welcoming smile. He stared at her, also remembering the distant past. So, this charming, composed beauty with the lovely eyes and tender mouth was the woman whom Hadleigh had wanted to marry. For the first time he wished that he had met her all those years ago for, had he done so, perhaps his attitude to their marriage might have been different.

'Delighted to meet you,' he muttered. 'I am told that you are a gifted mathematician. I believe that my son has some interests in that direction.'

Mary raised her eyebrows and said coolly, 'I would scarcely describe Lord Hadleigh's gifts as lightly as that, m'lord. My late husband was greatly impressed by his prowess and he has been helping me to develop the notion of a clockwork calculating machine. In some respects his abilities are in advance of those of myself, my late father and my husband.'

The Earl stared at her, dumb-struck. Her voice was even more lovely than her face and her graceful body. 'I am most pleased to hear that, madam,' he offered at last.

It took Mary all her strength not to say, And so you should be. She contented herself, however, with

a small bow and then listened to her aunt and the
Earl recalling that, in the even more long ago, when
neither Mary nor Russell had been thought of, they
had been part of a merry crowd of friends, now long
since dispersed.

'It is years since we last met,' ended Aunt
Beauregard, 'and I trust that you will forgive me for
calling you Jackie Chancellor—but that is what I always knew you as.'

'Pardon granted,' smiled the Earl, who was beginning to recover himself after the shock of meeting
the woman whom his son had wanted to marry and
finding her very different from the idea he had of
her. It did not hurt that he knew through his associ-
ation with the Royal Society that Henry Wardour had
been the last of a very rich family and that his widow
had inherited everything.

That certainly put a different complexion on
things! If only that scamp, Hadleigh, had not rushed
back to enjoy himself in London.

They all sat down again. Shaw, who had recovered
his equanimity a little, rang for refreshments. When
they arrived he was so busy ingratiating himself with
all the company that he failed to notice that Chard's
secretary had disappeared on his master's errand.
Mary found herself next to Lord Bretford, who was
making great efforts to entertain both her and Aunt
Beauregard.

She was so exercised by another matter that she
could scarcely pay attention to m'lord's gallant at-

tempts to mend fences between them. Where was Russell? She had understood at their meeting with Lord Chard that he would be accompanying him to Eddington. Instead he and George Russell were absent and Lord Chard appeared to be on reasonably friendly terms with Arthur Shaw. What deep game could he be playing?

'Yes,' she found herself saying distractedly to the Earl when by his subsequent expression she should have been saying 'no'! The Earl was thinking that nervous excitement must be infectious for the lovely Mrs Wardour was showing distinct signs of having caught it.

'And now,' said Lord Chard, 'I believe that we may resume our discussion of the lawlessness obtaining locally and what we ought to do about it. I take it that we are all agreed that we must stamp it out wherever it occurs and whoever indulges in it. Agreed?'

'Agreed,' said everyone. Shaw was particularly loud in his approval of m'lord's statement.

'Excellent,' said Chard. 'And that goes for the ladies, too, I believe.'

'Certainly,' said Mary in a strong voice, thinking of poor Russell and of the would-be murdering monster sitting opposite to her who was virtually licking Lord Chard's boots in his efforts to agree with him.

She was beginning to get an inkling of what Chard might be up to.

'In that case then,' said Chard, 'we may proceed to the next part of the meeting. My secretary should be back shortly with my two assistants.' He turned an ear towards the double doors. 'I believe that I hear them coming.'

He was right. Without benefit of the stunned under-butler the doors opened to admit not only Chard's secretary, but two men at the sight of whom everyone in the company but Lord Chard and Mary stared with dropped jaws and aghast expressions.

They were Viscount Hadleigh and Mr George Russell!

Not only that, but behind them were three large grim-faced men wearing a dark blue livery.

After a brief, somewhat shocked pause, everyone began to speak at once, but not before Briggs, who had gone an odd yellow colour, had pointed at Russell and squeaked, 'You can't be here, you're dead!'

Lord Bretford's exclamation was more commonplace. 'What in the world are *you* doing here, Hadleigh? You are supposed to be in London,' while Aunt Beauregard's lament was,

'Why are you wearing such odd clothes, Russell?'

It was, however, Briggs's anguished cry which had the most effect. Shaw, glaring at the weak fool who had betrayed them both by his inability to keep his silly mouth shut, and knowing that the game was up, bolted for the little door which opened on to the back corridor of the house.

He never reached it. Russell, delighted by Briggs's give-away which meant that two of the uniformed men had made for him immediately, and burning for revenge on the man who had tried to kill him, chased after Shaw and caught him even as he reached for the door-knob.

'I'll teach you not to try to murder me!' he roared and landed him a facer of which Gentleman Jackson would have been proud. Shaw fell to the ground, moaning and clutching at his bleeding nose.

'Damn you, Hadleigh, you've broken my nose,' he moaned thickly.

'Be grateful that it wasn't your neck I did for,' Russell ground out, straightening up and blowing on his bruised knuckles. This was all a great deal more damaging than playing about at Jackson's salon. One of the men in blue began, most roughly, to haul Shaw to his feet.

His father was staring at his son as though he had never seen him before. Mary clapped her hands together in delight at seeing Russell avenge himself on his betrayer, and Lord Chard, intrigued by the turn events had taken, had risen to his feet.

'Well, well,' he drawled. 'Matters have developed even more swiftly and pointedly than I might have hoped. I had not imagined that things would be settled so quickly. Burgess,' he ordered the man in blue who was now holding Shaw in a head lock, 'you may inform your prisoner of what he is accused, and after that you may charge Briggs.'

Briggs, quivering and shaking, began to try to save himself. 'It wasn't me,' he almost wept, 'it was him,' and he pointed at Shaw, who, having had the charges against him read out, was still trying to stanch his bleeding face. 'I didn't want to hurt m'lord, he made me.'

'If you will allow,' Chard said, ignoring Briggs and turning to Lord Bretford, who was trying to come to terms with the fact that Russell had been behaving as though he were Ritchie, 'I will designate this room a magistrates' court and since all witnesses to the crime of which this pair are accused are present, they may give their evidence to me, and to Lord Bretford, who, I believe, is also a magistrate, as to whether or not they should be consigned to prison to await the next Assizes. My secretary will act as clerk to the court.'

The man holding Shaw, disregarding his captive's plea for his nose to be treated, had manacled his wrists behind his back, and pushed him behind a reversed chair. The now sobbing Briggs, also manacled, was shoved beside him. A side table was pulled forward so that the two Earls could sit behind it facing the prisoners. Chard's secretary sat beside them, a ledger open before him, ready to keep a record of the proceedings.

Russell watched them with a grim smile on his face. He had already gone over to speak to Mary and Aunt Beauregard. Aunt Beauregard quavered at him,

'Is it true that they tried to murder you? Were they only pretending that you had gone to London?'

'I suppose that now we are in a courtroom I ought to reveal as little as possible before I give evidence,' Russell replied. 'But I think that I may say that you have come to the right conclusion.'

'How dreadful! And that man with you. Who is he? I think that I have met him somewhere before, but where I cannot remember, except...' and she began to tremble.

Mary who had been registering her pleasure at seeing Russell safe and well, even if he did look like one of his own under-grooms, asked her gently, 'What is it, Aunt?'

'Nothing, except that he reminds me strongly of someone I knew many years ago.'

'He was until recently the hermit who lived in the woods and his name is George Russell,' Russell told her.

The day's surprises were not yet over. Aunt Beauregard gave a little cry and hid her face in her hands. She dropped them to mutter, her face now ashen, 'No, it cannot be, I must be mistaken.'

At this point Lord Chard, who had been privately conferring with his fellow Earl, called the room to order.

'This magistrates' court is now in session. The accused are present and the charge is that they attempted to murder Russell Chancellor, Lord Hadleigh, by attacking him and throwing him into the quarry off the by-way to Ancoates. All the necessary witnesses to the crime of which they are accused are here present.

'Shaw and Briggs, listen to me carefully. How plead you?'

'Not guilty, m'lord,' Shaw blurted out defiantly. Briggs's reply was almost inaudible, made as it was through his sobs.

'In that case I will call upon the principal witness, Lord Hadleigh, to give evidence. Stand up, Lord Hadleigh, and face the Bench.'

Russell did so. He was happy to note that everything was being carried out in proper form so that none might later claim that Lord Chard had carried out his magistrate's duties incorrectly.

He described, as accurately as he could, the attack made on him by Shaw and Briggs up to the moment when he had been thrown into the quarry. 'After which,' he finished, 'I have no recollection of anything until I recovered consciousness in Mr Russell's cottage. I have no doubt, from what they said and the manner of the attack, that they intended to kill me.'

'It's all a lie,' howled Shaw. 'It's only his word against ours and there are two of us. Who's to say he wasn't larking about round the quarry on his way back to London?'

'Be silent, Shaw,' said Chard severely, 'until you are asked to speak. May I, before you incriminate yourself further, remind you that if Lord Hadleigh was truly on his way to London it would have been exceedingly odd of him to have taken the by-way north past the quarry, rather than the one leading south which joins the main road to London.'

'May I speak to that, m'lord?' asked Russell, who was beginning to enjoy watching Shaw twist and turn in his doomed efforts to defend himself.

'Yes, Lord Hadleigh, continue.'

'I understand that it was given out and can produce witnesses so to confirm that Shaw and Briggs told everyone that I had left Eddington to return to London.'

'Thank you, m'lord. Which brings up another point. The question of his lordship's missing chaise, does it not, Shaw? The constables have already confirmed that it is not in Eddington's stables. One would wish to know where it is, seeing that whatever else he did, Lord Hadleigh did not travel to London in it. We will leave that for the present.

'You may stand down, Lord Hadleigh. I call upon Mr George Russell to give evidence.'

The hermit rose. Like Russell he was still dressed in the clothes in which they had arrived at Loudwater. Lord Chard had decided that their story, which really needed no confirmation, was further supported by Lord Hadleigh's unseemly attire of which his secretary had already made note.

'You, sir, are Mr George Russell, a gentleman who resides in the county of Northumberland.'

'That is true, m'lord.'

'Please describe to the court the circumstances in which you came to find Lord Hadleigh in the quarry.'

'My home is on the edge of the wood in these parts. I was engaged on my daily walk when I heard loud voices and the sound of a scuffle. Through the trees I could see two men attacking a third. I am an old man, m'lord, and to my shame I allowed that fact to prevent me from assisting the poor victim. They overcame him and began to carry him towards the quarry. I watched them throw over the edge the man whom I later recognised as Lord Hadleigh, whose acquaintance I had made shortly after he arrived in Northumberland.

'When I reached the quarry I saw that the villains' victim was caught on some bushes above a ledge in the quarry wall. I was, by great good fortune, able to assist him. Fortunately, although he remembers little of it, he was sufficiently conscious to be able to assist me before he collapsed at the quarry top.'

'Thank you, Mr. Russell. Were you able to see and identify the two men who attacked m'lord?'

'Yes.'

'And are they in the courtroom today?'

'Yes, m'lord, they are standing over there,' and he pointed at Shaw and Briggs.

'Thank you, Mr Russell. You may stand down. I now call on Mrs Henry Wardour to give evidence.'

Aunt Beauregard, who had been making little moaning noises all the time that Mr George Russell had been giving evidence, hissed, 'Why you?' in Mary's ear.

'In a moment,' Mary whispered back before walking over to stand before the two Earls. She passed Russell on the way and, since he was shielded from all the others in the room, he mouthed 'I love you' at her.

It was an odd thing for a lady to give evidence in a court of law. Had she been Russell's wife she would have been unable to do so, but since she was not Lord Chard had chosen to call her as further evidence.

'Mrs Wardour, please tell the court of what you know about this unfortunate affair. You may take your time in answering if you so wish.'

Mary needed to take no time to think of what she ought to say. She had been waiting for some days to give evidence which would help to trap the men who had wished to kill the man she loved and was eager to begin.

'Simply that I understood from Mr Shaw when I called at Eddington House, because Lord Hadleigh had failed to visit me on a day on which he had promised to do so, that he had suddenly left for London. This surprised me because Lord Hadleigh had said nothing of this to me on his last visit.'

She spoke in a clear, unflustered voice and her manner was such that the watching Lord Bretford was sorry all over again about his past conduct towards her.

Lord Chard knew that what Shaw had said to Mary, if repeated at the Assizes, would not have been evidence because it was hearsay, but since everyone around Eddington had been told the same thing by both Shaw and Briggs he allowed it to pass.

'What happened next, Mrs Wardour?'

'I went riding alone several days after that conversation. I was stopped by Mr Russell who asked me to visit his cottage. He would give me no reason and told me that I must not inform anyone else of what I found there. Greatly puzzled I accompanied him, to find Lord Hadleigh in bed, recovering from his injuries, which I later learned he had sustained when he was thrown into the quarry. They asked me to say nothing of his survival, or that he had not gone to London in case the two miscreants came to finish off the villainy which they had already embarked on.'

'Why were the authorities not informed at once?'

'For the reason I have given you and also that Lord Hadleigh was not fit to travel. I did as they asked, secretly brought them food and some old, but clean, clothing, which had belonged to our grooms, that they are wearing now. As soon as Lord Hadleigh had recovered sufficiently to be able to ride, I joined them in leaving secretly for Loudwater to inform you, m'lord, of the attack upon him.'

'Thank you, Mrs Wardour, most lucid, as I am sure, Bretford, you would agree.'

'Yes, indeed,' said Russell's father who had been staring bemused at the poised, beautiful and clever young widow whom he had once summarily dismissed as a possible wife for his heir on the grounds that she was an unmoneyed nobody unfit to become a Viscountess, let alone a future Countess.

Mary bowed gracefully and resumed her seat next to her aunt, who had also been gazing at her in some surprise, having had no notion of the secret life which Mary had been following since Mr George Russell had accosted her near his cottage.

'What a minx you are, my dear,' she muttered at Mary, 'concealing all that from me.'

'For your protection, dear Aunt,' replied Mary.

Once her evidence was over Lord Chard leaned over to Lord Bretford and had a quiet conference with him, after which he spoke to the two defendants in their makeshift dock.

'Do either of you wish to say anything before I order you to be committed for trial at the next Assizes in Newcastle?'

'Yes,' roared Shaw, 'it's all a pack of lies, made up because Lord H. knew that I didn't agree with all the changes he was making at Eddington—and without his pa's knowledge too, as his own man said—'

'That will do,' said Chard severely. 'The evidence against you is overwhelming and you do not help yourself by blackguarding a man whom I understand gave you a second chance after he had discovered that you had been deceiving and cheating his father. You, Briggs, have you anything to say?'

'Yes, m'lord,' wailed Briggs falling on to his knees. 'I only did what Shaw told me because he was my superior. I never meant to kill m'lord, as God's my witness, I didn't.'

'I find that difficult to believe,' said Chard. 'You do not help your cause by lying about your involvement. On the evidence given we have heard that you helped to throw Lord Hadleigh into the quarry and only Mr George Russell's fortunate intervention saved him.

'All rise: constables, remove the prisoners and convey them to Newcastle Gaol to await trial.'

It was over.

The two Earls conversed confidentially with one another for a few moments. The secretary rose, closed his ledger and put the chair, which had stood in as a temporary dock, back in its proper place.

Russell ran over to Mary and, regardless of everything and everyone, threw his arms around her.

'There's my brave girl,' he said. 'Now we can be married!'

He didn't care whether his father, or Lord Chard, or half-Northumberland including Newcastle, heard him: this time he was going to make sure that they ended up in bed together—to enjoy themselves there rather more than they had done in the one in George Russell's cottage!

All Mary knew was that she was at last where she ought to be, but common sense and the public nature of their reunion had her pushing him gently away, murmuring, 'Later, my love, later.'

Meanwhile, Aunt Beauregard had risen and walked hesitantly towards Mr George Russell, who, without his long hair and beard, and even though clothed as a groom, still looked a fine figure of a man.

'George, is it really you?' she asked. 'I recognised Jackie Chancellor with whom I was not greatly friendly, so you may judge how much more easy it was for me to recognise the man whom I was engaged to marry. As that wretched man said of poor Lord Hadleigh, I thought that you were dead—and for over thirty years, too! Was that a cock-and-bull story or are you really not my George at all?'

A look of anguish passed across the hermit's face. 'Not here,' he murmured, 'not here. When we can be alone, I shall explain. Oh, my dear, when I think of all the wasted years...' He dropped his head.

'But why?' Aunt Beauregard was suddenly as distressed as he was. 'No, I must not trouble you. Later will do,' though she privately thought that whatever explanation he cared to give her, nothing would ever do, since nothing could give back to them the years they had lost.

Fortunately for them both, at that moment the door opened and the harassed under-butler walked in.

'M'lords,' he faltered, not quite sure how to address such a distinguished company. 'A young man and a young woman have just arrived and have asked to speak to Lord Hadleigh. Shall I announce them—

or shall I tell them that it is not convenient for them to be entertained today?'

'Oh, announce them, by all means,' exclaimed Russell, quite forgetting that now that his father had arrived he was no longer the master at Eddington. 'Two more members added to our party can only serve to enliven it the further.' Belatedly recognising his father's seniority, he turned to him, smiling, adding, 'If that is agreeable to you, sir.'

'Oh, quite agreeable,' said Lord Bretford, who was showing more friendliness to his son that he had done for years. 'Come one, come all, today, apparently. But before you do so,' he said, addressing the butler, 'my friend, Lord Chard, also has an announcement to make.'

He stood back to allow Chard to speak.

'I have nothing to say as momentous as our late proceedings,' said Chard, his smile as broad as Russell's, 'but it occurs to me that, under the circumstances obtaining, Lords Bretford and Hadleigh would find it difficult to entertain us all at Eddington House. In consequence I am inviting you all, including Mr George Russell and the two ladies, to stay at Loudwater for as long or as short as you individually please. I have no doubt that you both...' and he bowed at Russell and his father '...would wish to be near enough to Eddington to begin to restore the place even further now that Shaw has been dealt with, and Loudwater would make a convenient base for that.'

'If I may be allowed a rider to your kind invitation?' said Lord Bretford. 'While I would be delighted to accept your hospitality, the task of continuing the restoration of Eddington and its house must be left in the hands of my son, Lord Hadleigh. I have been informed by Lord Chard that he has been responsible in a very short time for returning it to some of its former glory after many years of neglect. If he is willing to carry on the hard work he has begun, then I am happy to make him my deputy here—if that is what he wishes, of course.'

He paused; Lord Chard had been nodding agreement to his statement about Russell's hard work. Russell himself, thus publicly and kindly acknowledged by his father, who had always previously lost no opportunity to demean him, scarcely knew what to say.

'Certainly, sir. It is, indeed, my dearest wish to be allowed to remain at Eddington as deputy and agent for I have discovered here a way of life which suits me—and which, I hope will also suit the lady who has promised to be my wife. It is most kind of you to allow me to do so.'

He had begun by stammering a little, but as he gained confidence he finished on a high note, and, tenderly turning, took Mary's hand and kissed it.

'Excellent,' said Lord Bretford, before going over to congratulate his son and his bride-to-be. 'You, sir,' he ordered the under-butler, almost as an afterthought, 'may introduce our visitors to us.'

The under-butler disappeared. Conversation, from being formal, became general. The company began to finish off the Madeira and biscuits whose provision had been the last act of Shaw's reign. They were all thus, after the harsh proceedings of the morning, in a much jollier mood, when the under-butler returned.

'M'lords, ladies and gentlemen, I have the honour of presenting to you Mr and Mrs Thomas Bertram.' It was plain that he was beginning to enjoy his new role in which he was no longer subservient to the late Briggs.

'Good God!' exclaimed Russell. 'Where in the world have you popped up from, Tom? And Angelica, too—you both look blooming.'

'Everyone on their honeymoon should look blooming,' declared the Honourable Tom in the tone of one making a witty *bon mot*. 'Can't say the same of you, old chap, not in that odd get-up. I know the butler fellow made a kind of general introduction for us, but I should dearly like to know in whose company I have found myself. Not that you don't all look eminently respectable,' he hastened to add.

The Hon. Tom's artless charm, together with that of Angelica, who had rushed over to Mary and begun to kiss her as though she were renewing an acquaintance with her dearest friend, thoroughly broke the ice. Even Aunt Beauregard, who had suddenly realised that she was in the same room as the two runaways of whom her old friend had written such piteous letters, was captivated by the Hon. Tom. The other members of the party, by contrast, were amused by him.

Mary invited Angelica to sit beside her. She immediately began to stare at Russell in his shabby clothing. 'I can't tell you how pleased I am that I refused Lord Hadleigh,' she began, 'so old and so under-dressed compared with my dear Tom. He's quite the Corinthian, isn't he? Have you received any proposals yet?'

This last sentence came out belatedly, more as something polite to say than if the speaker really believed what she was saying.

'Lord Hadleigh,' said Mary, amused by Angelica's naïve frankness, and deciding to make her answer as unadorned as possible to spare Angelica embarrassment, 'has asked me to marry him. I have consented and, from the manner in which his father received the news, I am delighted to say we have his blessing.'

It was, apparently, almost impossible to embarrass Angelica. From scorning Russell as both elderly and ill dressed, she now went on to congratulate Mary effusively on having made such a great catch.

'They say he will be enormously rich when his father dies,' she ended, 'which is why Pa and Ma wished me to marry him. But money isn't everything. *I* accepted Tom out of pure love, of course. Wild horses wouldn't have made me marry a man for his money.'

'But I gather,' Mary could not help replying, 'from a letter from your mama that, before you decided to elope with him, Mr. Bertram had recently inherited a reasonably large fortune.'

'Oh, that!' exclaimed Angelica. 'That really made no difference to my decision to marry him—none at all!'

Her voice took on a sharper note. 'Do I understand that you have been corresponding with my mama—how odd!'

'No, she wrote to my aunt, Miss Beauregard, asking us to inform her of your whereabouts—she was quite worried about you.'

Angelica tossed her head. 'I do hope that you won't. Inform her, I mean. I have never been so happy in my life. At home it was always nag, nag, nag. Tom never nags at me.'

Lord Bretford, overhearing this conversation, couldn't help being relieved that his son had had the good sense not to propose to such a featherbrained piece—however pretty she was. It was beginning to look as though Hadleigh had far more to him than he had previously thought. Certainly Mrs Wardour had been something of a surprise.

He was astonished at the regret which swept over him when he thought of his treatment of his son, particularly when he took into consideration the fact that he had been right to query Shaw's accounts and right to come north to find out what was going on. The whole business meant that he had been an absentee landlord of the worst kind and a poor father to his son. As soon as he could have a private word with Hadleigh, he would try to mend the fences which he had spent his life destroying.

And George Russell. Where had he sprung from? How had he been transformed from the heir to Eddington and its lands into a hermit living in a wretched cottage on the edge of the wilderness? At least, if they were all to spend a few days together at Loudwater, some mysteries might be cleared up. He would give his coachman immediate orders to drive there in Chard's wake. The others, particularly his son, would need to return home to collect their luggage for a few days' stay at what was reputed to be one of the most beautiful mansions in the north.

Aunt Beauregard, still in a daze after encountering a man she had thought dead for many years, and for whom she had mourned inconsolably, could also scarcely wait to reach Loudwater and George.

As for Mary and Russell, it mattered little to them where they were so long as they could be together as much as possible.

Living at Loudwater was a little like living in heaven. It was a house of the most tasteful beauty which was so well run that even those visitors who had previously thought themselves pampered by life were surprised by it.

Russell was once more dressed in his usual clothing. Briggs, desperate not to hang, had tried to gain some commutation from his almost certain sentence to do so by continuing to claim that he had been bullied into helping Shaw to attempt to murder Lord Hadleigh. He had also told the authorities where they had hidden his chaise. Not only that, but he had ratted on Graves, telling how he had conspired with Shaw to cheat Lord Bretford. As a result Russell's father, on being informed of this, had decided to leave Loudwater as soon as possible to return south and hand his secretary over to the law.

This revelation made him even more humble vis-à-vis his heir when he remembered how he had reprimanded him when he had claimed that there was something amiss with Eddington's accounts.

'I feel almost human again,' Russell confessed to Mary while they were walking one afternoon in Eddington's neglected park, so different from Loudwater's beautifully kept grounds. 'Life has ceased to be one long worry that I am not living up to my father's expectations—particularly the one in which he wished me to marry the fair Angelica.'

Mary began to laugh. 'I think that he changed his mind when he met her. She and Tom Bertram are well suited. I was most relieved, though, when they did not take up Lord Chard's invitation to stay at Loudwater. She told me, in confidence, that the idea of being cooped up with a lot of old men did not attract. I tried to persuade her to go home and make peace with her family, but I fear that idea didn't attract either!'

'Agreed,' said Russell. 'Had we married I think that I might have strangled her in the week. Whatever should we have found to talk about?'

'Not chess and calculating machines, that is for sure,' Mary returned, which set him laughing again.

They had spent the morning at Eddington: Russell had been going over the books and had begun advertising for a bailiff while Mary was directing a new housekeeper and her staff in the business of continuing to refurbish the interior of the House.

She had previously brought down more of the paintings from the attic, in particular the portraits of Serena Cheyney and Margaret Russell, which now hung in the little drawing room. Lord Bretford had spent part of the morning at Eddington and on seeing those of his wife and her cousin, had obviously been extremely struck by them. When Mary, showing him the room, told him, quite casually, unaware of any deeper undercurrents, that Serena Cheyney was now a widow and lived not far from Ancoates, he had said nothing, but shortly afterwards had excused himself and left.

'I thought that he had agreed to go over the accounts with me,' Russell said to her over their simple nuncheon. 'Have you any idea why he left so suddenly?'

'Only that I showed him the portraits in the small drawing room, and informed him that Serena Cheyney, now a widow, lives nearby.'

'That explains it, I think. You remember that, according to both Aunt Beauregard and Sir Ralph Cheyney, everyone thought that, when my father came north after his father had inherited the Earldom, he was going to ask Serena to marry him, but instead he proposed to and married her cousin, the Eddington heiress, Margaret Russell, my mother.'

They were both silent for a moment. Mary said slowly, 'Is it possible that his father, your grandfather, compelled him to marry your mother instead because she was the heiress?'

'I am beginning to think so—which would explain many things.' He fell silent and did not enlarge on the matter further.

Mary respected that silence and said, 'Aunt Beauregard told me something yesterday which might throw further light on the business. When your father was a young man visiting in the north Margaret Russell was not the heiress. George Russell was then the heir. Apparently, shortly before his ailing father died and when he was betrothed to my aunt, Margaret's father discovered that he was illegitimate and consequently had no claim either to be the heir, or to the Russell name.

'It seems that it was discovered that, quite unknowingly, George's father had married a woman whose husband was then living, although in some sort of asylum, so the marriage could not be valid. To avoid scandal Margaret's father and his lawyers confronted George with the truth. They could not allow him in law to inherit, but they were prepared to set up a trust for him which would provide him with a small income if he would disappear. To explain the disappearance they would pretend that he had died suddenly and been summarily buried elsewhere.

'George was something of a scholar. He obtained a post in the Bodleian Library at Oxford University. He never married, becoming a recluse and took the name of William George. A few years ago he had some sort of nervous fit, retired from his post and came north again to where he could, from a distance, see Aunt Beauregard whom he had lost so many years ago.'

Mary's eyes filled with tears. 'It is such a sad story and, oh, Russell, ours might so easily have been the same as George and Aunt Beauregard's and your father and Serena Cheyney's. I shall never think myself unlucky again because, although we have lost so many years together, we have found each other in time to marry and have children.'

Russell sat silent for a time until Mary began to wonder what she had said to disturb him. Finally he came out with, 'You are not the only one who has been the subject of strange confidences. Allow me a moment's thought and I will tell you of them.'

'As many moments as you like,' she said gently, wondering what was coming next.

Russell was remembering the early evening of the previous day... He had arrived from Eddington, tired, but exhilarated to have Chard's butler greet him in the Entrance Hall.

'Your father, m'lord, is in his suite of rooms and has asked that you visit him as soon as you have recovered from your journey.'

Now, what could that be about, he wondered. His father had been uncommonly civil to him ever since the scene in the impromptu magistrate's court and more than civil to Mary, to whom he had taken a great fancy.

'Inform Lord Bretford I will be with him shortly,' he said, and kept his word as he always did. He found his father standing in a window, looking out over Loudwater's beautiful Park. When he turned to greet him Russell thought that he looked tired.

'Ah, Hadleigh, you are prompt: an excellent virtue. I have asked to see you this evening because I need to speak to you and I must not linger in the north much longer: I have duties to carry out in the south. Watching you, talking to Chard and to Mrs Wardour, and thinking of the past, it has been borne in upon me that I owe you an explanation and an apology.

'I have become unhappily aware that I have not behaved to you as a father ought to behave to a son. Only your good nature has prevented you from resenting your brother Richard because of the favour which I have always shown him as opposed to the distance which I have kept between the pair of us. I owe you an explanation and I can only hope that when I have finished you will forgive me a little—I cannot hope for more than that.

'First let me tell you something of my early youth. Like my friend, Ralph Cheyney, I had no great expectations from life. My father was the cousin of the heir of the Earl of Bretford who was years younger than he was, and my branch of the family had little money. I had half-determined to enter the Army, but decided on one last fling before I did so. Ralph, as you know, lived not too far distant from Eddington and he invited me to stay with him after we went down from Oxford. I accepted his invitation—we had been part of a rowdy set—and the result was the most golden summer of my life. I was one of a crowd of young people and we seemed to be perpetually laughing and enjoying ourselves as only the young can do.

'I shall never forget the first time I saw his sister Serena. I had laughed at the notion of love at first sight, but it held true for the pair of us. There seemed to be no reason why we should not marry—once I was gazetted into the Army—so I proposed to her. She was poor, as was Ralph, who was the younger son; his brother was the heir to the baronetcy, and they came from a good family. She accepted me, and I went home with my head in the clouds, dreaming of the future.

'When I reached there it was to discover that my father's cousin had died suddenly from some sort of summer fever. Not only that, but his father was dying, too, and that meant that in a short space of time my father would be the Earl of Bretford and I would be Lord Hadleigh. Any pleasure I might have gained from that flew away when I told him that I wished to marry Serena: he would have none of it.

'''What! Marry a poverty-stricken girl when you could have any heiress that you wanted! No, no, I have other ideas for you. My friend Henry Russell, who inherited Eddington when it was found that his brother's heir was illegitimate through a bigamous marriage, has an only child, a daughter, Margaret, who is his heiress. I met him again recently and he has intimated that he would look kindly on a marriage between you. I have given the notion my blessing and I expect you to return north to offer for her as soon as decently possible, given that we must carry out the due mourning rituals for my cousin.''

'In vain I told him that my dearest wish was to marry Serena and join the Army. He told me that I was a fool, that the Bretford heir must marry money and land and Margaret Russell would possess those in abundance. "She's a pretty girl, too," he said. "Her father gave me her miniature to give to you. I believe you must have met her." I had met her, and although it was true that she was a pretty girl, my heart had already been given to Serena.

'She was never to receive it. My great-uncle died shortly afterwards and as Lord Hadleigh I was sent to Eddington to meet and marry the Russell heiress. To my eternal disgrace I did as I was asked. Your poor mother was delighted: it seems that she had worshipped me from afar. Serena I did not see. The word was that she had heard that I was coming to propose to Margaret and went to stay with relatives. I never saw her again. My marriage to your mother was happy enough, although I fear that she soon came to realize that she was always second best.

'The trouble was that my grief at losing Serena was made even more bitter when her brother Ralph inherited and she became so greatly dowered that I could have married her—but alas, that came too late, I had been married a year by then. It was when you and Ritchie were born that the major damage was done.

'The older he grew, the more he looked like Serena, which was not surprising given that she was our blood relative. The more you grew, the more you began to resemble your mother and the Russells in your looks and your tastes. As a result you were the one who suffered the most of my displeasure at being forced to marry against my wishes, and Ritchie received my love in lieu of that which I couldn't give to Serena. I was grossly unfair to you, I now know— and to your poor mother also. You have your own talents, which are different from Ritchie's, and he recently reproached me for my behaviour to you. I can only ask you to forgive me for the many unnecessary unkindnesses which I inflicted on you. I will quite understand it if you cannot forgive me—and also forgive me for colluding with Dr Beauregard to prevent you from marrying the girl you loved.

'I wanted you to marry an heiress because my father had made me marry one, and Dr Beauregard thought that if his daughter married you she would most likely give up his mathematical work through which he hoped to gain posthumous fame. Her marriage to Dr Wardour was supposed to ensure that. I fear our plans went badly awry. She told me when I asked her what had happened to her father's research that Dr Wardour destroyed her father's papers, but used her to continue and support his own work.

'I offer you a heartfelt apology for the wrongs I have done you and ask you to forgive me so that we may try to be a father and son in the truest sense. I will quite understand if you find it difficult for us to be reconciled.'

Russell remembered that he had immediately offered his father the forgiveness which he had asked for, adding, 'Let us agree to forget the unhappy past, Father, and not let it poison the relations between us. Today is a new day for us and so shall it be henceforward.'

His father had said, his voice shaking a little, 'I know now that I do not deserve your forgiveness, Hadleigh, nor the kindness with which you have just spoken. I agree that the past must die—a lesson which I should have learned when I was younger than you are now.'

All of this he now told Mary, ending with, 'It explains why he was so determined that we should not marry. He would not allow me the happiness which had been denied to him. Hence his determination that I should find an heiress—in my case, Angelica Markham—and marry her whether I loved her or not.'

'I am so pleased that you and your father have become reconciled,' said Mary, 'and only fancy, if you had done as he wished and not refused him, you might have been the lucky man who won Angelica's hand!'

'Wretch,' said Russell, rising from his chair and coming over to her where she had retired to the sofa after their meal. 'You deserve a kiss for that, and another and another. Thank God we are here where there are few servants to interrupt us, unlike Loudwater. I'm afraid that I shall burn for you so hard that I shall be ashes before I reach the altar.'

'And I, too,' sighed Mary, as he took her into his arms. 'I never knew in the past why poets spoke of the flame of love and of burning for the loved one, but I do now.'

The next few minutes saw the flames of love, or of passion, whichever one might like to call them, burn high and bright. Mary traced his face with her hands as though trying to learn it so that she might know him, even if the heavens turned permanently dark.

Russell for his part stroked and caressed her until his impatient body brought him near to fulfilment without him ever having possessed his love. The dishevelled nymph and her equally dishevelled satyr finally drew apart, gasping.

'Now I know why young ladies are never allowed to be alone with a man,' Mary laughed, her eyes alight, 'not that I could ever imagine myself making love to a man other than yourself, but, oh, the wicked temptation of being alone with you exceeds my delight in figures, algebra and geometry!'

'So pleased to learn that you prefer me,' Russell teased her, 'otherwise I should be quite cast down to find that one of Newton's equations excited you more than myself. What a naughty wench you are, to be sure, and who would have thought it?'

He took her in his arms again and in their exalted state who knew where *that* might have ended had there not been a hammering on the door which signalled that the under-butler was tactfully informing them of his presence.

Some hasty rearrangement of stock, buttons and bows was necessary before Russell bellowed, 'Enter,' and the under-butler came in and brought the outside world with him, with some tale of one of the tenant-farmers wishing to see m'lord urgently.

'I regret to have need to disturb you, sir and madam,' he ended.

But a damned good thing he did, was Russell's conclusion as he made for the Entrance Hall, or we should certainly have anticipated our wedding night. Never mind, we can have a stroll in the grounds this afternoon, and with luck might even take up where we left off!

At the same time as Russell and Mary were celebrating the love they had rediscovered after so many years, his father was alighting from his coach before a pleasant house not far from Ancoates. From thence he was shown into a room where a woman, still beautiful and strangely resembling his second son, was waiting to receive him.

'So you have come to me at last, Jackie,' she said softly. 'I always thought that, one day, you would.'

'I am here for your forgiveness,' he told her. 'I gave you up in exchange for an easy life and God has been punishing me for it ever since.'

'But not any more,' she murmured. 'You have my forgiveness and I quite understand why you acted as you did.'

'I cannot hope that you love me still, but I have never forgotten you and that last summer which we shared.'

Her smile for him was a sad one. 'Nor I, and now we are old and may, if we wish, enjoy all that lovers in the autumn of their loves can hope for.'

'Which is more than I deserve,' he replied, and for a moment in the pleasant room it almost seemed that time had turned back as they remembered the past...

Russell's luck held, however; no one came to interrupt them, and though, regretfully, they both agreed that final consummation must be left until after their marriage, which was being arranged to take place in London as soon as possible, he was able to initiate his dear love, if not into the wildest shores of passion, at least to somewhere near them.

Lying on a grassy bank among the golden and scarlet colours of autumn they took their fill of one another, Mary discarding Russell's unwanted shirt and Russell loosening Mary's dress so that he could caress the glories of her body even as she celebrated his. Only the memory of their vow to remain virtuous until their wedding day prevented them from consummating their love on friendly mother earth as so many lovers had done before them.

'If I had my way,' Mary gasped, 'I would rather become your true wife here in the open than after a long and arduous day in church—but we must remember those who will be coming to celebrate our long-overdue marriage and will like to think that we have behaved ourselves.'

'We are at one in that as we are in everything,' replied Russell, reaching for his shirt, 'but if we do not stop now, my rosy nymph, we shall be unable to.' So, regretfully, they rose from the grassy bank on which they had been reclining and walked back to the House, passing on the way the workers in the Park who were engaged in trying to restore it to its former glory.

'I meant it when I told my father that our marriage must not be long delayed,' Russell said when they were in the chaise which took them back to Loudwater. 'I asked him not to let the lawyers maunder on overmuch while working out the settlements, for not only am I impatient to make you my wife in the fullest sense, I shall also not be happy until I am back at Eddington.'

'Nor I either,' Mary said. They had reached the top of a small rise from whence they could look out not only over the Park, and the far pasture where Russell's newly acquired sheep were grazing, but also the wilder scenery of Northumberland in all its majestic splendour.

Her eyes suddenly sparkled with mischief. 'I never thought to love a place so much. The only proviso I have to make is that when we finally settle here you must set aside a quiet room where we may work together on our project to design a calculating machine. Since our meeting again has revived your talents I am in hopes that you will not waste them, and that you will be more than another ignorant squire. After all, you have Lord Chard as a splendid example of what may be achieved. I believe that as a young man he was very like the Lord Hadleigh you were in the years when we were apart—and look at him now.'

Russell turned to take her hand in his.

'Anything you want, my darling, anything you want. Ask—and it shall be granted unto you.'

'Hold to that, sir,' she said, merrily, 'and we shall not go far wrong!'

'Minx!' he exclaimed, and took her in his arms to run with her down the little hill, to their shared delight as well as that of the watching workers.

Lord Hadleigh's rebellion had brought him, and those around him, happiness, and Eddington House had found a loving man and woman to guard it and secure its future.

Epilogue

'I half thought that we might be attending a double wedding,' said Ritchie Chancellor, who was helping his brother to prepare for his marriage. Russell and Mary were not being married in London, but in Lord Chard's private chapel at Loudwater. 'What with Father having found his lost love and they being nearly as besotted with each other as you and Mary are.'

'To say nothing of you and Pandora,' retorted Russell. 'Why is this damned stock taking so long to tie?'

'Well, you did send your new valet away because he was being so clumsy,' replied Ritchie reasonably. 'Perhaps I ought to lend you a hand,' which he did, creating a thing of such magnificence that Russell stared at it in the mirror before saying gloomily,

'Why are you so damned good at everything and why do I no longer mind that you are?'

'Because you are so damned good at so many things now yourself,' retorted Ritchie, 'and also because it is quite plain why Father made so many mistakes when rearing us. You reminded him of the woman he didn't want to marry and I reminded him of the woman he did, so he favoured me and demeaned you. To crown all that, like the Russells you resemble, you are a countryman while I, God help me, am any damned man you please.'

'Not quite,' said Russell with a grin. 'The cream of the jest is that each of us secretly resented the other, and now, suddenly we don't.'

'No need,' said Ritchie practically. 'Father's so busy making amends to both of us for the past that I feel inclined to tell him to shut up every now and then. Do you intend to dress like this in Northumberland?' he asked, before swinging the big standing-glass round for Russell to see himself in all his glory.

'Good God, no! That's one of the things I like about the place, no one minds if I look like my own gamekeeper!'

'Does Mary mind?' Ritchie's expression was sly. 'Is she going to look like the gamekeeper's wife?'

'What a tongue you have on you, younger brother, and the answer to that is I don't know. What I do know is that she graces everything with her presence whatever she wears.'

'Agreed as to that,' said Ritchie. 'So, after all these years we have come to terms with Father's past and you need not mount any more rebellions. I was so happy to learn t'other night that you had taken my advice and learned that lying occasionally answers.

Theoretically honesty may be the best policy, but in reality it does not always answer. The trick lies in knowing when to abandon it, and not too often at that.'

'As I have learned,' Russell said. He knew, though, that he would never be quite such an iron man as his brother. He had shown mercy to Shaw, where Ritchie would not have done, and in return for his kindness he had nearly lost his life. Even so, he had to be true to himself, and the new man he had discovered on and after his journey to the north was a different one from the discontented fellow who had idled around London.

He pulled out his hunter. 'I think that it is time that we went downstairs. My bride will be waiting.'

'And that would never do. Give me your arm, brother, and we'll be off.'

So far as Ritchie was concerned it could not be said that they were reconciled since they had never really been at odds, but time and chance had revealed to them that, beneath their outward differences, they were really very much alike.

Downstairs Mary was being dressed by Jennie, her maid, Aunt Beauregard, Serena Lascelles and Pandora Chancellor, Ritchie's wife. Since Mary was a widow it had been decided by all of them that deep cream would be the most suitable colour for the bride.

'I cannot understand why I feel so nervous,' Mary was saying. 'After all, this is my second wedding, but I really feel more overset than at the first.'

'Quite natural,' said Aunt Beauregard. She and George had decided not to marry—at least, not yet. Companionable friendship would be the best at first, they had thought, like Jackie and Serena. Aunt Beauregard found it difficult to think of him as the Earl. George had bought a pretty little cottage in Ancoates and she had helped him to furnish it so that it did not look at all like the one in which he had played the hermit.

'After all, your first was a marriage of convenience. I never forgave your father for handing you over to that old man. It must all have seemed like a bad dream—if not a nightmare. Now this marriage is quite different. Stand still, love, and let me crown you with this wreath of cream silk rosebuds. It's a pity you weren't married in the spring or summer, but I quite understand why you didn't want to wait until next year.'

'All very true,' sighed Mary. She looked at herself in the mirror Jennie held up for her. Her cream dress, its waist slightly lower after the new fashion, was charming in its simplicity. Her slippers were of silver, and Serena, whom everyone had learned to love, was handing her her small bouquet—again of cream silk roses.

There were times when she felt like pinching herself to prove that this was no longer a happy dream:

that she was really about to marry her first and only love.

'Now,' said Pandora in her jolly way, 'you must take these four things and bestow them around your person.' She and Mary were getting on famously— so much so that from their very first meeting they had become bosom bows. They were as unlike as Russell and Ritchie were, but this had not prevented them from establishing an instant rapport.

'Something old,' she announced and she handed Mary a small linen pocket-handkerchief.

'Something new,' said Aunt Beauregard, and she decorated the collar of Mary's dress with a small gold pin.

'Something borrowed,' and Serena handed her a garter to hold up one of her stockings.

'Something blue,' murmured Jennie shyly and she handed her mistress a length of blue ribbon to tie around the little finger of her right hand.

All her attendants stood back and exclaimed at her.

'Now you are ready,' said Aunt Beauregard. 'Let us go downstairs. We must not keep the groom waiting.'

Nor did they. The chapel at Loudwater was not overlarge and it was quite full. Russell and Ritchie stood by the altar waiting for her, but when she entered the chapel Mary only had eyes for Russell.

So much so that when they at last stood side by side, she breathed gently, 'At last!' to feel him squeeze her hand in return.

Aunt Beauregard began to cry: Pandora, ever resourceful, handed her a handkerchief. The groom, looking at the bride, thought that he had never seen anything quite so beautiful. And to think that he had had to wait so long to make her his—but finally he had, and that was all that mattered. Neither of them could remember the ceremony at all. It passed in a dream, not like the nightmare of Mary's first wedding day and, when later they were at last alone, only the ring on Mary's finger was there to prove that the dream was true.

Not all of us achieve our dreams, but Mary and Russell's not only came true, but in the doing they made of Eddington House a place of love, where all the ghosts of the unhappy past were finally laid to rest in the presence of the pair who had found one another against all the odds.

*   *   *   *   *